Praise for Erin Nicholas's
She's the One

"This sexy romance provided me with plenty of laugh-out-loud moments as well as a few heart swooning ones. [...] This is one great story that I highly recommend."

~ *Night Owl Reviews*

"In *She's the One* you can't beat the intriguing characters, the witty yet emotional dialog, and the plot that has set in motion a series that is very, very promising."

~ *Guilty Pleasures Book Reviews*

"I absolutely adored this book! [...] I can't wait to read the next in the series, and am so glad to have found a new-to-me author who has a lot of books I can go back and glom onto."

~ *The Book Pushers*

Look for these titles by *Erin Nicholas*

She's the One

Erin Nicholas

SAMHAIN
PUBLISHING

Samhain Publishing, Ltd.
11821 Mason Montgomery Road, 4B
Cincinnati, OH 45249
www.samhainpublishing.com

Editing by Lindsey Faber
Cover by Angela Waters

First Samhain Publishing, Ltd. electronic publication: June 2013
First Samhain Publishing, Ltd. print publication: June 2014

Dedication

To Lindsey, who uses words like *delightful* and *charming* and *refreshing* when she talks to me and who says things like, "Let's make this even more amazing"…and then does. Thank you for everything.

Chapter One

Babysitting had gotten a hell of a lot harder since she was sixteen, Amanda Dixon thought. For one thing, her charges were a lot older—never mind old enough to know better—and she sure wasn't making five dollars an hour at this gig.

Of course, she couldn't drink mojitos at any of her teenage babysitting jobs. So there was that.

Watching her younger sister, Emma, pass out congratulations—or so she called the kisses she was laying on each guy—to the members of the Omaha Hawks football team, Amanda chugged the last of her drink and signaled the waitress for another.

The team and their fans were celebrating the big win at Trudy's bar.

Of course, they also came to Trudy's after a loss. And after practice. And every Thursday.

Screw being the designated driver—she'd pay for a cab. Because she could not handle tonight's party without some more lime juice and rum.

"Wilson, you big stud!" Emma called to a man across the bar. "Come give me a hug."

The three-hundred-pound man who played center for the Hawks whirled at the sound of her voice and quickly strode to where she stood and caught her up against his broad chest. She gave him a big, smacking kiss on the lips.

"This is why I play ball, girl," he told her when he set her down again. "All the sugar I get."

"That's why we show up," Emma told him with a laugh. "The Dixon girls have a lot of sugar to give."

I love my sister. I love my sister. I'm proud of her. She's beautiful, smart and confident. And I love her. Amanda took a long, steadying breath, like Emma had taught her in yoga class. Then she repeated her mantra. *I love her. She's a grown woman, capable of making her own decisions. I love her and I'm proud of her. Even when she's acting like a hooker on the docks after the ships just came in.*

The Hawks had won a big game that afternoon. Amanda got that. Everyone was excited. Everyone was in a celebratory mood. Inhibitions lowered as blood-alcohol levels climbed. And this was definitely not Amanda's first time at Trudy's bar with this crowd.

But everyone was extra exuberant tonight as the Hawks were moving on to the playoffs to defend their championship title for the third year in a row. And extra exuberant around here was...something. Like headache inducing.

Amanda watched Emma get dipped back by another of the Hawks before he laid a kiss on her.

As she tipped her newly refilled mojito back for a healthy swig, Amanda could admit that her irritation with her sister was pretty much pure jealousy. She'd like to be Emma for one night. Or even fifteen minutes. Emma was well known as the fun Dixon sister. Everyone liked Emma.

Amanda glanced around the bar. Okay, all the *guys* liked Emma. Most of the women felt a lot like Amanda did—like they hated Emma at the same time they wished they could *be* Emma.

"Ladies and gentlemen, the man of the hour, our fearless leader, the man who made it all happen...Conner Dixon!" someone called out in an announcer's voice. A loud cheer went up as the quarterback for the Hawks entered the bar.

Amanda sighed. They all knew him as the man of the hour. She thought of him as the only reason she was really here.

Her brother had played spectacularly today. He deserved his moment in the spotlight without worrying about getting his toes stomped on by their younger sister. Emma loved to be the center of attention. Keeping her from embarrassing Conner—or herself—was almost a full-time job for Amanda.

She slid out of the booth, intent on grabbing Emma's arm and making her sit down and leave the guys alone for a while. But *her* toes almost got stomped on by Ryan Kaye, the Hawks' star running back.

"What's a guy gotta do to get one of those?" he asked Emma as she was set back on her feet by one of the benchwarmers. "I made the spectacular winning catch."

"You sure did." Emma gave Ryan a huge smile, then launched herself at him. He caught her against his chest and she wrapped her legs around his waist—a sure sign her brother was watching—and kissed him. And kissed him.

As Emma finally lifted her head from the hot French kiss, Amanda heard her whisper, "I think there's smoke coming from his ears."

"Good." Ryan squeezed her ass, then set her back on her feet.

Amanda rubbed a hand against her forehead. Emma and Ryan *loved* riling Conner up.

"Seriously?" Conner demanded behind her. "*Seriously?*"

And it was really easy to do. Dammit.

Ryan turned, dragging his thumb over his bottom lip. "What? I don't deserve some sugar after that catch?"

"For God's sake," Conner muttered. He grabbed Emma around the waist with one arm and hauled her up against his side, turned, and deposited her out of Ryan's reach.

"I thought I explained this to you," Conner said. He pointed at Ryan. "No dating my sisters." Then he pointed at Emma. "No dating my friends."

Emma sighed. "We were *kissing*, not dating."

"Kissing leads to dating," Conner said.

Emma giggled as Ryan gave her a wink. "Not always."

"Emma," Conner growled in warning.

"Well, it's your fault," Emma told her brother, crossing her

11

arms. "You have so many friends, there's hardly any guys left in Omaha to date."

Conner rolled his eyes and Ryan laughed out loud. Emma had no trouble finding guys to take her out in spite of Conner's alleged likeability.

"I don't know every guy in Omaha, Em. Don't be dramatic."

Of course, telling Emma to not be dramatic was like telling the sun not to shine.

"You don't know any boring, ugly guys," she conceded. "But you know the hottest, nicest ones. And those are the ones I want to date."

"Too bad. I do *not* need to think about the guys on my team being hot. And they definitely aren't always nice. You've never seen them break up a bar fight or deal with a guy who put his girlfriend in the hospital."

Emma sighed and batted her eyelashes at Ryan. "Hot and heroic. You're not helping me here, Conner."

"A chastity belt might help," Conner muttered.

Amanda's thoughts exactly. She reached for Emma. "You're in a time-out."

"Whew," Emma exclaimed as she slid into the booth across from Amanda and reached to gather her long blond hair on top of her head with both hands. "I swear that man could ruin me for all other men."

Amanda frowned at her sister from across the table. "You only kissed Ryan because Conner was watching." If it had just been to congratulate Ryan on the catch, she would have given him a simple kiss like she had the rest of the team. But because her big brother was watching, Emma had kissed him like he was returning from the war. "That's hardly enough to ruin you."

Now, the one-night stand Emma had with Ryan last year was probably another story.

Emma reached for Amanda's mojito and took a drink. "Have you ever kissed Ryan Kaye? I'm telling you, the guy sets the bar high for all the other guys."

Amanda shifted on her seat. No, she'd never kissed Ryan Kaye. Not in person anyway.

In her dirty dreams, however—oh, yeah. And yes, he was the best she'd ever had.

"That hasn't stopped you from kissing lots of other guys," Amanda said, knowing she sounded bitchy. Emma had a way of bringing that out in her.

"Well, Ryan and I aren't going to end up together so I have to keep looking. But Ryan did me a favor—the guy who can outdo him is the guy for me," Emma said nonchalantly.

"You know it makes Conner nuts when you flirt with his friends," Amanda said. Of course Emma knew that. It was why she did it.

Emma grinned "It's like playing a video game," she said. "If I do something that makes the *tips* of Conner's ears red, I'm not going far enough. If his whole neck gets red, I've gone too far. It's fun."

And that was why Amanda was at Trudy's with the postgame football crowd when she really should be home going over her students' midterm reports. Sure, Conner could look out for Emma and their other two sisters, Isabelle and Olivia, but he shouldn't have to.

Keeping his blood pressure down was Amanda's self-appointed mission in life. This quite simply meant keeping track of their three younger sisters so he didn't have to. Which wasn't simple at all.

"And *this* is why Mom said no margaritas on Olivia's birthday."

Emma frowned. "What do you mean, 'no margaritas'?"

Amanda shook her head. "Mom wants to do a spa day instead."

"But margaritas are tradition," Emma protested. "What happened?"

"You happened," Amanda said. "You and Isabelle."

It was always Emma and their sister Isabelle who were

making a spectacle, drawing attention and driving people crazy.

"What do you mean, 'I happened'?" Emma straightened in her seat. "What did I do?"

"Well, gee, let me think," Amanda said. It had been Emma's birthday, and as the birthday girl she'd felt that anything went. Of course, Emma often thought anything went. "Maybe it was the tequila shots at the bar with the cowboys, or the dirty dancing in the center of the dance floor, or the impromptu kissing booth they set up when they found out it was your birthday."

"We were having fun," Emma said, sitting back in the booth and crossing her arms. "Nobody got hurt."

"Mom was embarrassed," Amanda said. "So she wants no margaritas and no guys for Liv's birthday."

Emma rolled her eyes. "Olivia's not exactly the type to do body shots and make out on the pool table."

"But *you* are," Amanda said, her blood pressure rising. "Just because it's Olivia's birthday is no guarantee that *you* won't be the center of attention again."

"You think I'm going to get plastered and have sex on the pool table at Olivia's party?"

"I think you'll do whatever strikes you as a good time at the moment," Amanda said. "As always."

"No one's stopping you from chugging some schnapps and getting up on that table yourself," Emma said.

Amanda was the one stopping herself. She couldn't do it. If she gave in to those temptations, she'd be Emma times ten.

"In fact, we all know you want to," Emma said.

Yep, they knew that. They were her sisters. They all knew one another inside and out, for better or worse. They also knew she'd never do it.

"In fact, I wish you would," Emma went on. "I know the idea freaks you out, but I swear, it would be good for you. It would be good for *me*."

"And it's all about you," Amanda said.

"If you let go a little and pulled that stick out of your butt, maybe you'd get off of *my* butt."

Olivia, their youngest sister, chose that moment to slip into the booth. "Sorry I'm late." She looked from one sister to the other. The tension was palpable. "Oh boy, what did I miss?"

"Nothing much," Emma answered, leaning her forearms against the table. "Amanda's informing me that I'm the biggest slut she knows and that I can't be trusted out in public with our mother anymore."

Olivia looked at Amanda. "I'm sure that was word for word."

"No. But 'pull that stick out of your butt' is a direct quote," Amanda told her.

Emma sighed heavily. "You're pissed because I know how to have a good time."

"That's not why I'm pissed," Amanda said. "And you know it."

"Okay, how about we take it down a notch?" Olivia said. "Before somebody says something she doesn't mean."

"No," Emma said, "I'd love to hear what Amanda has to say here. What would you do, big sis, if you let yourself do whatever you wanted? I'd *love* to know. Spike your hot chocolate? Maybe wear three-inch heels instead of flats? Oh, I know, you'll get a Brazilian instead of a regular bikini wax?"

Amanda felt her cheeks heat, and it wasn't with embarrassment. She had three younger sisters. Three. Isabelle was almost as daring and sassy as Emma was. Almost. But no one—*no one*—could make her as crazy as quickly as Emma did.

"You really think you invented drinking games and flirting?" Amanda had done her share of partying and had gotten into plenty of her own trouble. But it had only taken one time of getting in way too deep for her to pull back and grow up.

That didn't mean that she never wanted to push the limits now, though. She did. On a regular basis. She wanted to be like Emma. She wasn't proud of it, but she was honest. "For God's sake, Emma, what you do doesn't exactly take brains or talent."

"That's not what Ryan said," Emma shot back. "Or Derek or Tom or Justin or—"

"I've decided what I want for my birthday."

They both stopped and looked at Olivia.

"You want to hear it?" she asked them.

Emma sighed. "Really? Amanda and I were kind of having a moment here."

Amanda couldn't help it. She smiled. When Emma got mad, it was like every other emotion she felt—she wanted to experience it fully, revel in it even.

"Well, you both have said more than your share and I want a chance to talk," Olivia said.

Amanda took a deep breath. It was for the best. She didn't want to hurt her sister. "Okay, fine, Liv. What do you want for your birthday?"

"For you and Emma to trade places. For one weekend."

Amanda glanced at Emma. Emma looked at Amanda.

"It will help you to walk in each other's shoes for a couple of days," Olivia said. She looked earnest as she explained. "You'll see what's good about what the other one does and maybe you'll find out something that you didn't know about their life."

It wasn't like they knew *nothing* about each other's lives. They squabbled and disagreed, but they still liked each other and spent time together.

Olivia went on. "I want Emma to do everything Amanda needs to do this weekend and Amanda to do everything Emma would normally be doing."

Amanda felt a surge of...something. It was surprise, shock even. But there was an unmistakable swell of adrenaline too.

Emma, on the other hand, looked worried. She sighed. "Okay, let's hear it. What do you mean exactly?"

Amanda worked on not looking excited.

"Emma, tomorrow you're going to take Mom to lunch, then grab Amanda's laptop, pretty up her PowerPoint presentation for Tuesday, make all the copies she needs and put them in nice folders, call to confirm the catering for the meeting and then watch movies with me Saturday night," Olivia said. "On Sunday, you're going to take Mom to church with me, you're going to do Amanda's laundry and then make me lasagna for dinner."

Amanda watched Emma process Olivia's instructions and had to fight a smile. Liv had the details of Amanda's weekend down. Not that she was going to let Emma touch her presentation, but it was a nice idea to have her do the copies and folders.

Emma glanced between Olivia and Amanda. "She makes you lasagna every Sunday night?" was all she said.

Olivia laughed. "No. But I love lasagna and these are my rules."

Emma rolled her eyes. "And what does Amanda do this weekend?"

Olivia turned a huge smile on Amanda. "Well, Emma doesn't have carefully laid plans and schedules."

That was an understatement.

"So, I'd say you just go through your day asking yourself 'what would Emma do?' in every situation."

Emma was frowning. "'What would Emma do?' What's that supposed to mean?"

Olivia looked triumphant. "Exactly what it sounds like. In every situation Amanda asks herself 'what would Emma do?' before she makes a decision."

"And then she does whatever she thinks I would do?"

"Right." Olivia picked up the strawberry daiquiri the waitress set down in front of her.

Emma frowned at Amanda. "What if she doesn't know what I would do?"

That wasn't going to be a problem.

"Amanda?"

She'd been so engrossed in her sisters and Olivia's crazy

request that she hadn't noticed Tim's approach.

"Hi, Tim."

"Want to dance?"

Amanda knew that Tim had a thing for her. He was one of Cody Madsen's fire crew, and she'd met him a few times when she'd gone to pick Olivia up from work. Olivia was the chief's administrative secretary so she knew all the firefighters well, and she liked Tim. She'd even tried to talk Amanda into going out with him. But Amanda didn't want to start anything with anyone. Especially a nice guy like Tim.

She didn't have time for dating. And certainly not a nice guy who would want a relationship that would last more than a weekend or two. She was way too busy keeping track of her family.

She knew that Conner considered himself their safety net. For everything. He'd been seventeen when their dad had died, and Conner had immediately taken over the fatherly role for his four sisters, ranging from age eleven to fourteen.

But he'd done so much already. They all owed him. Amanda was going to be the one to take care of Emma and Isabelle and Olivia now. She was a grown woman, she made a good living, she had connections and resources. She could help her sisters with whatever problems they had now.

Even the ones they created themselves.

"Oh, sorry. We're in the middle of planning Olivia's birthday," she said to Tim.

She instantly felt a sharp kick in her shin. She glanced at Emma, then Olivia. Her youngest sister was looking at her.

What would Emma do? Olivia mouthed to her.

Amanda swallowed. Right. Emma would dance with Tim. Absolutely. Not only did she choose dancing with a cute guy over almost anything else, but she would definitely choose it over a deep, emotional conversation.

"On second thought, Tim, I'd love to dance."

He took her hand and led her to the dance floor. They were

playing a series of slower songs and Tim pulled her close.

They swayed together for half of a song without talking and Amanda let her mind wander. She liked the song and she liked the feel of Tim's strong arms around her. She felt...appreciated. And that was something she didn't feel very often.

She didn't like feeling sorry for herself. She had a limited social life, but it was purely by choice. She could join Emma and Isabelle at any time. They would love it and, frankly, she knew that Conner would be there for her. If she ended up in trouble, he'd be there to bail her out. But that was the whole point of her *not* getting into trouble. She didn't want him to have to do that. She didn't want him to be embarrassed or frustrated or to have his coworkers or boss think less of him because of his sisters.

Tim pressed her closer with his big hand on her low back and she let him. She hadn't been up against a guy in a long time.

And not because she didn't want to be.

She shared genes with Emma, after all. And she could make Emma blush if she tried. So she had to *try* not to.

She loved men. She loved dancing and singing karaoke and flirting and throwing caution to the wind. *Loved* it.

Like the game she'd played at camp one summer, where she stood with her arms crossed and let herself fall back, trusting those behind her to catch her. That freedom, that confidence, that ability to let go of control. She'd loved it.

And she knew that Conner and her mom and Olivia and even Isabelle and Emma would be there if she let herself go.

But just because they'd catch her didn't mean they wouldn't be disappointed.

She knew because she'd been disappointed in Emma and Iz more than once.

She also knew because she'd disappointed Conner. One time. One big time. She'd never forget it. And she'd never do it again.

So, if nothing else, she'd learned from her mistakes. She was not invincible and she was never going to have her brother—or anyone else she cared about and respected—see her out of control and in trouble like that again.

"I'd love to take you out this weekend."

Tim's voice jerked Amanda back to the present. And the very nice guy she was dancing with.

"Oh, um..."

"I really like you, Amanda. You're sweet and sexy and I'd love to get to know you better."

Which was the perfect thing for him to say. The perfect thing for her to say yes to. But as she opened her mouth, she knew she wouldn't.

She was leading Tim on. She hated women who did that.

She couldn't get involved with anyone right now. She really did still feel like she needed to watch out for Emma and Isabelle until they settled down. She'd think about her own life once the girls had these wild streaks out of their systems. Which, Lord willing, would be before she was eighty.

"Tim, that's very nice. And you're a great guy."

She saw his disappointment and felt a twinge of regret. She didn't want to hurt him or make him think it was something he'd done wrong. He'd been nothing but a gentleman to her, and if the timing were different, or if her *sisters* were different...but they weren't.

Still, she couldn't hurt him. It wasn't about him. Not that he'd understand that. No one ever believed the "it's not you, it's me" routine.

"Tim, I have to tell you something and you have to promise not to say anything to anyone."

He nodded. "All right."

"I...have feelings for someone else."

As she said it, her gaze landed on Ryan Kaye—as it often did. Ryan drew her attention whenever they were within a hundred yards of one another, it seemed.

Of course, Ryan drew the attention of a lot of women.

He was good-looking, sexy and charming. And he knew it. But that wasn't the biggest draw.

He had a laid-back, easygoing, everyone's-friend thing that made him very approachable. Then once the women did approach him, he made them feel like he was just so flattered by their attention.

Along with the attention of the other fifty-two women in the vicinity.

He could have a freakin' harem if he wanted it. There were certainly enough women, and none of them seemed at all offended that he might be running his hand up and down another woman's back while he spoke to them.

Women really needed to have more self-esteem. Couldn't they see that he just enjoyed the way they stroked his ego—and the other things they were willing to stroke?

It was so irritating that Ryan Kaye was the one guy who showed up in her naughty dreams. It couldn't be someone nice like Tim, or some hot guy from TV that she'd never actually meet, or, better yet, some nameless, generic hot guy. No, it had to be Ryan. Every damned time.

And, to herself only, Amanda could admit that most of her irritation with Emma's fling with Ryan was that her fling had been with *Ryan*.

Her sister was beautiful, sexy, funny, smart and could have any guy. *Any* guy. But, of course, she had to hook up with Ryan. The only guy that Amanda had dirty dreams about.

She should look on the bright side. Ryan was a guy who could potentially get Amanda to let go and get wild, but now that he'd been with her sister, *that* wasn't going to happen. So really, Emma had done her favor.

It didn't feel like a favor though.

"Oh. I had no idea," Tim said. "Are you dating someone?"

"No, not dating. We..." Her gaze drifted to Ryan again. He was in the midst of three women—a common place to find him—his usual cocky smile on his face. "It was just one night," she said without thinking.

"But you're not over him," Tim said.

"Right." She focused on the man she was dancing with. "It's very possible Ryan ruined me for all other men." If Olivia wanted her to live by the "what would Emma do?" motto, then why not borrow some of her sister's lines too?

Tim frowned and stopped dancing. "Ryan? You mean Ryan Kaye?"

Amanda froze. Crap. She hadn't meant to give a name. She'd meant to play it as being so brokenhearted she couldn't even talk about whoever-he-was.

Dammit.

"Um, no, I..."

"It's Kaye," Tim said. "Fuck. Of course it's Kaye."

Of course it was Kaye?

"Ryan didn't mean to hurt me," she said quickly. She did not want this spreading beyond her and Tim. "He's just...so..."

"Yeah, yeah," Tim said. "I know. He's Ryan Kaye. Enough said."

Amanda tried again. "Ryan wanted—"

"I know exactly what Ryan wanted," Tim said. "You can spare me the details."

Okay, great. That definitely made fibbing a little easier. "I wanted more than he could give."

Like one night of screaming orgasms in every position I can come up with.

Whoa. Amanda bit her bottom lip. Where the hell had that come from? That wasn't what she wanted from Ryan. She didn't want *anything* from Ryan, she corrected quickly. Ryan was off limits. He was way too wild, way too hot and way too familiar with her sister's bedroom. Three very good reasons to steer very clear.

Ryan could totally deliver on those orgasms and you know it.

The stupid voice in her head was especially obnoxious tonight. She focused on the voices from *real* people.

"Ryan Kaye needs to learn some manners when it comes to women," Tim said. "I doubt he even knows how to spell 'consequences'."

Uh-huh. Which was why he and Emma were a perfect pair.

"Ryan's a nice guy," she felt compelled to say. He was, and she was painting him, unfairly, as a one-night-stand kind of guy. Not that it wasn't accurate. She'd heard the stories. Ryan was a love-the-one-you're-with guy and was rumored to have a pretty short attention span.

Ryan would be perfect then. You could have a hot, quick fling but not worry about him wanting to stick around long term and get in the way.

She needed to get a grip.

"I'll get over it," she told Tim. It would be easy to get over a love affair she'd never even had. "But I need some time. I'm sorry."

Dammit. This had not turned out the way she'd planned. She'd wanted to let Tim down easy and stay friendly. Instead he looked pissed.

"I'm sorry too, Amanda."

"Thanks, Tim."

He leaned in and kissed her cheek. Aw. He was a nice guy. Why couldn't she be in a place where she was ready for a nice guy?

She watched him push into the crowd around the dance floor before she headed back to the table with her sisters.

She put her hand against her cheek where Tim had kissed her. She hadn't been kissed on the cheek in a long time. She hadn't been kissed period in a long time.

And that sucked now that she thought about it.

Chapter Two

Ryan put Becky, the drunk, clingy brunette, into a cab at the curb and promised he'd call her.

He wouldn't. He wadded up her number and tucked it in his pocket.

He appreciated the Hawks' rabid fans and loved flirting with women of all types. But he didn't take them as seriously when they were stumbling drunk and had accidentally called him Cody twice.

Ryan grinned. Cody wasn't a bad guy to be mistaken for, but when Ryan made a woman scream, he wanted her screaming *his* name. Call him picky.

Turning back to the bar, he was startled to find a guy standing behind him.

"Hey, Kaye."

He looked vaguely familiar, but Ryan assumed he was a cop or a firefighter if he was at Trudy's bar. There wasn't a rule that you had to work at St. A's or otherwise protect the city to drink at Trudy's, but it seemed that was the way it went.

"Hey," Ryan answered. "If that was your girl, nothing happened."

Well, she'd squeezed his ass and tried to kiss him repeatedly—succeeding in meeting his lips with hers twice—but that didn't really count. To him anyway. This guy might feel differently.

"That's not the girl I'm worried about."

The next thing he knew, Ryan was on his butt on the pavement and his jaw hurt.

He bounded to his feet, rubbing his face. "What the hell,

man?"

"A girl like Amanda deserves better than you."

"What are you talking about?" Ryan wasn't the type of guy to hit back. Or to hit first, for that matter. If he was getting hit, he assumed there was a good reason. But he sure as hell wanted to know what it was.

"Amanda Dixon. You should have just left her alone."

Ryan was way too distracted by Amanda's name to worry about dodging a swinging fist, so he stepped forward and grabbed the guy's wrist. "I don't know what you're talking about."

The guy didn't try to pull away, but stepped forward, getting right in Ryan's face. He was a good three inches shorter, so he had to stretch and tip his chin belligerently. But it was clear he wasn't intimidated by the size difference. He was pissed. He clearly believed that Ryan had messed around with...*Amanda.*

"How do *you* know Amanda?" Ryan asked, dropping his hold on the other guy.

"I'm crazy about her," he said, stepping back and shaking his wrist.

Amanda had dated *this* guy? The kind of guy who would take a swing at a stranger? Who wore faded blue jeans, an Old Navy T-shirt and a ball cap?

Ryan rubbed a hand over his own faded T-shirt. That was interesting.

"Who are you?" Ryan asked.

"Tim. Winters. I'm over at Firehouse Three."

Ah, one of Cody's guys. Cody Madsen was the Hawks' star running back and the chief at Firehouse Three. Amanda's youngest sister, Olivia, worked for Cody and knew all the firemen. Made sense how Amanda might have met Winters anyway. "And what do you think I did?"

"Fucked her."

Ryan eyebrows shot up. He would have definitely

remembered that. "Come again?"

"Seduced her, fucked her, made her fall in love with you."

Ryan's hand dropped and he frowned. "What the hell are you talking about?"

And why had his heart sped up at hearing all of that? He would love to—

"She told me."

"She told you what?"

"That she's in love with you. That you ruined her for other men."

Well, if he had Amanda in his bed for even a night, he'd certainly do his best to make her never want to leave.

"Sorry, man," Ryan said. "I didn't know about you."

True enough. He hadn't known Tim's name until a minute ago and definitely hadn't known that Amanda was dating him. He still found it very interesting that Amanda would go for a guy who...didn't dress or act like Nate Sullivan or any of the other doctors or administrators at St. A's. The only place Ryan ever saw Nate without a tie was on the football field. Even at Trudy's he looked like he'd mugged a *GQ* model on his way over. Amanda could have any of those classy, sophisticated men. What was she doing with Winters? Or pretending she was with Ryan?

"I want her," Tim said.

Ryan didn't know what was going on exactly, but she surely had a good reason for the story, and if Amanda had told Tim she was with Ryan, he wasn't going to be the one to tell the guy the truth.

"Too bad, man. She's made her choice."

"But—"

"Dude, she doesn't want you, and going around hitting guys who are bigger than you isn't a great way to handle it. Especially bigger guys who know your chief."

Tim's eyes narrowed. "She should be mine."

Ryan laughed. "You don't know her very well if you think

Amanda Dixon is anybody's but her own."

"You—"

"Go home, Tim. Before I go back in there and tell my cop buddy that I was assaulted."

Tim's jaw tightened and Ryan prepared to duck, but finally the other man pivoted and stomped away.

It was good to have friends who carried badges. He could have taken care of himself with Tim, but his hand would have been sore tomorrow. He hated that.

He headed back into Trudy's. He had a Dixon to find, and it wasn't the one who had thrown him the game-winning pass that had made Ryan the man of the hour.

But he was looking forward to this even more.

Amanda was with her sisters in a booth against the far wall. They were a hard group to miss.

Emma and Isabelle were enough to have Conner wondering what sin he'd committed in a previous life to be the older brother to such beautiful, outgoing, sassy, intelligent women...who had given him an ulcer at age twenty-four. But then there was also the oldest, Amanda, and the baby, Olivia. Emma and Isabelle were the most gregarious, by far, but Conner had been watching men—friends of his and complete strangers alike—make fools of themselves over all four girls nearly his entire life.

It was exhausting for Conner. And entertaining for his friends.

Conner Dixon was a pretty laid-back guy for the most part. He was calm and cool in a crisis, which, as a paramedic for one of the busiest trauma centers in the area, was a good thing. But his sisters could suck the laid-back right out of him in the blink of an eye.

As Ryan approached he heard Isabelle say, "I'd pick Mac. He's got that big, badass thing going on."

Ryan knew without looking that the Mac she was referring to was Mac Gordon, a paramedic for the best crew in Omaha.

He was the only Mac around, and the big and badass thing definitely applied. And, sure enough, when Ryan did glance over toward the tables, he found Conner surrounded by Mac and his crew, including Sam Bradford, Dooley Miller and Kevin Campbell. But it was Mac who sat right next to Conner and had his arm draped over the back of Conner's chair.

Mac had appointed himself Conner's mentor. Not because the younger guy needed a mentor exactly, but because Conner had a thing for Mac's wife and Mac loved torturing him. He took every opportunity to call Conner in for extra shifts, to make him do the crap work, to criticize his work. And he never missed a chance to remind Conner that Mac was the one going home to Sara, the woman Conner had put on a pedestal as the epitome of all women. Sara Bradford Gordon had caught Conner's eye the first time he'd seen her walk into the ER at St. Anthony's. He'd hit on her...and had been putting up with shit from Mac ever since.

Ryan turned his attention back to the Dixon sisters. He knew Sara Gordon and she was beautiful, sweet and sassy, but she couldn't compare with the Dixon Divas as far as Ryan was concerned.

"I'd be all over Sam," Emma said. "No question."

Ryan raised an eyebrow. That fit. Sam was the ladies' man—or had been according to the stories—and had tried everything at least once. Emma would definitely be able to keep up with him.

"Kevin's the sweetest," Isabelle said. "Perfect for Olivia."

"I think there's more naughty under Kevin's sweetness than you might think," Emma said, studying Kevin Campbell, the ex-NFL defensive lineman. "Okay, how about you, Amanda?" Emma tipped back her beer bottle.

Ryan perked up. Ben Torres, the trauma surgeon who had married Sam's sister, Jessica, was probably more Amanda's type. Ben was a nice guy and a brilliant surgeon. He hung out with these guys—the group was tight—but he wasn't rumored to have been the badass or the playboy that these other guys were.

"Probably Dooley. I like a guy who can have a good time," she finally said.

Ryan felt his mouth drop open. Dooley Miller? He was the...goofball. Out of uniform, he wore exclusively blue jeans and T-shirts that said things like *The police never think it's as funny as you do*. Amanda would most likely go out with *Dooley*?

If that was the case, Ryan was so in.

Emma snorted. "Since when is having a good time a criteria for you for anything?"

For some reason, that annoyed Ryan. Emma had enough fun to cover all her sisters, her brother and all of his teammates. Amanda was fine just as she was.

He stepped forward and took Amanda by the elbow. "I need to talk to you."

She looked up at him and her eyes widened. "You do?"

"Yes. Now." He wanted this story that she'd given to Tim Winters and to know why *he* had been the one she'd used as the pretend boyfriend.

"I, um...thought you left."

He tugged her out of the booth. "Why'd you think that?"

"I saw you leave with that brunette."

She'd been watching him. Ryan felt a smile curve his lips. "I put her in a cab." Then he frowned. "Did you tell Winters you were with me because you thought I'd left and he wouldn't be able to confirm it?"

Fuck. That wasn't nearly as nice as thinking his name was the first to come to mind when she thought of guys she'd like to fool around with.

"You talked to Tim?" she asked. Then she muttered, "Dammit."

"What did you tell Tim?" Emma asked, taking in their exchange with interest.

"Nothing," Amanda said quickly.

"That she was with me," Ryan said right over the top of her.

Emma leaned closer. "With you as in *with* you?"

She was a nosy little thing. Ryan signaled Carrie, the waitress. "Two of whatever each of the ladies want," he said, pointing to Emma, Isabelle and Olivia. He looked at the girls. "Stay here and mind your own business. Or at least mind someone's business other than mine and Amanda's."

Emma grinned. "You and Amanda have business in common?"

He looked down at the woman beside him. He still held on to her elbow, and he became aware that she smelled really, really good. Yes, it appeared that he and Amanda had business in common. How interesting. "Just stay here," he finally said to Emma.

He tugged Amanda through the crowd to the corner near the back door. It wasn't exactly private, but it would work for a few minutes. That was all he would have, he was sure, before Conner realized one of his friends had one of his sisters off in a dark corner alone.

"Yes, I talked to Tim Winters," Ryan said when they were as alone as they were going to get. "Right after he clocked me and knocked me on my ass."

Amanda gasped. "He *hit* you?"

"Yeah, because I slept with you."

"I... Oh... Um..."

Ryan fought a smile. "But it's weird. That really seems like something I'd remember."

She rolled her eyes. "We all probably blend together after a while." She said it quietly, more of a mutter really, but he heard it.

"What's that mean?" he demanded. He put a finger under her chin and tipped her head so she had to look at him. "Amanda, what does that mean?"

She shrugged and pulled her chin away from his touch. "It means that it's got to be difficult keeping track of everyone in and out of your bed without making them all wear name tags."

He grinned. He couldn't help it. She was sassy too. He liked that. And liked even more that it didn't show all the time. Emma was pretty much what-you-see-is-what-you-get. He liked knowing that there might be layers to Amanda Dixon to discover.

"Where would they pin the name tags?" he couldn't resist asking.

For a moment, Amanda seemed surprised. Then she smiled. "You'll have to get the adhesive ones, I guess."

"Might cover up something I need to see."

"You could try only dating women named Jennifer or something."

He smiled. "But then Tim Winters wouldn't believe whatever you told him about you and me."

Amanda pressed her lips together. Then said, "I'm really sorry he hit you."

"I'll live. What I want to know is why he did it."

"I thought he...told you."

She actually blushed and Ryan wondered if he could remember the last time he'd seen a woman blush. Not off the top of his head.

"I want to hear it from you."

She looked at the collar of his shirt instead of his eyes. "I told him I had a one-night stand with someone and had feelings for him."

"Me."

"Yes."

"How'd I get to be the lucky one?"

She snorted.

He hated that she thought he was messing around. "Amanda."

She finally looked up into his eyes.

"Why me?"

She swallowed. "You're...the type, I guess."

He frowned at that. That was what she thought of him?

That he was the type of guy to screw around with another man's girl?

"I don't touch what isn't free to be touched."

She sighed. "Tim and I are not dating. We haven't done more than chat and dance. I was trying to let him down easy without the whole 'you're a great guy, but—' routine. I thought another guy was the easiest way."

"Especially if the other guy ruined you for all other men. Who can argue with that?"

Her eyes widened and she blushed again, but then she laughed. "That's what I thought. Ruined is ruined, after all."

He'd love to be the one to ruin her.

The thought snuck up on him, and Ryan had to take a quick breath before saying casually, "Clearly he's a little more into you than you thought."

She shrugged and gave him a small smile. "The one time I think 'what would Emma do?' and I end up with an honest-to-goodness nice guy. Figures."

"What does 'what would Emma do' mean?" Ryan asked.

Amanda laughed softly. "Well, I guess what *wouldn't* Emma do might be more accurate. As you know."

Ah, and there was the jab about him and her little sister. He'd been expecting it.

Okay, maybe she had a point. Emma was a bit notorious and yeah, okay, Ryan knew Emma's naughty side personally. Still...

"Why are you thinking about what Emma would do or not do when it comes to Winters?"

"He's been flirting with me and he's good-looking, so when he asked me to dance, I thought 'what would Emma do?' Emma's never turned down a dance with a cute guy. Ever."

"Why are you doing things just because Emma would do them?" Though knowing what kind of things Emma would do, the idea sounded pretty good to him. He'd love to see Amanda in some skimpy lingerie. Or do some role-playing with her. His gut tightened and his palms itched. Oh, yeah. They'd start with the pirate and his slave girl.

"Let me ask *you* a question," Amanda said instead of answering his question. "Is Emma sexy?"

Ryan was pretty sure he was going to get himself into trouble, but he answered, "Yes."

"You notice her as soon as she walks into a room?"

Well, not *just* him but... "Yes."

"And she's fun? Someone people want to spend time with, someone people look forward to seeing?"

Ryan felt like he was even closer to screwing up as he nodded. "Yes. Emma's...Emma."

Amanda didn't look insulted. "Exactly. Emma is Emma. She's the girl all the guys want to be with and all the girls want to be." She swallowed hard and crossed her arms. "Even me."

Ryan felt a kick in his gut. "Emma also drives a lot of people crazy."

Amanda nodded. "I know. I'm at the top of that list. But there's no denying that Emma has a lot of fun. She's sexy, and people want to be around her, people pay attention to her—who wouldn't want to be her? Or like her? Even if just for a little bit?"

"Okay, I'll grant you all of that. So, you thought you'd flirt and dance a little, but Tim took it the wrong way."

"Right."

"And when you had to let him down you thought 'what would Emma do?'"

"Something like that."

"And you picked me because?"

"Because you're..." She trailed off and her cheeks got even redder.

Ryan couldn't help his grin. This he had to hear. "Because I'm...?"

"Something Emma would do."

He couldn't stop the laugh that escaped. No one could

really argue with that, he supposed.

Amanda wet her bottom lip and looked up at him and said softly, "Sorry."

He didn't want an apology. He didn't want her to be sorry for having the idea of the two of them burning up the sheets one night. He wanted her to keep that idea firmly in mind, in fact.

But Winters had mentioned something that Emma wouldn't do—he'd said Amanda had fallen in love with Ryan.

"Did you tell him it was a one-night stand?"

He liked the idea that she would think he was so amazing that one night would cause her to be head over heels. Even if it was only in her imagination.

Amanda took a deep breath. "Yes, just one night."

Ryan moved in closer, wanting her full attention on him. "Okay. Make it up to me."

"How?"

"Give me that night."

"What night?" she asked carefully.

"The one we allegedly had. And whatever it was that ruined you for all other men."

Amanda stared at him as if he were crazy. Which he probably was. She'd made up a fling. It was simple and innocent—mostly—and nothing he really needed to worry about. Winters had slugged him and gotten it out of his system. It was probably over. And if it wasn't, Amanda had plenty of people—including him—who would step in to dissuade Tim from trying to win her over. It wouldn't require any of them pretending to be her lover.

But Ryan didn't want it to be that simple. Obviously.

"What do you mean?" she finally asked.

"I mean, I got hit for this. I think it's only fair I get to actually do whatever it is that I got hit for."

"He thinks we..." She frowned. "You know what he thinks."

"He thinks we slept together."

She nodded.

"That's what I want."

He could see her fingers digging into her arms where she had them crossed. "Basically, you want me to sleep with you to make up for the fact that you got hit."

"Seems like the decent thing to do." He fought his grin at her outrage.

"What's *decent* about that?"

He leaned in closer. "Apparently it's something that's occurred to you as a possibility. I came to mind when you needed someone to have an imaginary fling with."

She opened her mouth, then snapped it shut. "It was subconscious," she mumbled.

"Even better. Subconscious desires say a lot about how you really feel." Oh, this was fun.

"I can't sleep with a guy who's slept with my sister."

"Good thing I haven't then."

She arched an eyebrow. "You are aware that *Emma* is my sister, right?"

He grinned. "Very aware, actually. And your sister and I have done some heavy-duty flirting, we've kissed and we went skinny-dipping one night. But that's it."

Amanda looked seriously shocked. "What?"

"Skinny-dipping. I've seen her naked," he admitted. "But there was no sex."

"You expect me to believe that *you* and *Emma* got naked together but didn't have sex."

Ryan lifted a shoulder. "Yeah."

"But..." She glanced toward the table where her sister Isabelle had joined Olivia and Emma. She looked up at him. "Really?"

"Really."

"So..." She trailed off, seemingly still processing the information about him and Emma.

He knew most people thought they'd had a one-night

stand. They let them think it because it drove Conner crazy.

Ryan tucked a hand in his front pocket. "So...a guy you're obviously attracted to is asking you to spend a hot night with him having the best sex of your life. There's only one question you should be asking."

She sucked in a quick breath.

"Come on, Mandi, ask me what the question is." She wanted to, he could tell. He also liked the way her eyes widened slightly at the nickname he'd just given her. No one called her anything but Amanda, or Dr. Dixon.

He waited. He'd wait all night for her.

Finally, she said, "What question should I be asking?"

He grinned. "What would Emma do?"

Amanda groaned. They both knew the answer to that question. Emma would jump in with both feet and big old loud *yee-haw*.

Oh, boy.

But worse—it didn't matter that Emma would definitely do it. Amanda wanted to do it, and it had nothing to do with Emma.

"What are you suggesting, *exactly*?" she asked.

Ryan grinned and she knew she was in trouble. She'd basically just admitted that she was interested. A firm "hell no", maybe punctuated by a good scowl, would have possibly talked him out of it. But she hadn't done any of that.

"You, me, some whipped cream and twenty-four uninterrupted hours."

Yep. That sounded just about perfect.

"Only twenty-four?"

In a blink, Ryan's grin dropped and was replaced by a hot, hungry look. "I'll give you twenty-four *days* if you want them."

She was very afraid that she did. She swallowed hard. "That's a lot of whipped cream."

"Yeah. We'll probably have to use some chocolate syrup and some marshmallow cream too."

Amanda fought the smile...and the "yes, now, let's go" that threatened. "Marshmallow cream?"

"Ever tried it?"

"For sex? No."

"You'll never want it on ice cream again."

"Well, that will save me a ton of calories."

"And, trust me, you'll be burning up a bunch too."

"Then how can I say no?"

Nothing bad would happen. It was Ryan. He was dangerous in a sexy, he-can-make-me-do-anything-he-wants way, and there was, of course, that risk of him ruining her for all other men. And she wouldn't have to worry about embarrassing herself or anyone else. Ryan would be discreet. In fact, her brother was the last person who'd ever find out about anything between her and Ryan. Ryan wouldn't risk telling Conner he'd hooked up with *another* of Conner's sisters. No way.

Ryan took a deep breath and shook his head. "I can't believe I just made a date for sex with Amanda Dixon."

"Did we set a date?"

"How's right now?"

Right now sounded pretty great, actually. And it might be a good idea not to think about this too hard or too long. "I happen to have the next twenty-four hours free." That was true only since Olivia had announced her birthday wish, but, well, if Emma was going to take care of the rest of Amanda's to-do list, then Ryan was the only thing she needed to do.

Ryan lifted a hand to her face, running his thumb over her cheek, staring at her.

"What?" she finally asked, the heat from his touch radiating through her body—though some parts warmed more than others.

"I'm just mapping out in my mind how to see, touch and taste as much of you as possible all at one time."

Tingles exploded through her body. Oh boy. He was *such* a good choice if she only had one wild weekend. And he hadn't slept with Emma. That was...amazing. Amanda sucked in a quick breath and licked her lips. She didn't intend for it to be seductive, but judging by the look on Ryan's face, it was anyway.

It was that look, that combination of fascination and heat, that made something click deep inside her. This was her one weekend, the one chance to let it all go, to do a few—okay, as many as possible—of the things that made her envy Emma. And this was the perfect guy. She could trust him. And there was no denying the attraction.

What would Emma do? She'd make every minute really count.

"I changed my mind," she said.

Ryan frowned. "No way. That's not an option."

She smiled. His eagerness made every ounce of feminine power that she possessed flare to life. "Oh, I promise to make it up to you," she said. "All I want it a chance to figure out which things on my list we can get to in twenty-four hours. And what supplies I need to bring."

He moved in a little closer, the heat from his body touching her from head to toe. "What kind of things?"

"Well, just because I don't flaunt it all over doesn't mean I don't have some...*needs.*"

"Say fantasies," he urged in a husky voice. "Please call them fantasies."

"They're fantasies," she agreed. "But there's a bunch."

She had a feeling she was going to spend the next few hours worked up over all of this. She wouldn't mind if Ryan spent some time thinking about it as well.

"Such as?" he asked.

"I think it will be more fun if you wait and find out. But here's the thing with this weekend. I want to be in charge. I don't do this kind of stuff, ever. So if I only have one night, then

I want to make the most of it."

Ryan's indrawn breath was a little shaky. She *loved* that. This guy could have any girl do anything for him, but he was turned on by *her*. And this was only the beginning.

This was supposed to be Olivia's birthday. So why did Amanda feel like her sister had given *her* the gift?

Ryan stared at the woman in front of him. Was this a dream? God, if it was he hoped it was recurring. Forever.

Amanda looked up at him, a sexy smile curling one corner of her mouth. "Will you agree to some rules?"

Rules. Hmm. That was a new one. But he said, "Like what?" instead of no.

"Like, my brother can't find out about this."

That was a good one. Ryan loved giving Conner a hard time about his fling with Emma, but that was...different. Somehow. This was going to be a fling too. Not even. Just one night. But this was Amanda. He had a feeling Conner would actually hit him for this, where he'd only threatened to with Emma.

"Okay," he agreed, somehow moving his hand from her face. He wanted to keep on touching her. And keep on and keep on. His whole body felt strung tight with the idea that he'd soon have Amanda Dixon in his bed. Even if it was only one night, it was going to be something.

"And we'll spend the weekend at a hotel. That way no one's going to accidentally show up and find out. And so we won't be uncomfortable at each other's apartment when this is over."

Ryan wasn't worried about being uncomfortable around Amanda afterward because, well, he didn't do that. If a woman ended things with him, he moved on. It was easy. As soon as one person was done—for whatever reason—then they were done. There were no hard feelings, there were no screaming matches, there was no begging to give it one more try. If he'd liked a woman enough to spend time with her and sleep with her more than once, then he figured there was a good chance he'd still like her after that was over, so he stayed friends with all of his ex-girlfriends. But if the relationship was over, Ryan figured it had run its course and that was that.

But he'd agree to anything to have her.

"I'll do this wherever you want to," he told her honestly. He didn't really care what bed he had her in, as long as it was sturdy. He had a few fantasies himself.

"Great. So, I'll get the hotel room and figure out what all I want to do."

She gave him another sexy smile and Ryan wondered if she had any idea how much those affected him. He didn't care what she wanted to do--he was up for it.

"Then I'll text you the hotel and room number and meet you there tomorrow at...nine?" she asked. "That gives us until nine on Sunday."

That wasn't going to be enough time. That was all Ryan could really concentrate on. He was going to have Amanda all to himself for twenty-four hours, specifically for the purpose of being naked the entire time, and it simply wasn't going to be enough time. How he knew that already was beyond him, but he *knew* it.

Ryan looked at his watch. "That's a long time from now."

"Well, you should probably go home and get some sleep," she said. "And hydrate. And stretch."

He knew he was staring, could feel that his mouth was actually hanging open, but...holy shit. "What can I do to get twenty-four more hours?" he asked.

She grinned. "That's the nicest thing anyone's said to me in a long time."

But she didn't answer the question.

So Ryan decided to show her a little bit of why she might want to expand their timeline.

He cupped the back of her head and pulled her in for a kiss. She was clearly surprised at first, but as he pulled her hips against his and tipped his head, her hands went from his chest to the back of his neck, and she stretched up on tiptoe to meet his lips more fully.

He ran his tongue along her bottom lip, and her little whimper was enough to make him part his lips and go deeper. She opened willingly for him and his tongue stroked hers as possessiveness flashed through him. This was all his. Whatever she wanted this weekend, whatever she had planned, it was all his.

Ryan slid his fingers into her hair, the warm, silky mass making his hand ache with the need to slide it over all the warm, silky parts of her.

Amanda gripped the front of his shirt and arched closer. Ryan moved a hand to the sweet curve of her ass and brought her against his fly. He needed her with an intensity, and a suddenness, that stunned him.

Amanda ripped her mouth from his, breathing hard. "Ryan."

He didn't let her move back when she tried. "Let's start the time now."

She stared at him and pressed her lips together. "There's..." She had to stop, breathe and start again. "I'm not ready."

She'd felt damned ready when she opened her mouth, moved against him and groaned. He grinned. "You sure?"

She took another deep breath. "I'm *ready*, but...I have a lot I want to do in those few hours. I don't want to go in unprepared."

"I told you I'd give you more than that. You can have days. As many as you want."

She shook her head and pulled back, and this time he did let her go. "One will be more than enough."

Ryan's eyebrows shot up at that. Was that right? Well, he might just have to work on proving Miss Amanda wrong on that one.

She glanced around. "And we've been noticed."

Ryan followed her gaze. The guys who'd been sitting with her brother were still there, but Dooley Miller had moved to block Conner's view of the corner, and as Conner tried to stand—which would have definitely given him an eyeful of one of his best friends and his sister—Mac Gordon clamped a hand on Conner's shoulder, pushed him back into the chair and signaled the waitress. Sam Bradford then made a production of moving his chair in closer to Conner and seemed to be confiding something very important, taking Conner's full attention.

Ryan grinned. Looked like he owed some guys some beer.

"Those guys are cool," he told Amanda. "Mac got involved with Sam's little sister. They know what's going on and they won't say anything."

She moved back. "I don't want anyone having to run interference," she said. "This is going to be the best night I've had in a really long time. But it's one night, and no one's going to end up upset, embarrassed...or worse by it. Okay?"

Ryan frowned. What the hell did that mean? "Why would anyone end up upset, embarrassed or worse?"

"I need to know that whatever happens, it's just you and me. Okay?" she asked again.

He had a feeling he was missing something here, but the whole best-night-I've-had-in-a-long-time bit made him nod. "Of course." Whatever Amanda wanted, he would give, for as long as she wanted him to give it.

Her smile was bright and she gave him a final quick kiss. "Thank you, Ryan. I can't wait."

He watched her head back for the table with her sisters, grab her purse, say something that made three pairs of beautiful eyebrows rise, then turn to go.

Anticipation tightened his gut as the door bumped shut behind her. Screw the best night in a long time. It'd be the best night of her life. He'd make sure of it.

It had been a long time since she'd been *out* like this, but skimpy dresses and killer shoes never went out of style. Mostly because no one paid that much attention to the outfit when there was that much skin showing. Amanda turned in front of the mirror. The dress was jade green and clung in all the right places. She'd put her hair up in a sexy twist, then taken it down, then put it up again. Well, if it was up to start with, she could always take it down later.

She practiced in her heels for a few minutes on the tile in the bathroom. The dance floor would probably be even slicker, but hopefully she'd have someone to hold on to.

Like Ryan.

Amanda stopped and pressed her hands to her stomach, breathing in and out.

Yeah, Ryan.

She was definitely going to be holding on to Ryan. For dear life.

They were going to spend the night together. One hot, sexy night in this very hotel room. And she was definitely ready for it. She'd been ready since last night when he'd kissed her.

Even now she felt a flush wash over her body.

Wow, that guy could kiss. She couldn't wait to see what else he could do.

But before that, she needed to live it up, throw caution to the wind, do all those things she'd been repressing for a long time now. Ryan was her chance for really letting go and having Emma-type fun. And, after all, she'd promised Olivia.

Besides, what she had planned for the night would very nicely combine some fun and crazy with getting up against Ryan as much as possible. He was the one guy she knew for sure would have no problem going to the club, Frigid, with her, and once there, he was the only one she was going to let get close.

Well, that probably wasn't entirely true. At Frigid there was close, too close and *way* too close. Ryan was the only one getting way too close. But there was a wide spectrum of activities between walking in the door and way too close.

Feeling a flutter of excitement in her stomach, Amanda looked at the clock. Half an hour before Ryan was supposed to be here. Damn. She was ready now. Really ready. Beyond ready.

She grabbed her purse and headed for the lobby. She'd meet him down there. They could get going sooner, and getting him away from the huge bed in the ritzy room she'd reserved for the night was a good idea—if she actually wanted to go out tonight.

Which she did.

The elevator arrived and she started to step on but happened to glance at the two passengers already inside. They were both older gentlemen, easily in the seventies, and their eyes were wide, their mouths open.

She looked down. And giggled. Yeah, this dress was made to get exactly that reaction. But she didn't want to be responsible for any cardiac emergencies.

"I'll catch the next one," she said, stepping back.

"Oh, no," one of the men protested, lunging to put his hand against the elevator door before it could close. "There's plenty of room."

She grinned. "I appreciate it. But there's a little draft. I think I need a coat."

"It's eighty degrees outside," the other man said.

"I think I'm a bit conspicuous," she said, appreciating their enthusiasm but definitely feeling a niggle of doubt about her plans for the night. Dammit. She didn't want any doubts.

"A girl doesn't buy a dress like that if she doesn't want to be conspicuous," one of the men said with a wink.

"Right. I definitely need a coat." She waved at them as the elevator door swished shut and they headed for the lobby.

But she didn't have a coat.

As they said, it was eighty degrees outside. Why would she have a coat?

Dammit. She couldn't very well sit in the lobby of the Britton Hotel in this skimpy thing. And the more she thought about it, the more sure she was that she couldn't meet Ryan in her room—their room. They'd never make it out. And she needed this night out.

She let herself back into the room and grabbed the bathrobe from the back of the bathroom door. It wasn't fashionable, but it would cover her while in the lobby.

She stepped off the elevator in the lobby and started for the couches that were clustered near the front doors.

"Amanda?"

She turned, and nearly slipped on her heels on the polished marble floor.

Ryan's hands caught her by the elbows before she went down.

When she looked up he was grinning down at her. "Love the bathrobe. But with that hair and makeup, I'm not gonna believe you're just out of the shower."

He set her back on her feet.

Being this close to him made her hot all over. In fact, way too hot for the bathrobe.

She stepped back and shed the robe.

Ryan's reaction was better than the guys on the elevator.

Because along with the wide eyes and the gaping mouth, there was a heat in his eyes that made her catch her breath.

"What the..." His gaze roamed over her from head to toe and back again. Twice. The second time slower. "Not that I'm complainin', but honey, you went to a lot of work considering I'm gonna be messing you up real soon."

Desire flashed through her. Yep, not meeting him at the room had been a really good idea.

"Later." She grabbed his hand. "Let's go have some fun."

"Uh." Ryan didn't move as she started for the doors. "Fun's exactly what I have in mind."

She looked back at him. He honestly looked confused. She

turned to face him. "Fun like dancing and drinking and making out?"

"Fun like stripping you out of that thing and licking you from toes to nose."

That wave of heat rippled through her again. They were going to do that. Exactly that. But later.

"We're so on the same page there, Ryan."

"Well, the licking is best done on a horizontal surface, preferably one with feather pillows and maid service to worry about cleaning up the whipped cream."

She smiled in spite of suddenly wanting to do some licking of her own. "That is the plan. I swear."

"Then let's go this way." He inclined his head toward the elevators and tugged on her hand.

"Ryan, we'll never leave if we go up there now."

"That's kind of the idea." He frowned. "Isn't it?"

"Well, yeah, after we go out." She frowned too. Why was he frowning?

"Go out? Go out where?"

She frowned harder. "Out. Anywhere fun. I thought maybe we'd go to Frigid."

"*Frigid*?" he repeated. "Are you kidding?"

"No." She stepped close. "Ryan, this is my night to be wild, to do all the things that make my blood hot and my heart pound. You are on that list too, trust me. But I have twenty-four hours and I want to live it up."

"At Frigid?"

"To start."

Frigid was hands-down the hottest club in the city. And it didn't get its reputation from the music, the drinks or the people who showed up. Sure, you could just drink and dance. That was fine. No one would question or pressure you to do anything more. But it was also perfectly acceptable to make out with a total stranger—or two—in the middle of the dance floor. Or lose your top on one of the couches that encircled the dance floor. Or give someone a blow job on the upper balcony. Or head all the way upstairs, grab a condom or two or three from the bowl inside the door, and find the nearest naked body. You didn't have to have sex there, but everything went, nothing was off limits and you were guaranteed to get an eyeful no matter what *you* chose to do while inside.

What happened at Frigid stayed at Frigid. And just about everything happened there.

"Have you ever been to Frigid?" Ryan asked, still clearly stunned by her request.

"Yeah, once," she admitted.

It had been when the club first opened and Emma had more or less blackmailed her into going. She'd been propositioned several times and had actually been talked into some dirty dancing, but that was as far as she went. She suspected Emma had made it to the second balcony while Amanda was sandwiched between two hot guys looking for a threesome for the night, but she'd never asked and Emma hadn't volunteered the information.

They'd both made it out still wearing all the clothes they'd worn in, so Amanda counted it as a success. But she hadn't been back since.

"You've been there, haven't you?" she asked. She really wanted him to say yes, she realized. She had an image of Ryan as the wild party guy who would try anything—and had. That was who she was counting on being there with her tonight. She'd heard the rumors about Ryan and his numerous girlfriends. She'd certainly seen him in action with women at Trudy's on more than one occasion. But she knew how stories could get blown up and tales could get taller the more they were told.

Dammit.

That hadn't even occurred to her. She needed the Ryan from her dirty dreams. He *had* to be that guy.

"Please," she said, slapping her hand over his mouth before he could speak. "Please tell me you've been there. I need a wild night out. I do. I *really* need it. And I need someone who can be there with me, keep up and keep me from doing anything I'll regret in the morning. Please tell me that's you."

If it wasn't, she had no idea who she would call.

No one. There was no one else she could go out with like this. It had to be someone who wouldn't be scandalized, who wouldn't try to talk her out of it, who wouldn't judge...

Ryan pulled her hand from his mouth. "I've been there," he said, looking directly into her eyes. "I can keep up. I can do whatever you need me to do." He said it with a strange intensity that made her feel tingly. Then he pulled her closer. "I'm just gonna need to know exactly what it is that you want."

"You. Right there with me. I want to do shots, but I need someone to make sure I can get home if I have too many. I want to dance and flirt and have hands all over me, and feel sexy and hot and in charge. But I need someone to make sure that it doesn't go any farther. I need to know that you're the only one who's going to touch me under this dress. You're the only one who's going to need a condom with me tonight."

Ryan's voice was low and firm when he said, "I can *guaran-fucking-tee* that no one else is going to need a condom with you tonight."

She stared up at him. He made her feel safe. At the same time she wanted to let him know she wasn't wearing any panties. Wow. This was going to be...interesting. And perfect.

"Thank you," she whispered. Then she leaned in and pressed a kiss to his lips. Her three-inch heels put her closer to his mouth than last night, and she knew that she was going to be taking advantage of that a lot in the next few hours.

He put a big hand on the back of her neck as she attempted to pull back, and kept her still while he prolonged the kiss, then urged her lips open and swept his tongue along hers in an erotic, possessive gesture.

When the kiss broke, it was only because Ryan let it.

She tried to steady her heart rate. And her balance on her heels. "A couple other rules for tonight," she said, her voice husky.

"Yeah?"

"I don't want you putting your hands under anyone else's dress or using a condom with anyone else for tonight. Is that okay?"

His hand was still on the back of her neck, and he held her motionless as he leaned forward and rested his forehead against hers. "Are you asking me if it's okay that you want to be the only one to fuck me tonight?"

Her bones melted a little.

"Yeah, Mandi, that's okay. That's absolutely okay."

Well, then. Great. They were on the same page.

And their room was right upstairs. A short elevator ride to the twenty-first floor.

"Maybe we don't need to go—"

But that was as far as she got before Ryan straightened, took her hand and started for the doors.

"Oh, we're going," he said as she tripped after him on her high heels. "This is something I've *got* to see now."

Adrenaline surged and Amanda felt goose bumps erupt all over her body.

Happy birthday, Olivia, she thought. You are a very, very good sister.

Chapter Three

He was her fucking babysitter.

Ryan sat at the bar at Frigid—of all the fucking places—and watched Amanda dance.

She hadn't sat for more than two minutes since they'd walked in the door.

Which didn't surprise him one damned bit. She was easily the most beautiful woman there. Sure, she wore a green dress that hit above midthigh, left her stomach bare and plunged low in back—too low for her to be wearing a bra. But she didn't look slutty. She looked like…sex. That was all he could think as the silky material glided over her body as she moved. The silk caressed her hips, cupped her ass, clung to her breasts and shimmered as she swiveled to the music.

It also shimmered when people ran their hands over it.

And lots of people were doing a lot of that.

A person didn't come to Frigid—or at least they didn't stay once they found out what the place was all about—if they didn't want to be touched. Touching was not only accepted, it was encouraged. The seats at the bar were for those who liked to watch, but the dance floor was all about touching. And rubbing. It was for introductions, foreplay, working up to the other levels. The couches around the dance floor were for the exhibitionists. The couches in the dark corners were for a bit more privacy—and more nudity. As you moved up the levels of the club, things got wilder.

He'd never been to the fourth level and didn't know anyone who had. But he'd heard. He liked some of the level-four activities, but preferred to have them in his own condo and bed.

The gorgeous woman who had claimed Amanda four songs

ago pressed against her from behind, nudging her forward into the guy who had joined them for the past two songs. The man's hands settled on her hips, rubbing up and down enough to lift her skirt into scandalous territory while the woman's hands came around and cupped her breasts.

Amanda sure didn't push them away. She let her head fall back and the man kissed her throat, then her collarbone, then her lips. Their hips continued to move in rhythm and Ryan clenched his beer bottle tighter. Amanda was into this. He couldn't believe it. And it was hot. That he could believe. Watching her let her sexy side out was a true pleasure. A tighter-in-his-jeans, almost-couldn't-breathe pleasure.

Watching her do it with someone else was torturous.

But that wasn't going to last much longer. She'd had plenty of foreplay and Ryan knew that her partners were keeping track too. Rarely did anyone dance all night. Not someone who danced like Amanda was. She was letting them touch her, press against her, say who-knew-what to her. And she was clearly loving all of it. Pretty soon the brunette and her guy were going to want to move things to the couch.

Amanda's rule was no one but him under her dress. Which he was more than okay with. He was fighting to keep his ass on his barstool even as she swayed her hips in an upright position fully covered. Or as covered as that dress would allow her to be.

The only thing that kept him from storming onto that floor and hauling her out of here—or to level two or three—was that she was so damned hot. And it was how much she was enjoying it that added to the heat.

Amanda was into every bit of this. Including the two shots she'd had at the bar before hitting the dance floor, the two the brunette had bought her and the one she'd tipped back when she'd taken her one and only break to come to the bar, give him a smile that said she was having the time of her life, kiss him—hot and long and tasting like the raspberry liqueur in her shot—and then head back to the dance floor.

So far he'd resisted joining her. For one thing, watching her was good. Really good. But also because, if he went out there and started touching her himself, it wouldn't end until she was spread out on the nearest firm surface. Just him and her. One thing was certain—he wasn't inviting anyone else. Not even the stunning brunette who had clearly claimed Amanda for herself.

With anyone else, he'd definitely consider it. The shorter woman was sexy and obviously into this whole the-more-the-merrier scene.

But he didn't want to share Amanda.

It was strange and he chose not to dwell on that confusing and unexpected thought. He didn't want to share her. Period.

So he didn't join her dancing. Yet. She was having a great time and nothing had happened yet to risk that. Her dance partners were sexy and hot, clearly making Amanda feel the same way, but they hadn't broken any of Amanda's rules.

Just then the man's hand drifted to the bare skin of Amanda's outer thigh before sliding higher, definitely under the edge of her skirt, heading for the back of her leg and up to her buttock.

Thank God.

That was Ryan's cue.

He was by her side in five strides. He grasped the other man's arm. "This is where I come in."

The guy looked up, clearly read Ryan's claim in his eyes, and took his hand from Amanda's leg. "Damn," was all he said, but he moved off to another dancing pair. Whatever he wanted that night, he'd be able to find.

Amanda smiled up at Ryan and he leaned in to kiss her. He held her face in both hands and moved his mouth over hers soft and thoroughly, making sure anyone looking on would know that she was his.

But the brunette wasn't ready to give Amanda up. She reached out and ran a hand up and over Ryan's chest. "Ooh, now this is going to be fun."

He pulled away from Amanda's mouth and looked over her

shoulder at the other woman. "I'll take that as a compliment."

"Oh, you should." She licked her lips and curled her fingers into his pec. "And so you know, you can have me, but I get her first."

Ryan looked into the woman's big brown eyes. She was gorgeous. And any other time, any other guy would have had a raging hard-on from simply looking at her, not to mention her offer.

But his eyes immediately went back to the blond between them. *She* was the one he wanted. She was the reason he was aching.

"I'm not sharing her."

The brunette narrowed her eyes and her fingernails dug in a little. "Then maybe you need to move on."

He gave her a little smile. "I don't think so."

The woman's other hand rested on Amanda's waist. She moved to stroke across Amanda's stomach. "I don't think it's up to you," she told Ryan.

Ryan had to admit that the sight of one beautiful woman touching another was provocative. But the thought that wouldn't leave him was that all that smooth, tanned skin should be under his mouth, not under another woman's hand.

He moved in even closer, his hand going to Amanda's hip. He rubbed over the silky material and looked into her eyes. Okay, the hot girl had a point. "What do you think, Mandi? You want this gorgeous girl all over you?"

She gave him a sexy smile. "Kind of."

He raised an eyebrow. *Kind of.* Okay. And he still wasn't sharing her.

"If you hadn't had four shots and told me to be sure you don't do anything too crazy, I might go for that." Or maybe *he* was crazy for not going for it anyway. "But I think you're stuck with me."

"I had five shots," she said with a smile. "You need to keep better track." Then she turned to face the brunette. She cupped the back of the woman's head and brought her close to whisper in her ear.

The woman was still breathing hard when she looked at Ryan. "You sure?"

"Completely."

"He's got what you need?"

"Definitely."

Damn right he did.

The woman nodded. Then leaned in and kissed Amanda before stepping back. "You better," she said to Ryan.

He watched her walk away, then looked down at Amanda. "Now what?"

"I need your hands on me."

His thoughts exactly. "We could—"

But she was already tugging him toward the couches in one of the corners. It wasn't right on the dance floor, but it was hardly as private as their hotel room would have been.

"I have some big plans for this touching," he said as she pushed him to sit on the middle cushion. "We might be better off at the hotel."

"Can't wait that long." Amanda straddled his thighs and leaned in to kiss him again. The position pulled her skirt up, and he immediately cupped her butt in his hands to block anyone else's view. And because he couldn't help it.

His hands met bare skin and he was lost. In her kiss. In the smell of her, the feel of her, her heat. All of it wrapped around him and fueled a number of fantasies he either had only imagined subconsciously or that had only now materialized. Either way, he wanted her, over and over again, in every position there was.

"Touch me," she murmured against his lips. "I'm burning up."

He knew, in the back of his mind, that he wasn't the sole reason for her burning, but at the moment, with her tongue stroking his, he couldn't really work up any protest.

He slid his hands forward on the smooth skin of the back of her thighs and moved his mouth to her neck. He didn't want her mouth to be too busy to gasp his name, after all.

He caressed from the curve of her ass to just inside her thighs, making himself go slow.

She wiggled against him. "Here too." She leaned back slightly and his fingers made contact with hot, wet skin. Bare skin. No soft curls. Just bare skin.

"Jesus, Amanda," he groaned.

"I need you, Ryan. I need something. Make this ache go away."

But it wasn't going to go away. It was about to get much worse.

His fingers glided forward to meet her slick clit. His thumb circled, as his middle finger pressed into the wet heat that showed exactly how into all of this she was.

She gripped the hair at the back of his head, arching closer, gasping and moving against his hand. "Yes. Ryan."

He stroked deep and looked up into her face. God, she was something. And she could easily reach down, undo his fly, and they could finish this right here and now. But before he could say a word, the brunette from before materialized behind Amanda. She gathered Amanda's hair up in one hand, tipped her head back and kissed her, cupping Amanda's breast.

Ryan felt Amanda's inner muscles clamp down again and he was at war with himself. He could move his hand, pick her up and get her out of here. But she was clearly enjoying herself. A lot. He moved his finger in and out again, feeling the ripples of pleasure the movement created.

"Damn, you are good together," the brunette said, lifting her head. "I'm all in."

Before he knew what she was doing, Amanda lifted herself from his lap. And his hand. "Mand—"

The brunette took her place. "I'm Jennifer."

"I, uh..." He looked at Amanda, who had climbed up on the

cushion next to him, her knees under her.

"Go ahead," she said with a smile. "It's okay."

What was okay? What the hell? Hands on Jennifer's waist, he started to lift her off of him. "No. We're good. Let's go."

"Come on, Ryan. It's okay. I want you to have fun too."

He stared at her. What the fuck was that supposed to mean? "There are about thirty ways I can think of to have fun right now and none of them involve Jennifer."

Amanda rubbed her hand over his chest. "Come on, Ryan. It's fun. It doesn't mean anything. We're just messing around. I figured you'd go for this."

He would. Typically. And he hated that that was why she had him here with her.

Jennifer's hands were busy against his fly. She rubbed up and down the length of his erection—the erection that was all about Amanda—and he resisted the urge to dump her on her ass on the floor. He did, however, toss her, fairly gently, to the other couch cushion.

He stood and rezipped. "No," was all he said when Amanda opened her mouth.

She frowned and scrambled to stand as well. "I'm trying here, Ryan. This isn't enough? What do you want? To go to the balcony?"

He scowled at her. "I didn't even want to come over *here*."

"Did Emma go straight to the third level?"

He stared at her. Had she just mentioned her sister? *Now*?

He couldn't even speak. He took her upper arm and started for the door.

They were out on the sidewalk, several paces from the front of Frigid, before he dropped his hold and shoved his hands into his back pockets. He wanted to yell. And he *never* wanted to yell. If there was yelling to be done at work, Conner took care of it. And if there was yelling that needed to be done on the football field, Shane, Cody and Conner were well ahead of him and Nate.

But he really wanted to yell right now.

"What is going on?" Amanda asked him, hands on her hips.

He wasn't going to yell. This was Amanda Dixon. This was Conner's sister. He was not going to swear either. Then he looked at her haughty stance and the look of affront on her face and decided that, on second thought, he probably was going to swear.

He advanced on her, backed her up against the hot bricks of Frigid, and slapped his hands onto the wall on either side of her head. "What does all of this have to do with Emma?"

Amanda's eyes narrowed. "Why are you so pissed?"

"Just what the *fuck* do you think happened between me and Emma?"

"Emma said she and a friend came to Frigid one night. I assumed it was you considering it's—" She gestured at the building "—you know."

"A place where anything goes and people can get kinky?"

She nodded.

Ryan gritted his teeth. "I didn't know Emma had ever been to Frigid."

Amanda's eyes widened. "Does that bother you?"

"What?"

"That Emma might have come here with someone else?"

He frowned. "Why would I care if Emma came to Frigid with someone else?"

She frowned too. "Why are you mad that I thought you and Emma came to Frigid together?"

"Why are you so determined to paint me and Emma as nymphomaniacs?"

Amanda looked surprised at that. "I don't mean to paint you as anything. You're just both so...free and daring."

He looked into her eyes for a long moment. She was sincere in that she hadn't been trying to insult him or her sister. But she really did think of him and Emma as wild and, apparently, without boundaries.

He pushed himself away from the wall and took a deep breath. "I'm going to say this once, Amanda and you're going to remember it. You listening?"

She nodded, her back still pressed against the bricks.

"Your sister and I were messing around one night and we lost our clothes and we kissed. Actually, we kissed, *then* we lost our clothes. Then we went skinny dipping. It was nothing more, nothing less. We've let everyone believe it was more than that because it's fun to rile your brother, but it was just *swimming.* That said, your sister is a sweet woman who has more going for her than a smokin' bod. I think if you really want to do everything Emma would do, you might be surprised where that lands you. And I'm not talking about inside Frigid."

Amanda was staring at him, her hands flat on the wall behind her, her breathing ragged. "You're...you're defending my sister."

"Damn right I am. And myself, by the way. Yeah, I like to have a good time and yeah, I've been to Frigid before and had some fun. But that doesn't mean that's what I want from you."

She was still staring at him.

"What?"

"I... How can you defending my sister to me be hot?"

He started to reply, then shut his mouth. She found him defending Emma hot? "Seriously?"

She lifted a shoulder. "Emma's made a name for herself and most of the time I agree she deserves it, but I still worry about her. Knowing that a hot guy took time to see past all of her..."

"Curves?" Ryan suggested.

Amanda narrowed her eyes. "No. Her..." But again she trailed off.

"Hotness?"

Her eyes narrowed further. "*No.* Her...shenanigans."

Ryan couldn't help it. He snorted. "Yeah, 'shenanigans' was never even on my list of possible words to use."

Amanda's mouth curled slightly. "It's the perfect word for Emma."

He moved close again, now past his urge to yell. "Emma's okay, Amanda. You don't have to worry about her. And you certainly shouldn't measure your own sexiness by her. You've got it all, babe. Doesn't matter who you're next to."

She looked up as he leaned in close. "Are you sure?"

He ran his hand from her waist, over her hip, to the bare skin of her thigh. "Absolutely sure."

"I mean about Emma being okay?"

He peered closely at her face. She really was sincerely in doubt. "Emma's always gonna land on her feet, Amanda."

"Emma's never been without a safety net to land in."

"How many times have you bailed her out of jail?"

"None," Amanda admitted.

"How many of her unwanted babies are you raising for her?"

"None."

"How many marriages has she broken up?"

"None. That I know of," Amanda added.

Ryan chuckled. "Emma's smart. Yeah, she's got an adventurous streak, but she's not hurting anyone, including herself."

"You sure you're not in love with her?" Amanda asked.

He nodded. "Completely sure."

"Why not? You think she's pretty great, obviously."

"She is pretty great. But Emma and I were seasonal." He took Amanda's hand and started for the car.

"Seasonal?" she repeated. "Like you were only together for Christmas or the springtime?"

He shrugged. "Kind of. My mom always told me that people come into your life for different reasons. Some are forever, but those are rare. Most people are seasonal—they're with you for a reason and when that reason is fulfilled, they move on."

Amanda didn't say a word as he held the car door open for

her and she got in. But once he was settled behind the wheel, she said, "And Emma's reason in your life was sex?"

He shook his head, pulling into traffic as he tried to explain this. "Emma was in my life to get me back in a swimming pool and, I think, to intrigue *you* into choosing me as your one-night stand to get rid of Tim."

She pivoted in her seat, and he was sure she was going to ask what he meant by Emma being in his life to get Amanda there. It sounded fanciful, but that's what happened when you were raised by a gypsy-hippie free spirit. His mother believed there was a reason for everything that happened and that all of those reasons were like threads that, over time, wove together into the pattern of a person's life. Every thread was necessary for the final pattern to be complete.

"Emma got you back in a swimming pool? What do you mean?"

He smiled. Maybe she was cool with his theory that they had been brought together by fate. Or maybe she hadn't really heard that part.

"I've been freaked out about swimming pools since I was fourteen and one of my buddies almost drowned. But Emma got me back in the water."

"How'd she do that?"

"Skinny-dipping."

Amanda swung around to face forward, and he could see in the dashboard lights that she was scowling.

"What's wrong?"

"I thought you just had a whole bunch of hot sex."

"And you're *bothered* that we didn't?"

"Yes." She was scowling at the road again.

"Why?"

"Because..."

But she didn't finish the statement.

"Amanda?"

"That's...not what I expected."

Ooookay. "What's that mean? You didn't expect me and Emma to become friends?"

"I didn't think either of you was really looking for a relationship. Or that you actually *had* a relationship with each other."

"We're friends," Ryan said. "We're also two human beings capable of intelligent thought and actual emotions."

He knew he sounded defensive, but hell, what did she think? That all he was capable of doing was screwing? That the only part of him that Emma might be interested in was below his belt?

Okay, so that had been the part that started it all, but yeah, he could say interesting things from time to time.

"So if everything is so wonderful between you, what happened? Why aren't you still seeing each other?"

Was that a note of jealousy in Amanda's voice? Ryan glanced over at her, but couldn't read her expression. He chose to believe it was jealousy because that made him feel pretty damned good.

"Emma was a lot of work."

She snorted. "No kidding."

He shrugged. "That's Emma. She needs a lot of attention. But I don't like to have to work at things all the time. There's a lot of stress and strife in this world. The people you surround yourself with intentionally, that you care about and share things with, shouldn't be part of that stress."

"You don't want to have to work at a relationship?"

He raised an eyebrow when he glanced at her. "When you say it like that, you make me sound like as ass."

She smiled. "Sorry. But you kind of said that."

"It wasn't the words, it was the tone," he told her with a little chuckle. "But yeah. I mean, if you love people, you want to be around them because they make you feel good and you can be yourself. They shouldn't make you worry constantly or *need* you all the time, right?"

Amanda was frowning when he looked over again. "You're right. I try to keep all of the stress and problems away from Conner because I don't want him to always think we're just a lot of work. If the girls need something, I try to take care of it so that Conner doesn't worry."

Ryan knew that Conner had become a father figure to his sisters after their dad died. Conner still took that role very seriously, according to everything Ryan had ever seen. But yeah, he could see Amanda taking over a lot of responsibilities. Amanda was organized, efficient, confident and poised, and a lot of people found her intimidating.

But not Ryan.

He thought she was...fascinating. She came across as a hardass, but he knew another side of her from Emma. He knew that Amanda had grabbed one of the firemen at Cody's station by the front of the shirt and threatened to make sure he would sing soprano for a month if he didn't stop harassing Olivia. He knew that Amanda collected old books because her father had read the classics to her as a kid and they reminded her of him. And Amanda was the first one Emma called when she was sick. Amanda had met him at the ER in jeans, a ponytail and no makeup when he'd taken Emma in because of a horrible migraine one night after hanging out at the bar.

Amanda Dixon was fascinating to him. He couldn't fully explain it. But he'd really liked seeing her in those jeans.

"Don't you deserve to be worry-free too?" he asked. "Why's it all your problem?"

She pressed her lips together, then turned slightly in her seat to look at him. "I know you think I'm hard on Emma."

Ryan shook his head. "All I know is that tonight you were jumping to a lot of conclusions about her. And me for that matter."

"I'm not a bitch," she said. Then she sighed. "I'm not *trying* to be a bitch. But sometimes it does happen that way."

Ryan couldn't help his little snort.

She scowled at him. "I might have a really good reason, you

know?"

"For assuming the worst about your sister?"

"No, for wanting to protect her. And Isabelle and Olivia. And Conner."

"Protect them from what?" He couldn't pinpoint why exactly, but he felt there was something here he wanted to know about.

"Themselves," Amanda answered. "And each other."

"You're protecting them from each other?" Ryan repeated. "I don't get it."

"I know how easy it is to be overconfident and to think you can handle yourself in a situation only to find out you're way in over your head," she said.

Ryan shook his head. "Babe, I'm still not following."

"Conner's never been anything but solid and dependable and responsible."

"Okay." *Solid and dependable* definitely fit his friend.

"I haven't."

He glanced at her again. "What?"

"I haven't always been solid and dependable and responsible."

That was a tempting statement. It wasn't even the words so much as how she said it. With a bit of hesitation and a hint of remorse. He absolutely wanted to know more.

"You're doing penance then?" he said, trying for a light tone.

"Kind of," she admitted. "And because...I want to save the girls from the embarrassment and guilt. And I don't want to put Conner through that. Again."

Maybe it was the five shots at the bar or the adrenaline or the darkness or that the whole night was way off from her usual world, but Ryan sensed that Amanda wanted to tell him the story.

Or maybe he just *really* wanted her to.

"So what happened?"

She took a deep breath. "When I was twenty, Conner walked in on me half-naked with his high school football coach."

Ryan was grateful for the bright red traffic light. He braked hard and turned to her. "*What*?"

She nodded, looking sheepish. "He was Conner's hero, the man he looked up to most with our dad gone. I was home one weekend to see Olivia perform on the dance team. I was waiting in the hallway outside the locker rooms for her to come out, and Coach walked by. He stopped and flirted, I flirted right back, one thing led to another and I ended up in his office with my top and bra off."

The light turned green, but there were no cars behind them, so Ryan stayed right where he was. "And?" He had to hear this. Holy crap.

"Then I noticed the photo of his *wife* on his desk and I changed my mind. But he wouldn't let me go. He kept talking about the importance of follow-through."

Ryan's grip tightened almost painfully on the steering wheel. "Tell me you took his head off." Amanda wasn't the type of woman to let a guy bully her, but he still itched to smash the man's face.

"I slapped him, but before I could do anything else, Conner walked in. He went to all the games, and he and Coach always sat around and talked afterward."

Ryan's gut churned. Conner had seen his sister in an embarrassing and potentially dangerous situation with the man he most respected. God, how horrible. And how awful for Amanda to be seen like that.

A car horn blared behind them, and Ryan coughed and turned back to driving. Neither of them said anything for several blocks. Finally Ryan said, "Okay, I can see where you're coming from."

"You understand why I'm kind of hard on Emma and how she behaves?"

He lifted a shoulder. "Yeah. But...you can't make Emma

care, Amanda. She has to come to that point by herself. Like you did. I assume you did some other...stuff...that you wouldn't have wanted Conner to know about before that night?"

She crossed her arms, hugging them to her stomach. Ignoring his last comment, she said, "Well, what do I do? Ignore all the stuff they do? Make Conner deal with it? Make him witness his sisters screwing up over and over again? How does that help him? He's already taken on so much and that would make him feel like he failed and..." She trailed off for a moment, then said quietly, "I can't kick them all out of my life because they piss me off and embarrass me."

Ryan shifted on the seat as a realization hit. She was out with him because she was living her sister's life for a night. The life that Amanda generally disapproved of and was embarrassed by. She was doing the things she assumed Emma did, which were the things that Amanda looked down on. And she was doing them with him. She sure wouldn't be proud of any of this in the morning.

Awesome.

"Listen, Amanda, I can't tell you how to have relationships with your family. It's just me and my mom, and my mom is the most independent person I know. She's the one who taught me that you accept people as they are or you don't. But if you don't, then you go your separate ways." Like maybe he and Amanda should right now before things went any further.

"So you don't see your mom?"

"I do. But we both know that we can harmonize for about a week. Then we need to separate for a while." Karmen Kaye could take care of herself. They got along better than most mothers and sons, but it was partly because they both knew their limits. She didn't give him advice unless he asked, she didn't nag him and he didn't fuss with her.

Amanda gave a little chuckle. "Well, that's definitely not my mother. And how do you avoid your siblings?"

He shook his head. "Never had any, so I don't know. Sorry." He looked at her again. "I'm not criticizing you, Amanda." He really wasn't. She was entitled to her opinions and feelings. He even understood where they were coming from. He just didn't have to share those opinions and feelings. "I'm telling you who I am. That's why Emma and I couldn't work. She needs people to be there all the time for her and I'm not that guy."

Amanda nodded. "Makes sense."

Ryan didn't say anything more. But there was a niggle of doubt as he thought about Amanda's words. He didn't know if it made sense. It was just how he was. He'd been raised by an incredibly independent woman who expected him to be incredibly independent too. It was what he knew. He wasn't sure how to handle people who *needed* him. It wasn't that he didn't care. If someone needed him to pick them up from the airport, move a heavy dresser or get drunk with them because they were pissed at their boss, he'd be there. But if he had to know when someone needed flowers to cheer them up, or that he needed to show up for something even though they didn't *tell* him to be there, or to remember something like the first time they'd eaten at a restaurant together, he pretty much sucked.

And then there was his need for quiet.

He'd grown up in a house fourteen miles from the nearest small town. His mother was a spiritual person. She loved nature, she loved meditating, she loved just *being*, as she put it.

Ryan loved running around and getting dirty with his friends, swimming in the pond, climbing trees and pretending to wage and win battles with everything from swords to guns made from sticks.

But he also had an appreciation for quiet and peace and...just being.

There was no low setting on Emma, and frankly, she exhausted him sometimes.

Then there was Amanda. If tonight was any indication, she could also wear him out. But he suspected that Amanda appreciated quiet. Or that she could if she ever let herself have any. She was outgoing and friendly. As a grad school instructor and physical therapist, she could hardly be shy. She had to interact with people all day every day, and these people needed to be encouraged and coached and even pushed sometimes.

But she was definitely not *exuberant* or *boisterous* or *perky* or any of the other adjectives used to describe Emma. Nor was she pushy or bossy or direct like Isabelle.

She was serious, though. Determined. Focused. There was something about her that made him think that Amanda Dixon would love meditation. If she didn't already do it, she absolutely should.

He pulled up in front of the Britton Hotel in the semicircular drive and got out of the car.

"I'll only be a minute," he told the valet who came forward.

The man nodded as he opened the car door for Amanda. Ryan moved in right away though. If Amanda forgot what she was wearing and swung her legs out of the car wrong, the guy would get an eyeful.

Ryan took her hand to help her out and keep her upright when she wobbled slightly on her heels. He hid his smile. He didn't know if it was the unusual amount of alcohol in her system or the unusual height of the heels, but she was at risk of falling on her face.

They didn't talk as they stepped onto the elevator and ascended to the twenty-first floor. Amanda dug the key card from her purse and handed it to him, and Ryan opened the door and gestured for her to precede him. He stepped in, hoping she'd kick the shoes off first so she would be steadier on her feet. But the first thing she did when the door shut behind him was press close and kiss him. With those heels still on, she could meet his lips easily.

Without thinking, Ryan took her chin in one hand, holding her still as he thoroughly tasted her.

He finally lifted his head, loving the look of dazed pleasure on her face. "Good night, Amanda."

She blinked. Then frowned. "'Good night'? You're leaving?"

"Yes." This wasn't at all how he'd expected the night to end either, but he was pretty good at recognizing when it was time to move on. Like whenever things got complicated.

"But I thought you wanted a night with me?" She looked adorably confused.

"I did." He also wasn't into lying.

"So why aren't you staying?" She pulled out of his arms, but stood facing him squarely.

"Let me ask you something first," he said. "What was with getting Jennifer involved when you and I were on the couch?"

Amanda didn't blush or stammer. "I was trying to make sure you were as into everything as I was."

"What made you think that would do it?" he asked with a slight frown.

"Because it wasn't until she was touching me that you came out on the dance floor."

He felt his eyes widen. "Seriously? You think she was the reason? *You* were the reason, Mandi. Because you asked me to look out for you and not let anyone touch you under your dress. Remember? The guy was going under your skirt."

"Oh." She seemed to be recalling the moment. Then she said, "But the only reason you interrupted was because I asked you to keep an eye on me?"

"Right."

"So, if he'd tried that, but I *hadn't* said that, you would have let it happen?"

Ryan looked into her eyes for a moment. See, this was one of those complicated, mixed-up emotions that just seemed like such a waste of time. "Are you asking if I would have been jealous? Yes. I'd envy anyone who got to touch you. But would I have interrupted it? Not if you were enjoying it. If you'd given any indication that you didn't want or like his—or her—touch, I would have stepped in. But if you liked it, then no. That would be your call, not mine."

She watched him equally as long as he had her. Then she said, "You're the kind of guy to step in if *any* woman needed some help."

"Yes."

He was. Sometimes people treated each other like crap and he didn't like it. If someone was being harassed somehow, he'd step in. Temporarily. That's why being a paramedic fit him so well. He could do a lot of very good work, but it was up to someone else to really dig in and figure out the long-term, complicated things, like what kind of surgery someone needed to repair their broken hip or what kind of social services they needed to get out of the abusive situation they were in.

His mom had taught him to "as far as possible, without surrender, be on good terms with all persons", as it said in the copy of Max Ehrmann's "Desiderata" she had hanging on their living room wall. But the poem also said "Be cheerful. Strive to be happy." He was happy with doing his part and trusting others to do theirs. His part was the upfront, in-the-moment, right-now needs. The long-term, later-on stuff was someone else's forte.

Amanda finally nodded. "I thought so."

He wasn't sure what that meant, and he'd learned a long time ago that it was often best to just leave it alone when women said something he didn't fully understand.

"So, I'm going to get going."

"But...this wasn't all that Tim thought we did together."

He nodded and turned back to open the door. The sooner he was in the hallway with a solid, locked door between them, the better. Eventually he was going to smack himself for walking away from Amanda. He could have her. She wanted it. She wasn't too drunk. But...

"The thing is, Amanda, I'm not into it now." It was only kind of a lie.

"You're not into it now?" she repeated. Then her cheeks got pink. "Okay." She swallowed hard. "Fine. Good night."

Part of him—a very big part of him—wanted to ignore her reaction, pretend it really was fine and walk out the door. He even took a step closer to the doorway. But he couldn't do it. His mom was a woman, and when she said she was fine, she was. If she wasn't fine, she also told him that. But he had learned in his thirty-one years of life that women like his mother were rare. Very rare.

"What are you thinking?" he asked, gripping the doorknob one final time before letting go and letting the door swing shut.

"Nothing." Now she did kick her shoes off and again hugged her arms tight across her stomach. "It's fine. I don't want you to stay if you don't want to."

"I don't want to," he said honestly. "The mood got lost somewhere along the way."

"You didn't want to go to the club in the first place," Amanda said. "And then I shocked you, right? You didn't think I had all of that in me?"

He hadn't analyzed when the mood change had actually happened, but now that he paused for a moment, he knew exactly what had done it. "It wasn't about the club, exactly."

"Was it Jennifer?"

"Not really."

"Was it what I said about Emma?"

He shook his head. "Not exactly. I didn't like that, but it was more..." He wasn't sure if he should say it.

"What, Ryan?"

He sighed. "It's that you clearly don't respect me. And I didn't realize that mattered. But turns out it does."

She stared at him. "Why do you think I don't respect you?"

"Because tonight, the club, me—it's all stuff you would never normally do. It's all stuff you frown about your sisters doing. And you were surprised to hear that I have conversations with the women I go out with, that I get to know them, even do things with them that don't involve getting naked. I..." He stopped and took a deep breath. "I guess I don't want to fit into the mold you've created for me."

Amanda didn't move. Didn't blink. Didn't swallow.

"Good night, Amanda. I'll see you around."

The door shut behind Ryan and Amanda finally let out the air she'd been holding. Then she deadbolted the door, shut off all the lights and went straight to the bed. She slipped out of her dress and slid, naked, between the sheets. Once her head hit the pillow, she covered her face with her hands and let Ryan's words replay in her mind.

Oh, God.

She was such a bitch.

She'd been living her life for so long so as not to embarrass anyone she cared about, and then she went and embarrassed *herself* big and bad. And with a guy that she *would* see again. A guy who knew her brother.

And she'd told him about Coach.

Oh, *God.* Why had she done that?

But she knew instantly—she hated the idea that Ryan thought she was an unreasonable, judgmental bitch, so she'd tried to make him understand.

She flopped over onto her stomach, glared at the clock and decided not to waste the perfectly good hotel room—hot sex with Ryan or not.

But an hour later when her mortification had failed to fade, she realized that she would need to make it up to him somehow. And an hour after that, she thought maybe she knew the way.

Four hours later, she was awake again. Not happy about it, but unable to reverse it.

So she got up and showered, dressed and tried to figure out how to see Ryan again. She knew where he worked, of course. But finding him there would be difficult without her brother knowing about it and wondering why. She didn't know where he lived, and didn't have his phone number.

But Emma did.

Dammit.

Emma would know exactly how to get a hold of Ryan. In fact, it seemed that they were *friends* on top of being a past hookup. After Ryan's clear offense the night before at her surprise over the friendship, she knew she should probably feel bad about not knowing he and Emma had been more than a one-night stand. But in her defense...how would she have known that? Emma never talked about Ryan in any way other than to say that he was amazing and had kept her up all night and that he'd likely ruined her for other men.

Really, what was Amanda supposed to think after all of that? Why would she have assumed that all they'd done was skinny-dip?

But she'd clearly hurt his feelings. So she needed to make it up to him. Somehow.

So to get the information from Emma, Amanda would have to tell her what had happened.

And it was Sunday morning. Emma was doing what Amanda was supposed to have been doing that day, which meant Emma would be at church with their mother in about an hour.

Church.

Hmmm... She couldn't get the third degree in the middle of church.

An hour later, Amanda slid into the pew next to Olivia, putting Emma and Olivia between her and their mother. "Amanda?" Olivia whispered. "What are you doing here?"

"I haven't been to church with Emma for a really long time," Amanda said softly as the music started. "I thought it would nice for Mom to have three of her four here." None of that was exactly *un*true.

They all stood for the opening hymn, and Amanda reached behind Olivia and pinched Emma's arm.

"Hey!" She glanced over with a frown.

Amanda held up the note she'd written on scratch paper in

the car, then handed it to her sister.

Still frowning, Emma took the slip of paper, but clearly figuring out that it was a secret if they were passing it behind Olivia's back, she surreptitiously read it. Her eyes widened and she gave Amanda a questioning look.

Amanda shrugged. The note simply said, *What's Ryan's number?*

Emma patted her dress, indicating she didn't have a pen. And truthfully, it was tight enough that no way could a pen have gone unnoticed.

Damn. Amanda glanced quickly at the front of the church and amended it to *dang*. She hadn't brought a pen either.

She sighed. Emma reached and pinched her. Three times quickly in a row.

Amanda shot an annoyed glance at her. Emma tipped her head and mouthed *three*. Amanda frowned and shook her head. Emma frowned and held up three fingers.

Ah, this was how they were going to do this.

Great. She was going to have to remember whatever numbers Emma gave her via code. Fine.

She motioned for Emma to go ahead. But Emma gave her a grin and faced forward as the song ended and the minister started the first prayer. Amanda sighed. Great. Emma was worried about Amanda staying through the whole church service. This was perfect.

Five minutes later, Emma coughed. Twice. It was clearly a fake cough and Amanda glanced over. Emma didn't look at her but she grinned again.

Okay, three then two.

Throughout the service Emma gave her one number at a time. She itched the cheek closest to Amanda with two fingers. She pointed to the five in the number for the third hymn. She reached behind Olivia and flicked Amanda's arm four times during the part where everyone stood and greeted those around them. She sneezed once, but quickly shook her head when

Amanda looked over indicating that the sneeze had been real. The second one was too. But then she crossed her legs and tapped the toe of her shoe against the pew in front of them six times. Then finally, at the end of the service as they all stood and gathered their purses and their mother began her social time, Emma looked at Amanda and said, "One."

"Three two two five four six one?" Amanda repeated.

Emma nodded. "You got it."

"We could have just done it this way after the service was over," Amanda pointed out.

"I know," Emma said, looking smug. "But this was way more fun. Plus now I can ask you why you need to know."

"What do you need to know?" Olivia asked.

"Nothing," Amanda said, knowing full well that wouldn't suffice.

"A phone number," Emma said easily.

"A guy?"

Amanda sighed. "Yes. Okay? Fine. A guy."

Olivia didn't say anything more as she was surrounded by three older ladies who were trying to talk her into teaching the second grade Sunday school class.

"Why do you need to talk to Ryan?" Emma asked.

Amanda looked at her sister. Ryan had said there was more there than she thought. He said there were things about Emma that might surprise her.

"Would it be possible for me to leave this as I just need to?"

Emma looked at her for a long minute, head tipped to one side. Then she nodded. "Okay."

That did surprise Amanda.

"Okay. Thanks."

"Let me know if you need anything else." Emma turned in time to link her arm with her mother's and lead Marla toward the social hall—and away from Amanda—where they would spend the next hour with cinnamon rolls and coffee.

That also surprised Amanda.

But she'd have to think about her sister being more than expected another time. It was Sunday, day two, the last day of her excuse to do whatever she wanted. Emma wasn't going to take over all of her responsibilities come Monday morning.

She headed for her car, dialing Ryan's number as she went. She had no idea if he'd gone straight home after dropping her off or not. Maybe he'd gone out, found another girl who didn't make him feel like she disapproved of everything he did.

Well, even if he had, she wanted a chance to show him that there was more to her than he was expecting too.

He answered on the fifth ring. "Kaye."

She took a deep breath and leaned back against the side of her car. "Hi, Ryan. It's Amanda."

There was a long pause. Then he said, "What did you tell Emma when you asked for my number?"

"How do you know I asked Emma?"

He chuckled. "Because you wouldn't ask Conner, Isabelle and Olivia don't have it, and you don't have the other guys' numbers to ask them."

She smiled, his voice making her stupidly happy. "I just told her I needed it."

He didn't seem as surprised by that as she had been.

"Well, now that you have my number, can I expect explicit text messages and inappropriate photos?"

She laughed. "I promise not to harass you like that."

"Damn."

Feeling lighter, she decided to be fully upfront. "I'm actually calling to apologize."

She heard a rustling on his end of the phone. "That's not necessary."

"It is. In fact..." She swallowed hard.

She hadn't asked a guy out in a really long time and she couldn't remember being nervous about it before. Typically she asked guys to be her date for various business-related events—awards dinners, Christmas parties, faculty get-togethers—never just a because-I-like you date. And there were only three men she asked to those events because she was comfortable with them, they were polite and could handle themselves in those professional situations without worry, and there was no pressure about sex.

Nate Sullivan was one of those guys. Nate had plenty of cocky, that was for sure. He was the lead orthopedic trauma surgeon at St. A's, after all. While most of the orthopedic surgeons did hip fractures and athletic injuries, Nate was the one they called in for the accidents that left patients with broken arms, legs, ribs and a vertebra or two.

Nate basically put people who had been turned into jigsaw puzzles back together.

But he was also a friend, a man she liked and could have good conversations with, who could handle himself in classy situations. Nate didn't have any time for romantic relationships. He was a nationally renowned trauma surgeon and a single dad to a teenage son. There was no time or energy left for maintaining relationships with women. Not that he slept alone if he didn't want to. Nate was good-looking, sophisticated and charming. He had as much female company as he wanted. But he didn't do *relationships*. So he enjoyed accompanying her to the various black-tie events she attended, and they were both happy with the kiss on the cheek at the end of the night.

She didn't want a kiss on the cheek from Ryan. And she wasn't going to take him to a faculty party.

"In fact?" Ryan prompted.

"I'd like to ask you out again."

There was no answer on the other end of the phone. For a long, long time. Her heart had already been pounding. Now it felt like it was being squeezed as it tried to pound.

"Ryan?" she finally asked.

He cleared his throat. "On a date?"

"Yes. But an Amanda date. Not a what-would-Emma-do thing. I want to show you that I can act civilized and not make embarrassing or offensive assumptions about people."

Another long, long pause. Amanda concentrated on breathing. If he said no, that would be...horrible. Not brokenhearted horrible, but how-will-I-ever-face-him-again horrible. After last night, she was worried enough about her cheeks burning off when she saw him again. If he turned her down for an honest to goodness, grown-up, noncrazy date, she didn't know if she could show up to any more football games. Which would be too bad. She enjoyed watching the guys play.

"The thing is," she said in a rush before he could say no, "I do respect you. You don't judge people, you don't give unsolicited advice, you don't make people feel uncomfortable because they might be different. You accept everyone."

There was no sound on the other end of the phone. She wondered if she'd shocked him. Because *she* was a little shocked that she knew these things about him. But she'd clearly been paying attention even if it wasn't on purpose.

"You make everyone feel good and...I would love to spend some more time with you. Time where I can do and say whatever I want and not worry about it disappointing someone or shocking someone or someone thinking I'm weird. I might be wrong, but you seem like the kind of guy to roll with things even if they seem a little nutty. I could use a little nutty time. What do you say?"

She stopped and had to breathe at that point, all the words having rushed out at once. She wasn't sure *exactly* what she wanted to do, but it was rare when she could do whatever she wanted without worrying about who was watching or who it would affect. With Ryan she somehow felt like she'd be...safe...to do whatever she wanted to.

But instead of answering that question, he asked, "When was the last time you asked a guy out on a date?"

She was the one to hesitate this time. "What do you mean?"

"I mean, the guys at the hospital talk. We know that guys ask you out all the time. We also know that you take Nate to most of your work things. If he can't go, you take some other guy who's only a friend. When was the last time *you* did the asking when it wasn't something you had to go to for work?"

"The guys at the hospital talk about me?"

Ryan laughed. "Of course they do. We only hire smart guys at St. A's."

That was really distracting. When she went to St. Anthony's, she spent a lot of time talking to staff, figuring out what opportunities there were for her students to observe other parts of the healthcare team working, what things her students needed to know or be able to do to impress those people, how her students performed when there, and so on. Yes, sometimes guys at the hospital asked her out. Sometimes she even said yes. But to think that they were all talking about her afterward or when she wasn't there was...distracting.

"What do they say?"

Ryan laughed again. "Oh, no. You're not sidetracking me. When was the last time you asked a guy out on a real date?"

She thought about it. "I don't remember."

"Good enough for me. I'll definitely go."

She straightened away from the car. "You will?" She felt a rush of relief, followed quickly by a rush of nerves. Where was she going to take him? What would she wear? Why hadn't she thought this out more fully before she'd called him?

"Sure. I can't wait to brag about this. The guys at St. A's are gonna keel over from jealousy."

"You can't tell anyone," she said quickly. "My brother can't know. And even if you don't tell him directly, someone will say something and he'll find out. Honestly, he's not going to like—"

"Amanda," Ryan broke in.

"Yeah?"

"Breathe."

She did.

"I'm giving you a hard time. I won't say anything."

She breathed again.

"I like your brother and I know this all stresses him."

"You say stuff about you and Emma all the time," she

pointed out. In fact, Ryan and Emma both seemed to specifically look for ways to flaunt their hook-up in front of Conner. Another reason she'd assumed it was more than a swimming lesson.

"Because we're just messing around and deep down your brother knows that," Ryan said.

"You don't think Conner will think we're just messing around?" she asked.

"I don't think Conner thinks you're capable of just messing around, Amanda. I don't think most people think you're capable of messing around."

She felt like maybe she should be offended by that, but when she thought about it, she realized he was right. And she should be glad about it. She wanted her students and her siblings to see her as upstanding and responsible. In fact—and she'd only admit this to herself—she would rather Conner think that of her than her students. The last thing she wanted to do was cause her brother more headaches than he already had. It was her way of protecting him like he did all of them.

She was capable of messing around, though. She just wasn't going to. "I want one day of being...not the usual me. I want to do something that I don't normally do," she told Ryan. "There will also be no falling in love and getting serious."

"What about near-public sex?" Ryan asked. "Is that on the yes list or the no list?"

Again, Amanda had to block the memories. She could still feel Ryan's hands on her when they'd been on that couch. His big hands cupping her ass firmly. His long fingers stroking her. The look of hunger and disbelief on his face.

She cleared her throat. "No near-public sex."

"Great."

Great? Amanda felt her eyebrows shoot up. "But completely private sex isn't off the table," she told him. For some reason.

Mostly because she wanted a reaction from him. Because she wouldn't be upset if he wanted to pick up where last night had ended. Well, before the whole you-don't-respect-me thing.

"After I prove to you that I can be a fun person and that I don't assume the worst about you," she added, when he didn't reply right away.

"Tell you what," Ryan said. "I'll go out with you if you promise there will be no sex."

She stopped, waiting for him to go on. Or to laugh. When he didn't do either she asked, "No sex?"

"Right. I think we both have some assumptions to disprove. You're going to show me that you're not going to base your opinion of me only on the things you've heard and imagined. And I'm going to show you that, while you should absolutely *want* to sleep with me, there's more reason than that to spend time with me."

She wasn't sure what to say to that. She really didn't like the no-sex rule. She believed there was more to Ryan than that. Of course there was. But, well, you didn't go for a ride in a convertible on a nice summer day and leave the top up. If something had a feature that attracted you, then you tried that feature out. Fully.

She'd come on strong last night. And she definitely knew what she liked when it came to men and sex. She'd been told she gave off a confident, sexy vibe. Maybe that was bugging Ryan. "Are you intimidated by the idea of being with me?" she blurted.

He chuckled in her ear. "Intimidated? No, that's not the word I'd use."

Hmm. He didn't *sound* intimidated. But why would he say no to sex? "So, the idea of me naked, lying back on your bed, ready and willing for anything, doesn't make you nervous?"

He cleared his throat and said gruffly, "It makes me harder than hell. Which you know. But it's not going to work."

"The idea that I'm expecting more than missionary sex in the dark doesn't bother you at all?"

"Mandi."

The nickname and the husky note in his voice made a shiver of pleasure trip down her spine.

"Missionary is only there for when I've worn you out to the point that all you can do is lie there and let me do whatever I want."

She pulled in a deep breath.

"And," he added, "it'll only be dark if we get so wild that we knock over and break the lamp. 'Cause I intend to be sure that I can see every single glorious inch of you."

Okay, maybe he wasn't intimidated after all.

"So," Ryan asked, his voice back to normal. "Where are we going and what time are you picking me up?"

Chapter Four

Ryan couldn't stop grinning. Amanda Dixon had called to ask him out. Something she *never* did. He shouldn't care. He shouldn't want to go. He should've said no.

She'd been pretty insulting to him last night after all.

But she wanted to have sex with him. That was hard to ignore.

Plus, he wanted to prove to her exactly what he'd said— that there was more to him for a woman to enjoy than his amazing skills in the bedroom.

He wasn't exactly sure why. Just as he still wasn't exactly sure why it mattered that she didn't respect him. Maybe it was that she was his friend's sister. Maybe it was that Amanda was a classy woman and he wanted her to know that he was good for more than the best massages—with flavored massage oil, of course—and to-die-for next-morning fruit smoothies.

Or maybe it was that he wanted to prove that to himself.

It had been a really long time since he'd dated a woman for reasons other than a good time. Not that he didn't think he and Amanda would have a good time. But he wanted to have...an important time. Which didn't even make sense to him. What was an *important* time? What made it important? And why hadn't the other girls been important? What made Amanda so important?

Or maybe it was that he also thought maybe Amanda needed him. For the massages and the fruit smoothies and the three-times-in-a-row orgasms. He didn't think she'd had a lot of any of those things.

But yeah, okay, he wanted to be more to her than that.

Ryan somehow kept himself busy for the next two hours.

She'd called him at nine thirty in the morning, but she'd also told him that she would pick him up at noon. Noon. Who went on a date—important or not—at noon on a Sunday?

But he was ready. He'd gone for a run, showered, cleaned up around the house, checked his massage oil stock and smoothie ingredients and was, as instructed, in jeans and a T-shirt at eleven forty-seven.

As expected, Amanda was a little early.

"Hi." She looked amazing. Happy. Excited even.

Which he really loved. "Hi." He couldn't help his grin.

She had her hair pulled up in a ponytail, and was dressed in light blue capri pants and a white-and-blue-striped sleeveless blouse. She had on only a touch of makeup and she looked young and natural.

He wanted to kiss her the moment he saw her.

Then he got a whiff of her lemony body spray and he wanted to do a lot more than kiss her.

But she simply turned on the heel of her white leather flip-flop and headed back down his front steps. "Let's go," she said breezily.

They took her car since Ryan still didn't know where they were going.

They chatted about nothing in particular on the twenty-minute drive, but Ryan lost all track of the conversation when she pulled into the parking lot of a big building with neon signs in the windows.

"Laser tag?" Ryan looked at Amanda, surprised and even a little impressed.

"I've only played once, but I loved it," she said. "I thought maybe you'd do this with me."

"Why would you worry about other people knowing you like this?" he asked.

She looked at the building. "It's not that I'd be worried about someone finding this out," she said. "It's that I don't take the time for it. It seems like I always have too many responsible things to do."

"Maybe you should let your sisters see you like this," he said. "Let them know you can have fun."

She shut off the car and pulled the keys from the ignition. "It's not the having fun I want to avoid with my sisters. It's the 'I told you so' that I'd get."

"You'd get 'I told you so' from them for laser tag?"

She got out of the car and he followed her. "Totally," she said over the top of the car. "I don't usually take the time to blow off steam, and then if I do and actually have fun, they would definitely say 'I told you so'."

"So you need me..."

"Because you won't think laser tag is dumb, you won't make fun of me for getting into it and you *won't* say 'I told you so'."

He grinned at her. "I definitely won't. Since I've never told you so." They both slammed their car doors and met at the front bumper of the car. "Your job is to make sure I have fun but to keep me from getting cocky and doing something stupid in there, okay?" Amanda asked.

It had to be a reference to the story she'd told him last night about Conner's coach. He was surprised. He'd attributed the confession the night before to the raspberry liqueur. But now she was bringing it up again, fully sober.

That was kind of awesome.

Immediately following that thought, a surge of anger and the need to punch something washed through him. It was unexpected and completely out of character for Ryan. But, dammit, the man had been a respected teacher and coach. A *married* teacher and coach. Who had to have been at least ten years Amanda's senior, if not more.

Ryan worked to keep calm. He didn't get angry. He didn't get protective. He didn't get riled up about other people's choices. He didn't really understand the need to get even.

Until Amanda.

Wow. He was going to need to do a lot of meditation with this girl around.

"I don't think you need to worry about making any life-altering choices while playing laser tag today," he said lightly.

She smiled up at him. "Promise?"

"Promise. Just fun. No trouble."

She took his hand and started for the front of the building. "That's perfect—and exactly what I need you for."

She needed someone she could have fun with, let loose with, who would understand, not judge and not let anything bad happen.

"I'm your guy." Ryan pulled the door open for her.

She gave him a smile that was cute and sexy at the same time. He didn't usually think of the women he spent time with as cute but...it fit.

And he was sure she would *hate* knowing he thought she was cute.

They stepped into the building and looked around. There were only four other people besides the people who worked for the laser tag place.

They signed in and paid for their game. Amanda chose *crazygirl1* as her player name and Ryan picked *CaptainAmerica*.

"How very patriotic of you," she commented.

He grinned. "Kicking ass and taking names for the red, white and blue."

She smiled back and tucked her hair behind her ear.

Cute. Definitely.

Ryan had played laser tag a few times and yeah, it was fun. But sneaking around in the dark suddenly seemed a lot more appealing.

"So why laser tag?" Ryan asked, content to simply watch her as they wandered the lobby, looking over the video games that lined the walls, waiting for the laser tag game in progress to end.

"It's dark so you're kind of anonymous, you get to run

around and hide and *shoot* people and you're *supposed* to."

He smiled down at her. "So you get to be bad, but no one really gets hurt. I get it."

And he loved the insight.

She wanted to be naughty but was afraid of the consequences. She didn't realize that the consequences of being a little wild could be *good* too. He'd have to help her figure that out.

As he strapped on the vest that would keep track of his shots and hits, he watched Amanda shrug into hers. He snagged the strap that was dangling just out of her reach. She looked up and he tugged on the strap, bringing her closer. She almost stepped on his toes, but she didn't protest the proximity or him reaching around her to buckle her vest.

"You ready to be a little naughty in the dark?" he asked.

"Yes." She said it breathlessly. "But before we go in there I need to know—are you for me or against me?"

He grinned and moved in even closer. "Against. Always. As much as possible."

"Then you better watch your ass."

He laughed, then swatted *her* ass. "I'll be too busy watching yours."

She was surprised for one second before her expression turned sexy. "Not in the dark."

"You're right. I might have to go by feel." He couldn't resist and ran his flat palm over her butt again.

She licked her lips. "Thought you said no sex."

"I said no sex on *this* date. But not on every date forever."

"So this is..." She trailed off, clearly wanting him to fill in the blank.

"Foreplay."

The buzzer sounded to signal the start of the new game and the inner doors swung open.

Ryan watched Amanda stare back at him, the single word *foreplay* hanging between them. She was the one to finally pull her gaze away.

"Then let's go," she said.

"Right *behind* you, babe."

She tripped a little as she turned and started for the game area.

Ryan followed her, a big grin in place that he didn't think was going to go away any time soon.

Everyone gathered around the computer monitor that listed all the players by their player names and waited for the signal to begin.

"And when you said 'against me', you meant like in a sexy, get-up-against-me way, right?" Amanda whispered.

He grinned. "Sure."

"You didn't mean 'against me' as in you'll shoot me if you find me?"

"Guess we'll find out." He raised his weapon.

"Ryan—" She was cut off by the starting buzzer.

The lights went down, plunging them into darkness but for strips of neon lights.

Everyone scattered but Ryan and Amanda. She turned and looked at him with wide eyes.

He raised his weapon. Her jaw dropped.

"You wouldn't."

"No consequences, remember?"

Her eyes narrowed. "Except maybe never seeing me naked."

He watched her for a long moment, trying to gauge if she was serious.

"I would so throw this game if you meant that," he finally told her.

She raised her gun and shot him.

As his vest beeped and blinked, she smiled. "Sucker."

"You're in trouble," he said simply.

They both knew that after being shot, the game would disengage his gun for a few seconds, so she had a little time before he would be able to shoot her back.

She gave him a wink and then turned and ran.

He was laughing as he gave her a head start. He *was* going to find her. And when he did, she was definitely in trouble. Good trouble.

Several minutes later, he had to admit she was good. He hadn't caught even a glimpse of her. He rounded a corner and suddenly felt someone grab the front of his shirt and yank him into a dark corner behind a padded column.

"Oh, my gosh, I'm in trouble," Amanda hissed.

"I should shoot you right now," he said.

She ducked behind his shoulder. "Some of my students are here."

"No way." What were the chances?

"They must have been in the game before ours too, so I didn't see them up front." She still hadn't let go of his shirt.

"I take it you don't want them to see you now?"

"Right."

"Why?"

That seemed to stump her for a moment. "Well...because."

It was dark, but he could see enough to know that she looked gorgeous. "You look like a woman who's having a great time. Nothing is wrong with that." He brushed a stray strand of hair away from her forehead.

"Yeah. Maybe you're right." She took a deep breath. "I just freaked out a little when I saw them."

"That's okay. You were surprised."

"Well...embarrassed."

"Embarrassed?"

"Yeah. I, um..." She pulled her bottom lip between her teeth.

"You what?"

"Kind of shot one of them. Repeatedly."

He raised an eyebrow. "Okay, well, that's what you're here for."

"I might have..."

"Yeah?"

"Yelled."

"Yelled," he repeated.

"Yep."

"Something specific?" He was fighting a smile now.

She sighed. "'Take that, maggot'."

He couldn't contain his snort. "Maggot? Wow. That's harsh."

She covered her face with her hands. "I know."

"I'm sure it's fine."

"As long as they don't see me it's fine. They'll think that it was a crazy woman who looked a little like their clinical director, but they won't believe it because I'd never do something like that."

"Obviously," he said dryly.

"So if they don't see me," she went on. "I'll be fine. But if they do then..."

"The world will still turn."

"But I'll be embarrassed."

"Which is *not* the worst emotion to feel."

She met his gaze. "I was thinking that maybe you'd be okay with hanging out in this dark corner with me."

Oh. He leaned in, bracing his forearm on the wall beside her head. "Well, it's probably best that these impressionable young people not find out that their director of clinical education would say something so horrible."

She smiled. "Exactly."

"Even worse would be for these kids to know that their director of clinical education is so hot and fun."

He leaned in and kissed her. She dropped her gun and wrapped her arms around his neck. He cupped the back of her head, holding her in place for a full, deep tasting. He stroked his tongue along hers, drinking in the sound of her groan and welcoming the feel of her pressing her hips into his.

Thankful for the wall behind her, he leaned in. Their vests

kept them from being breast to chest, but he felt every inch of her legs along his.

When he lifted his head, she sighed. "Wow."

He grinned. "Yeah, seeing you like this would definitely fuel some major fantasies for a lot of your students. It would be so distracting and so unfair to their learning process."

She smiled. "Thanks for thinking of all of them. Really generous of you."

"I feel strongly about the education of our future physical therapists."

"Uh-huh." She pulled him down for another kiss.

It was hot and made every cell in his body pulse. He wanted her and he *was* going to have her.

Amanda gripped his hips, her thumbs through the belt loops on his jeans, and pulled him closer.

Their height difference with her flat shoes and the laser tag vests kept him from getting close enough. Though he wasn't sure if he'd ever actually feel close enough.

He ran his hands over her vest, unbuckling the straps. "Gotta lose this, babe."

"Right with ya." Her fingers got busy on his vest, and within seconds both dropped to the floor with a thump.

Free of the plastic and electronics, Ryan ran his hands down her shoulders and over her back to her ass, and lifted her closer.

She gripped his shoulders, arching against him, kissing him again, her mouth hot under his.

Ryan curled his fingers into the firm flesh of her butt. He wanted to eat her up, lick her from head to toe, taste every sweet, soft, silky inch of her. He wanted to know how her lips tasted compared to her toes and how the back of her knee felt on his tongue compared to the skin on her inner elbow.

She pulled back and took a deep breath. "No-sex rule still in place?"

"Yeah. For now." It would be a good excuse to drag this

thing out. "But I never said no orgasm."

He slid his hand to the front of her capris, intent on loosening the buttons and getting inside. He didn't have to worry, or work too hard—Amanda undid the buttons for him. With a heartfelt groan, he slid his hand into the front of the cotton pants and the silky panties inside.

Amanda ran her hands up under the back of his shirt. Her hot hands made him want to strip everything off and have them all over him—some places more than others.

Ryan stroked his fingers over her sensitive flesh, and her breath hissed out.

"Ryan."

"Oh, yeah. Right here, babe."

He slid his finger lower, the heat incredible, the temptation to lunge and taste and thrust almost overwhelming. But he made himself go slow, enjoying every millimeter of heat and wetness.

She started to pull in a breath and held it as he pressed in, his finger sliding deliberately and deep.

Once he was as deep as he could go, he paused. "Breathe, babe," he told her.

"Can't," she gasped.

"Got to. You can't hold your breath for as long as I plan to be doing this." He stroked in and out, slow, pulling his finger along her inner wall, making her tremble.

She sucked in a deep breath.

"Good girl," he said gruffly.

He stroked in and out again, this time spreading the wetness up and over her clit.

She gripped his shoulders. "*Ryan.*"

"That's right, Mandi. That's right."

"Faster," she whispered.

"What was that?" he asked, stroking nice and slow and deep.

"Faster." She dug her fingers into his shoulders. "*Please.*"

"Oh, I like that." He picked up the pace a little. "*Please* is, after all, the magic word." He circled over her clit, then pulled the sweet nub between his thumb and the tip of his index finger, rolling it and making her cry out.

"I like that even mo—" He groaned as her hands found his hard, pulsing cock behind his fly.

"You're right. That's nice." She stroked up and down the length of him and he pressed closer.

"You're not distracting me." He slid his finger deep.

"It's payback," she said, her voice breathy.

"I love laser tag."

She laughed softly, then squeezed him through the denim that was becoming tighter and hotter by the second.

"I'd love to strip you down and put you up against this wall, your legs around my waist, spread open so I could thrust hard and deep."

He felt her inner muscles tighten. Ah, she liked dirty talk.

"You like words like 'thrust'?"

"And 'spread open'," she said.

Suddenly the buzzer sounded, ending the game, and the lights came up.

They jerked apart, Ryan's fingers bending back slightly as he tried to pull his hand from her pants. She yanked it free, then quickly buttoned up.

"All players please report to the console. Game two is about to begin," the girl said over the intercom.

Ryan grabbed their vests from the floor while Amanda redid her ponytail. When she'd taken a deep breath, he started toward the console.

She grabbed his arm. "I can't go over there. They might see me."

Right, the students.

"The game won't start until our vests register at the console," Ryan said.

"Okay." She glanced toward the computer, then toward the

door. "Maybe we should leave."

He nodded. "If you want to." They could absolutely pick up where they'd left off at his place or in her car. Or the hallway just outside.

"Yeah. I guess."

She glanced around. There were no other people outside of the hub area where the console would reset and register their vests for the next game.

They headed for the door, Ryan carrying both vests.

"Maybe we could come back sometime," she said casually as she reached for the door.

Ryan looked at her in surprise. "Are you asking me out *again*?" he asked. "Wow. You can't expect me not to brag about *that*. That's unheard of."

"Yes, I can expect—" She started as she stepped through the door into the outer room where the vests were stored between games. She came up short.

There were six other people in the room removing vests.

"Dr. Dixon?" one of the girls asked.

He heard Amanda sigh. "Hi, Stephanie."

Stephanie grabbed the arm of another of the girls who had her back to them. The girl pivoted and her face brightened as she saw her professor. She lifted a hand in greeting.

Amanda smiled at her. "Hi, Jill." Amanda spoke the words but also moved her hands at the same time, clearly using sign language. "How was your game?"

The girl spoke and signed back. "Okay. Confusing."

So she was hearing impaired. Interesting. Ryan hung up their vests as he watched them communicate. He was impressed by how well Amanda signed.

"What are you doing here?" Jill asked.

"Just having some fun," Amanda returned.

"Is he your boyfriend?"

Ryan grinned as Amanda glanced quickly at him and shook her head. "A friend."

"Too bad. He's cute."

Ryan's grin grew. He crossed his arms and leaned back against the wall to watch and wait.

"Yes, he is," Amanda agreed with her hands only. "But it's not like that."

She was going to be very surprised to find out that he knew sign language.

"Why not?" Jill asked.

Yeah, why not? Ryan wondered.

"He likes to have too much fun," Amanda told her.

"And you don't?"

No, she didn't, Ryan thought. Because of the consequences. And today—running into her students—would likely go on her list of negative consequences.

Dammit.

The three guys and two other girls headed out to the front, and Jill and Amanda followed.

Ryan wondered how Amanda would feel if she knew her lipstick was smudged and that the material across her butt was wrinkled.

Jill headed to the restroom and the guys in their group stopped in front of the snack bar. The girls—Stephanie and the other—stood off to one side.

"So...back to my place?" Ryan asked Amanda.

Amanda seemed distracted when she looked up at him. "Huh?"

"Do you want to go back to my place?" He said it and signed it at the same time.

Her eyes widened. "You know sign?"

"Yep."

"Oh."

"Yes, I totally understood when you agreed that I'm cute."

She rolled her eyes. "Like you didn't already know that."

"So, do you want to go back to my place?"

Her eyes went to the girls again. "It's weird that Jill's with them."

He glanced over at them. "It is?"

"Steph is in her class but the other girl is a pharmacy student and I don't know the guys."

"What's weird about it?" Ryan asked.

"She and Steph aren't friends that I know of. Her group is Karen and Allison and RJ."

He glanced at the group. "So?"

"So, I know Jill's been having some trouble at her current clinical site. There's a therapist there who's very uncomfortable with Jill's hearing impairment."

"What's that got to do with laser tag?"

"Things are different—a different group of people...makes me worry."

"She'll tell you if she needs you, right?"

"I hope so."

She frowned at something over his shoulder and he turned. Her attention was on the two girls again, and he focused on their conversation as it was clearly bothering Amanda.

"She's not as fun as I expected her to be," one of the guys told Stephanie.

"What do you think?" Stephanie asked the boy in the blue shirt.

He shrugged. "It's weird that she can't hear, you know?"

"I told you this wouldn't work," the other girl said to Stephanie. "How can he get to know her if they can't talk to each other?"

"Well, I can *talk* to her," the guy said. "It just won't do any good."

The group chuckled and Ryan felt the tension emanating from Amanda's body.

Ryan resisted the urge to grab the front of the kid's shirt and shake him. He glanced at Amanda instead. What was it about being with her that made him feel all these emotions so intensely? He didn't know the guy, didn't know Jill. It seemed like a shitty thing to say, but it wasn't Ryan's style to grab strangers. It didn't matter. Amanda had already stepped around him.

"Ladies," she said as she approached the girls.

They turned, the guys also quieting and focusing on Amanda.

"Just because she can't hear you," Amanda said, "doesn't mean that what you're saying isn't bitchy."

Ryan's eyebrows rose as the girls' eyes widened.

"What?" Stephanie asked.

"*My* hearing is impeccable. I heard what you said about Jill."

Ryan moved in close behind her. "Chill, Mama Bear," he muttered softly.

Amanda took a deep breath. "Stephanie, I'm disappointed in you."

The other girl stepped forward. "We just said that Jill didn't seem to be having fun."

"He said that she was weird."

"Hey," the kid protested.

The girl frowned. "This is a hard game to play if you can't hear. We didn't think of that."

"Well, you won't need to worry about that for the rest of the night. We'll be giving Jill a ride home."

"No, wait," Stephanie protested. "You can't take her home. She'll want to know why.

"Of course she will," Amanda said.

"That will hurt her feelings," Stephanie said.

Amanda crossed her arms. "*You* will have hurt her feelings."

Ryan wrapped his hands around Amanda's upper arms and leaned in. "Babe, we're going home. No Jill."

She tried to shrug him off. "I want to take Jill home."

"That's a bad idea." He turned her toward the door. "But I have a good one." He nudged her toward the entrance, then turned back and reached to grab the boy in blue by the arm. Ryan pulled him in close. "Here's how this is gonna go. You're going to be sweet, doting even. You're going to be so damned clingy that *she's* going to get sick of *you*."

The boy's eyes were wide, but he nodded.

"And if that's *not* how this goes," Ryan added. "I'm going to take away the only thing you have going for you—that pretty face."

He let the kid go as Jill came out of the bathroom.

"Nice to meet you," Ryan signed to her.

Clearly surprised, but pleased, Jill signed back, "Nice to meet you too."

Then he grabbed Amanda's hand and headed for the door.

They were at the car before Amanda said or did anything. But when she finally did, he really liked the result. Amanda turned him, pushed him up against the car, went up on tiptoe and kissed him.

Ryan responded the way any smart man being kissed by a hot woman would. He grabbed her butt and hauled her more firmly against him. The kiss got hot fast and then ended just as quickly. Amanda pulled back suddenly, breathing hard. "Thank you for standing up for Jill."

"Who's Jill?"

She smiled. "Seriously. Thank you. That was…"

"Nice? Sweet? Chivalrous?"

"Sexy."

"I like that one." He squeezed her ass once more, then let her go. Reluctantly. But he couldn't go any further than kissing and squeezing in the parking lot of the laser tag place, and he fully intended to go further.

Amanda glanced back at the building as he stepped back. "I can't believe they were acting like that." She unlocked the door and yanked it open. "I've always thought a lot of Stephanie. Why would she set Jill up with a guy like that?"

Ryan rounded the car and got into the passenger seat. "I

don't—"

"A true friend would be protecting her. They would have picked a better place to go and they would have prepared the guys for how to communicate."

"Jill's important to you," he observed.

"Yes. They all are. But I admire her. She's meeting her challenges head-on. I think she can teach us all a lot." Amanda started the car, frowning out the windshield. "But if she's having trouble, she has to let me know."

"When she's ready she'll come to you," Ryan said.

"Or I can *make* her talk to me."

Ryan reached over and took the keys out of the ignition, then got out of the car. He went around to the driver's side, opened the door and started to get in, forcing her to scoot over.

"Hey."

"You're too wound up to drive. You rant, I'll drive."

She took a deep breath and started in about how she was worried about Jill and a couple of other students and why.

By the time they pulled up in front of his building, she'd been talking nonstop for twenty minutes.

She looked up at the building. "Oh. We're here."

He grinned and got out. She slid over to the driver's seat, but he still held the keys.

"Let's go," he said, starting for the front door.

"Go? Where?"

"My place."

She got out but hesitated by the car. "What for?"

He looked over his shoulder. "You have a lot of emotion going on there, but it's all bottled up."

She blushed. "Yeah, usually. Sorry I went off like that."

He chuckled. "I'm flattered that you trust me enough to do it in front of me."

She seemed surprised by his words. "You think it's a matter of trust?"

He liked that idea anyway. It was either that or she didn't

care what he thought of her so she wasn't as careful with how she acted. "Yes. But you shouldn't bottle it up at all."

She quirked an eyebrow. "Is that right?"

"For one thing, that's not healthy."

"But yelling at people and calling them bitches is?"

"Yeah, okay, a professor calling a student a bitch is probably a bad idea," he said with a little chuckle. "But being passionate about things *is* healthy. And the way you stand up for the people you care about is one of the things I like best about you."

"There's a list of things that you like about me?" she asked, propping a hand on her hip.

He gave her a grin. "And I haven't even seen you naked. Yet. I'm sure that will add several delicious things."

Her cheeks got pink again, but he didn't think it was from embarrassment this time. She licked her lips. "What's the second thing?"

Distracted by her tongue and the wetness on her bottom lip, he didn't follow. "The second thing?"

"You said 'for one thing', it's not healthy to bottle things up."

"Oh." He gave her a wink. "It's also really hot when you get fired up."

"It is?"

"Definitely."

"So, I should keep yelling and threatening people and making a spectacle?"

"You really don't like that, do you?" he asked, sensing some frustration in her even though he knew she was saying it sarcastically. "You want to let it all out, but you fight it at the same time. What's up with that?"

"I don't like losing control. I don't like...the spectacle part of it," she said, using that word again.

"You were right to do what you did today. Jill needed you. Is it bad to make a spectacle if it's for a good cause?"

She sighed. "Of course not. I mean, standing up for the right things and people is a good thing. But I don't have to lose my cool."

Ryan really wanted to argue that she had hardly lost her cool. Sure, she'd been obviously pissed, but she hadn't slapped anyone or anything.

Suddenly he had an idea. There was no reason that convincing her she was completely fine couldn't take some time. Some time that she would be spending with him.

He was more convinced than ever that Amanda needed to experience his flavored-oil massages and morning-after smoothies. And a few other things.

"I think you need to learn to meditate. Get really in touch with your passion and then learn what to do with it."

"That sounds..."

"Like fun?"

She gave him a half smile. "A little weird."

"Yep. That's what a lot of people think. And then they try it."

"What do you know about meditating and getting in touch with passion?"

He felt heat flare in his gut. He wanted this woman. Badly. And he wanted her to be happy. Which was new for him. Not that he didn't care about the women he was involved with. But he wasn't even really involved with this one. Yet.

Yet? He paused and thought about that. Yet? That would indicate... He shut that down. One thing at a time. Amanda was his friend's sister. That was enough motivation to help her be happy. And she stood up for the people who depended on her. That was all more than enough to give her a little special treatment.

"I'll tell you all about how I know what I know," he told her. "While I show you what I know."

That sounded sexual—and it would be sexual—but it would also involve him telling her about his mother. Which sounded weird even in his head. He had to ease into that conversation.

"That sounds kind of sexual," she said.

He grinned. "Yep, and I've got exactly what you need. Inside."

There was a pause. Then she asked, "Does it involve me being naked?"

"Yep."

"I'm in." She slammed the car door and started after him.

Ryan couldn't help but appreciate her willingness where being naked with him was concerned.

He hoped she still felt that way after she tried his mother's tea and meditation techniques.

Ryan's condo looked nothing like her brother's. Or any other bachelor's that she knew. For Conner and his friends, furnishings were about comfort and getting as many bodies around the big-screen TV on game day as possible, great surround sound, and plenty of surfaces to hold the remotes, cans and plates. Conner's place was basically a big, slightly more expensively decorated dorm room.

Ryan's, on the other hand, was cozy, clean and...simple. His living room was divided from the kitchen by a long countertop. In the living area, he had a couch, an armchair and a coffee table. He also had several potted plants throughout the room. There was a desk near the door, which currently held his laptop, a pile of mail and a pen holder stuffed full of pens and pencils. There was a bookcase, full to the brim, a basic stereo system and a twenty-inch TV. It definitely wasn't the huge, cost-more-than-his-rent TV she'd expected. Which was too bad. Amanda appreciated a good home theater system.

Amanda was a closet television junkie. She loved everything from sports to sitcoms to cooking shows. She didn't like to admit it and knew that there were plenty of other ways for her to spend her time. But her TV addiction allowed her to be home in case anyone—sisters or students mostly—needed to find her, but be entertained at the same time. Besides, she learned things from the shows she watched. Some of them, anyway. Without her favorite shows, she would never have tried making baklava and she wouldn't have known anything about ice-road trucking.

She also found that staying up on pop culture helped her relate to her students. She wasn't much older than most of them and was actually younger than a few of the nontraditional students who had chosen another career first or had put off grad school for one reason or another. She knew that the school had taken a chance on letting her assume the position of director of clinical education at her age and with her small amount of clinical experience, but she was passionate about great clinical experiences and education, and as an alumnus of the program, the university president had agreed to give her a try. She was in her second year and was, so far, impressing everyone from the clinical instructors in the clinics, to the students, to the university administration.

But she knew everyone was always watching.

Which wasn't a problem. Not only did she take her job seriously, but she didn't have any reason to worry about people watching. The administration could watch, as could all of her students and her sisters. She was a good role model, responsible and dependable. She led a conservative—if somewhat boring—lifestyle.

Until the last couple of days.

She turned as Ryan came back into the room with two cups.

Until Ryan.

Sure, it was a one-time chance to blow off some steam, to live life on the Emma-side briefly. But she was already spending more time with Ryan than she'd intended. She really shouldn't have asked him out, but she'd been honest when she said that she wanted him to see a good side of her. Ryan knew things about her, but he didn't really know her.

But she definitely shouldn't have kissed him.

What the hell had she been thinking?

Okay, it hadn't been intentional, but that was part of the problem—Ryan Kaye made her forget where she was, even *who* she was. Amanda had gotten lucky that none of the students had caught them with Ryan's hand in her pants.

There were other reasons she shouldn't have kissed Ryan too. For one, she shouldn't be pursuing this whole thing with him. Yes, she'd wanted to apologize, show him that she did respect him and that she was a good person, maybe establish more of a friendship. But she didn't want a relationship with him.

For another, what was she actually going to do with him?

Of course, she had some ideas if they were going to spend a couple of hours together.

But what did they have in common? Ryan was the party guy. She was the couch potato. He was the love 'em and leave 'em guy. She was the one who stuck by everyone—even harder and longer than they wanted her to.

So a couple of hours was it. That's what she and Ryan would and *should* have together. All they should have.

Meditation wasn't the first thing on her list of things to do with two hours alone with Ryan Kaye though.

He handed her one of the cups. "First step, my mom's calming tea."

She sniffed the dark brown, nearly black liquid. It smelled slightly spicy, though she couldn't place which spices for sure, and sweet. She sipped. It reminded her a little of chai tea.

Then the aftertaste hit.

"What is this?" she asked, trying not to grimace too hard and insult his mother.

He had crossed to the stereo and pushed a few buttons before soft instrumental music filled the room. "Her own concoction. She sends some with me every time I visit. I don't ask. And I don't tell her that I toss about half of what she gives me. I drink it, but not daily."

"Are you supposed to drink it daily?" She sipped again, tentatively. The tea definitely gave a false sense of security. Everything was fine until you swallowed. Then the taste hit.

He grinned. "I know, it's tough at the end. Not everything she makes is like that. The cleansing tea she makes is bad from start to finish. The tea for better sleep is good all the way down."

It was strange. Even knowing how bad it would taste afterward, she still liked the initial taste enough to keep drinking. With a shudder she swallowed again. "She specializes in teas?"

"She specializes in holistic healing," Ryan said. "Among other things."

He motioned for her to sit on the couch. He joined her, draping his arm along the back.

"Holistic healing? Like herbs and natural medicine type things?"

He nodded. "Some of that. The holistic approach means looking at the physical, mental, spiritual and emotional parts of a person and making sure they all balance. She's into meditation, aromatherapy, whole foods, everything."

"And you practice all of this?" Amanda asked. That was definitely interesting and not what she'd been expecting.

He obviously drank and partied, but she had to admit, Ryan exuded calm. He was laid-back, easygoing, the one who could keep his head in any stressful situation. Conner wasn't the only one who said so and she'd seen it, though maybe on a simpler scale, on the football field. Ryan always seemed to be okay with whatever happened. He didn't get intense or mad or worried.

She actually did envy that. Maybe he could pass some of that on to her after all.

"I practice some of it," he said. "I try to eat well, I exercise, and I do meditate."

"Has your mom always been into all of this?"

"Here."

Ryan took her cup, which she was surprised to find was empty already, and set it on the coffee table. Then he pulled a spongy purple mat from under the couch and unrolled it on the floor.

"Lie on your back, with your knees bent."

She did. She was feeling mellow and interested and like spending more time with Ryan was a hell of an idea.

"We can keep talking, but I'm going to give you a massage."

Ooh, she could hardly complain or protest about that.

He took one of her hands. "I want you to close your eyes and focus on your breathing. In deep through your nose and out through your mouth."

Amanda let her eyes slide shut, and she took her next breath in as he'd instructed.

"Think about your lungs." A heavy, warm hand settled on her chest above her breasts. "Think about pulling air in and filling your lungs, then breathe out, letting all of it escape. Think about your diaphragm." He moved his hand below her breasts, resting comfortably but definitely making her aware of her body under his touch. "The diaphragm has to pull down to fill the lungs. Then it presses up to expel the air. Think about how it all moves together and breathe deep and slow and long."

He lifted his hand and she concentrated for three breaths before he started rubbing her hand.

He started on the pads of her fingers, working down each digit to the center of her palm.

"Yes, my mom has been into holistic healing, natural living, conservation, all of that for as long as I can remember. She's always been one of the most peaceful, happiest people I know. We had a radio and books, but no television, no video games. She's always gardened, made her own teas, medicines, and even beauty products."

"Beauty products?" Amanda asked, but it felt like a lot of

work to form a question. She wanted to just lie there and let Ryan continue rubbing her and talking in that low, soothing voice.

"Yeah, she makes face masks, hair conditioners, lotions, creams, anything. Some of them turn out great, some don't. She's always trying new things."

Amanda could hear the affection in his voice and thought she'd really like to look at his face. But lifting her eyelids seemed to be too much of an effort.

Ryan was rubbing his thumb over the heel of her hand, working into the palm, and she felt tingles of pleasure zinging through her body.

"She also loves to travel. We lived in twelve different states while I was growing up—a new one each year."

"What? Wow, that's a lot of moving."

"We had this old trailer that we lived in. We'd hook it up to the back of the truck and haul it to a new place when we were ready to go."

"You never stayed anywhere more than a year?"

"When I hit twelve years old, we stayed. Here in Nebraska. But now she's back to moving around again."

"What about your dad?"

Ryan's massage had moved up to her forearm and he was working his way past her elbow.

"My dad was around until I was three. Then it was Hank until I was nine. Then she met Larry here and he was with us until I graduated."

Amanda forced her eyes open for this. Ryan had finished with her left arm and moved around to her other side and started the heavenly massage over again. "What happened to these guys?"

"They agreed to part ways."

"They got divorced?"

He shook his head with a small smile. "They were never married to start with. Even Dad. My mom believes that not only can you love many different people in your life, but you should. She was truly in love with all three of them. And now she's with Neil and she loves him too. But all the guys know going in—and agree—that there will be a time when things are over and they'll all part as friends."

Amanda studied Ryan's face. He didn't seem upset or sad. He seemed to be completely accepting of it and content with it.

"So they stayed friends?"

"Yes, we still hear from them all."

"Your dad?"

"Yeah, we stay in touch. I've been out to visit him in Arizona and he's been back here a couple of times."

"And that's okay with you? That these guys have walked in and out of your life? That it's never been anything lasting?"

Ryan looked into her eyes and rubbed his thumb in tantalizing circles over her wrist. "It's okay with me. I'm completely okay. All of those men were good to me and my mom, loved us, taught me things. Then things changed for one or both and they parted ways. It seems healthy to me, actually. There are so many people living in toxic situations that they should get away from, or if one does leave, there's so much anger and animosity. Everyone suffers so much."

She couldn't argue with that. "But it doesn't sound like any of these situations or relationships were ever toxic. Why did they have to end?"

"They ended before they got toxic. If things got complicated or the feelings changed on one side or the other or the goals and plans didn't match up anymore or someone just wanted to try something new or do something else, they agreed it was better to let go."

Amanda turned her head so she was looking up at the ceiling instead. Ryan seemed fine. Who was she to judge the strange way of life—or of relationships at least? It didn't seem like anyone was unhappy in his life.

She closed her eyes and concentrated on the feel of Ryan's

hands on her. He and his past and his mother were certainly nothing she needed to think or worry about. They were fine. She loved when people were fine.

She was soon tingling all over and wanted his hands *all* over, yet she also felt like her bones had melted and her muscles would never again be able to move her.

He calmed her and excited her at the same time. Weird.

He moved to kneel behind her head and set his hands on her shoulders. He began kneading into the muscles that seemed perpetually tight. She let the music drift over her, the feeling of heat and perfect pressure seep into her muscles, and the scent of lavender from somewhere fill her senses.

"Turn over." His low, husky voice made goose bumps dance over her.

She did, of course, turn over. There was absolutely no reason in the world why she *wouldn't* do that.

Ryan continued running his hands over her shoulders, then over her shoulder blades and the muscles on either side of her spine. She wanted to purr.

"There's something else my mom promotes as a way to release stress and get in touch with your inner peace," he said softly.

She knew exactly where this was going, but she said, "Oh, really? What's that?" anyway.

"Orgasm."

Her entire body clenched. "How did I know you were going to say sex?"

His big hands pressed and stroked, working in the curve of her low back above her buttocks. Then he took a cheek in each hand, pressing his thumbs into the muscles and eliciting a soft moan from her. His touch was stimulating and relaxing at the same time. How did he do that?

"I didn't say 'sex'," he said, cupping her buttocks again, then stroking up to her midback, then back down to her midthigh. "I said 'orgasm'."

"But..."

"There's a difference," he said. "Sex is about two people. Good sex means you focus on the other person and tune into them. Orgasm is about you. You and your body."

She was thinking that he might get her to orgasm by just talking about it.

"My mom used to teach classes about it. And she had a hundred books on the topic of sex and health and healing. And she had a blog."

"Your mom had a blog about orgasms?" Amanda asked as he focused on a particularly tender knot under her right shoulder blade.

He chuckled and her toes nearly curled from the sound. "Among other things. Her blog was about the power of sex and how it affects the body."

"It's a little strange that you know a lot about sex because of your mother."

He chuckled again and switched to the muscle in the back of her left thigh. "I accidentally learned most of it. My mom had seminars three times a week at our house. She'd bring a group of women in and they'd talk about sexual issues they were having and so on. I was about thirteen, so...this was interesting eavesdropping for me."

Amanda laughed and then immediately sighed as he worked down to her calf.

"And, of course, she'd be working on the blog sometimes on her laptop when I was around. She often had me proofread it."

"That's..."

"My mom," he said before she could complete the thought. "She's very free-thinking, very open about everything. I knew about penises and vaginas when I was learning what a nose and elbow were. I knew how babies were really made in time to inform my entire first grade class. I also knew about birth control. I overheard my mother giving my favorite babysitter, Trina, a lecture about condoms and safe sex when she found

Trina and her boyfriend having sex in our kitchen while I was supposed to be in bed. I had a lot of questions after that."

"All of which your mom answered?"

"Yep."

Amanda wished she could see his face, but she could tell from his voice that he was still...fine. Very fine. He was very matter-of-fact, very comfortable with all of it.

"And I know that it seems strange," he went on. "But I was one of the last of my friends to have sex in high school. Because I knew, from Mom, that sex was a big deal. But it was an awesome deal. Something to treat with care. I've always taken very good care of the women I'm lucky enough to be with."

Amanda felt her breath catch. She'd been good about focusing on the pattern, the deep, long, calming breaths. But now she couldn't do it. She wasn't calm. She was excited. She was hot and tingly. And there was no way she could breathe easily with Ryan's hands all over her and his voice rough and low...

She turned to her back. Ryan's hands paused for a moment. Then his gaze met hers and his hands continued stroking, up and down the front of her thighs.

"So this orgasm thing," she said.

His pupils dilated and she smiled.

"Maybe you shouldn't have told me how much you know about sex," she said, absorbing the heat and pressure from his hands so she could relive it later. "My expectations are really high now."

He grinned a cocky, tempting, hot grin. "Good. You should always have high expectations for orgasms and sex and how men treat you." His hands stroked higher to the front button of her capris. He unsnapped, unzipped and pulled them over her hips, down her legs and past her feet, then tossed them to the side, watching her the entire time. "Maybe I should put my mouth where my mouth is."

He leaned in, braced a hand on either side of her hips and

then lowered himself like he was doing a push-up until his lips met the sensitive skin right below her belly button. Amanda felt her skin quiver and spirals of heat swirl out from that spot, warming her stomach and into her pelvis.

Ryan kissed her hip bone, then the spot where her hip flexed. He added a little flick of his tongue there and Amanda gasped.

He lifted a hand and reached down for her ankle, stroking his flat palm up the back of her calf to the dip behind her knee. He bent her leg and placed her foot flat on the floor. "I want you to think about all of your tension," he said calmly, kissing her inner thigh, keeping her knee bent. "Gather all the tension into your center, the bad tension and the good." He kissed the inside of her bent knee, running his hand up her leg again. "Think about the bad tension—all the frustrations, all the worries, all the things you want to control, but can't."

She tried to focus but he had now switched to her other leg, stroking and kissing, rubbing the arch of her foot—which made her want to sob with pleasure—then kissing her inner thigh where her panties crossed over her leg—which did make her moan his name.

"And combine it with the good tension," he went on, his voice a little rougher. "Mix the tension that's gathering here—" He laid his hand on her lower stomach. "And here." He ran his hand lower over the front of the pale-blue silk bikini panties she wore, pressing into her mound and making her ache. "And here." He ran his thumb over the silk covering her clit and she gasped, then lifted her hips, wanting to be closer, knowing that he was the only one who could release the pressure building.

When her butt lifted off the mat, he whisked her panties away.

He didn't move or speak for several seconds, and Amanda became more and more aware that he was fully clothed. *She* still had her shirt and bra on for that matter. But she was completely naked from the waist down. Exposed. At his mercy.

She started to wiggle, but Ryan clamped a big hand on

each hip. "I, um..." He cleared his throat. "Sorry. I'm really trying to make this all about you."

She lifted herself up on her elbows. He was staring at her. His cheeks were flushed and he was breathing raggedly.

"I'm the one half-naked. I'd say it's pretty much about me at this point."

He lifted his gaze to meet hers. "Babe, if you don't believe that being here, being allowed to see you like this, isn't about *me*, you don't know anything."

He did look pretty happy. "Just looking is that good?"

His gaze went back to the wet heat between her legs. "Oh, yeah."

She felt her whole body getting warmer. "Is it possible for you to give me an orgasm just by looking?" she asked, letting one of her bent knees fall further out to the side.

Ryan muttered a curse, then said, "I don't think so."

"Then get to work."

Chapter Five

His gaze flew to hers again, clearly surprised and very turned on. "Making you scream is going to be so fun."

She grinned. "I'm not really a screamer."

"You will be."

She started to reply to that, but he let her other leg fall open as well and then ran the tip of one finger over her clit.

One finger. Just one. And she was halfway there.

She let her upper body fall back onto the mat, gripping the edges of it in both hands.

"Good and bad tension," he reminded her. "So that when you come undone, it *all* leaves you. Your release includes *all* the tension, leaving only contentment and positive energy."

"Yeah, yeah. Just keep going." Whatever. Whatever he wanted, whatever she needed to do—she'd do it as long as he kept moving his finger like that.

He did.

He stroked up and down her cleft, spreading her wetness over her folds and her clit. He circled her sweet spot, pressing perfectly to take her closer to the brink, then slid lower and pressed two fingers into her, stroking her inner walls with an exquisitely frustrating, almost-there pressure.

Finally, when she was moaning and gasping his name, he leaned in and licked her.

Her hips bucked and the ball of tension—good, bad, whatever—knotted hard in her gut.

He stroked his fingers deep, his other hand holding her butt, and then sucked her clit. Hard.

"Ryan!" she cried.

"That's right, babe. Let it all go. Jump off that ledge."

Then he sucked again and she gripped his hair—and let it all go.

She didn't just jump. She frickin' launched herself off the ledge, arching through the air and reveling in the feel of the fall.

It was a long fall too. It took several minutes for her to come back to feeling the mat under her, the warm heaviness of Ryan leaning against her legs, the smell of lavender in the air, the sound of the piano from the stereo, the hum of the appliances in the kitchen, and the breathing of the man with her.

She opened her eyes and looked down the length of her body.

Ryan had rolled to one side. He grinned up at her. "So, that's what I know."

She felt the laughter bubble up. "Did any of those books or blogs talk about how fun it can be if *both* people get naked?"

He pushed himself up to sitting. "Babe, this was like chapter one. In a forty- or fifty-chapter book."

She gave him a naughty smile. "Oh, okay. 'Cause I thought maybe I was going to need to teach chapter two."

He smacked her bare butt, then tossed her panties onto her tummy. "See, I know you're trying to get me worked up, talkin' like that."

She frowned at her panties. She hadn't planned on needing them for a while.

He stretched to standing and held out a hand to help her up.

"Getting you worked up isn't a bad idea, is it?" she asked, allowing him to pull her to her feet.

"I've got practice in thirty minutes."

She stared at him. "Practice?"

"Football. The Hawks. Maybe you've heard of us?"

"You started *this* knowing you had practice?"

He smiled down at her. "I started and *finished* helping you relax. Which was my intention the whole time."

"But this was..."

"A great tension reliever."

She frowned at him. "That I could have done for myself with my vibrator."

His eyes darkened slightly, but he just said, "Self-pleasure is a very healthy way to get needed release."

She started to reply but realized he'd led her to his bedroom.

"I'd love it if you'd stay," he said, turning to face her in the doorway. "Now that we have all that healthy, positive, stress-release stuff out of the way, I'm thinking we could get on to chapters two and three. Maybe four depending on your stamina."

She wanted to. She was feeling incredibly mellow. Curling up in his big bed and anticipating his return sounded awesome. She glanced at the clock.

He wouldn't be back for at least two hours. Three if he went out with them for dinner like usual. And if he didn't, he might have to admit why he was anxious to get home...

"I can't," she finally said, clutching her capris to her chest. "It's Sunday night. I have to work tomorrow. This was all supposed to just be this weekend."

One weekend to let go. Then back to real life—with a better appreciation for why her sister was so fond of cutting loose.

Olivia's plan had worked, that was for sure. Amanda got it. Looking up into Ryan's dark blue eyes, she *definitely* got it.

"Stay. Make it more than one weekend."

Sure. With the guy who'd been raised to move on when things grew boring or routine. With her that would take like three days. But she liked that. Boring and routine never hurt anybody.

"I can't."

"Please."

Wow. Ryan Kaye was asking her—with a please—to stay in

his bed for the night. At least.

Why did she think Ryan didn't say please much?

Maybe because he didn't have to. What woman would say no to that?

"Listen, I get it." He lifted his hand to her cheek and stroked his finger over her jaw. "I know this is out of the ordinary for you. I want you to stay. I'll be thinking about it the whole time I'm gone, but it's your choice. If you go, I won't bug you about it. We'll still be friends. We had some fun. It's all good."

There he was—the Ryan who just lived and let live. No begging. No stress. Just whatever. That was his motto.

And suddenly it bugged her.

Ryan got his stuff ready, kissed her goodbye and then headed out with a little "see ya" as the door shut behind him.

She glared at the door.

See ya? As in, *see ya around maybe but it doesn't really matter to me one way or another?* Yeah, that was pretty much how he meant it.

And that really shouldn't upset her. They'd barely been friends before...all of this. It wasn't like not seeing him was going to leave a huge void in her life. Or vice versa.

Dammit. He'd given her an out. Like the nice guy that he was. She should take it and go. And he'd asked her to stay, so it wasn't quite the don't-let-the-door-hit-you-in-the-ass-on-the-way-out that it could have been.

So, fine. She'd take the out. Because what would staying really accomplish? Another amazing orgasm? Two? Sure, probably. And there was no denying that it was tempting. She hadn't had an orgasm, amazing or otherwise, in a long time.

But that would complicate things. Ryan Kaye was the kind of guy to make a girl want to drop everything with a simple text. The kind of guy who could talk her into shutting off her phone, climbing into his bed, and not worrying about things like work, family, food or wearing panties for days at a time.

And that was what she was afraid of. If he gave her those two or so amazing orgasms, she might do exactly that. And a bunch of other things she couldn't do. She was needed. She couldn't just say *damn the consequences*. Not for more than a weekend, anyway.

Plus, her life would eventually drive him crazy. There would be times—lots of times—when she'd have to leave again after just getting home, where she'd miss or have to reschedule dinner dates, where she'd say she could spend all of Saturday morning in bed with him but then she'd get called and have to leave at seven thirty, where she'd agree to go dancing and partying all night but then have a meeting scheduled the next morning, requiring her to go home at a decent hour.

Boring, frustrating stuff for someone who was used to doing whatever felt good at the moment and moving on when the good feelings stopped.

And would he understand driving her mother to six different stores looking for a certain kind of bath towel or buying chocolate cake for Isabelle after she had a bad day at work or staying up too late to watch a marathon of *White Collar* with Olivia—for the third time?

Those were the things the man in her life had to be okay with. They were boring, frustrating things that she did because she loved the people in her life. In her world, sometimes people needed things from her that were just about being there.

And that was the one thing Ryan didn't really do. He was in relationships for now. She was in relationships for forever.

Did he have less frustration, fewer arguments, more fun and more exciting memories with the people who came and went in his life? Yeah, probably.

Would she trade him? Not for more than a weekend.

Amanda pulled Ryan's front door open and came up short with surprise as a big guy stepped up onto the top step.

He looked as surprised to see her. "Well, hello, Dr. Dixon."

She groaned internally. Crap. "Hi, Mac."

What the hell was Mac Gordon doing here? Sure, he was a paramedic where Ryan was, but really? He had to stop by *now*?

"Ryan's not here. He has practice tonight."

"Was hoping to catch him before he left. I guess he *just* left."

"How do you know that?"

"I've seen *that* look on a woman's face often enough to know what you've been up to."

Amanda's hands flew to her cheeks. "You can tell?"

Mac chuckled. "I can now."

She glared at him and swatted his arm. "Not funny. You can*not* tell—"

"Dr. Dixon?" Dooley Miller came up behind Mac on the front steps.

She sighed. "Hi, Dooley." Before he could ask what she was doing in Ryan's house, she asked him. "What are you guys doing here?"

"Ryan's mom's been making some tea for Dooley's dad that's been helping his hip pain," Mac said.

Ah. The magical tea. What couldn't Ryan's mom's tea do?

"Ryan already left," Mac told Dooley.

"Not too long ago, I'd guess," Dooley said, studying Amanda's face.

"Oh, shut up," she said, stepping out of the doorway and closing the door behind her.

Dooley laughed.

"You'll have to come back later," she told them, pulling her purse strap up onto her shoulder.

"We don't want to interrupt—"

"You won't," she said as she pushed between them to head for her car. "It's fine."

Both men chuckled and followed her down the steps.

She swung back to face them. "You guys can't tell Conner."

"Tell Conner what?" Dooley asked. "We don't know anything."

Mac elbowed him. "That's true for one of us more than the other."

She gave them one of the frowns that she saved for students who weren't taking something seriously. "You guys can*not* tell Conner," she repeated.

Mac shook his head. "Trust me, Amanda, I've been in Ryan's shoes. I'm not telling Conner anything." Then he got a thoughtful look on his face. "Though, come to think of it, I'd love to torture Conner some. He's always telling my wife how nice she looks and it always gives her this little smile—"

Amanda stepped up close. Mac was a lot bigger than her. A lot. Of course, he was bigger than most everyone. But that didn't stop her from poking him in the chest and saying, "You are *not* telling Conner anything."

Mac's eyes got a little wide and he held up both hands in surrender. "I won't say a word."

She took a deep breath. In spite of Conner's not-so-secret crush on Mac's wife, Sara, Amanda knew she could trust Mac. "Thanks."

She headed for her car and was sliding behind the wheel when Mac called out, "You're going to have to tell him eventually."

She shook her head. "There's nothing to tell."

"Then you better be careful not to think about Ryan when you're with your brother. That little blush will give you away every time."

She put a hand to her cheek and glared at Mac. Because, yeah, her cheek did feel a little warmer.

She slammed the door and started the car, backing out and turning out onto the street without looking back at the men on Ryan's doorstep. And she practiced *not* thinking about Ryan all the way home.

By the time she pulled into her garage, two things were clear—not thinking about Ryan was going to take some real self-discipline...and a lot more practice.

"Kaye!"

Ryan turned to find Mac Gordon and Dooley Miller coming toward him. He and Nate were on the edge of the field, warming up with ball tosses. Ryan held up a hand to keep Nate from throwing to him for a minute.

"Hey, guys. What's up?"

"We stopped by your house to pick up more of that tea for Dad," Dooley said.

"Oh, sorry. Must have just missed me."

"Yeah, that's what Amanda said," Dooley replied.

The words hung in the air between them. Then Ryan grabbed each of the men by their sleeves and turned them away from the field where the rest of the Hawks were warming up.

"You saw Amanda?"

Even her name caused his gut to knot with need. Walking away had been so hard. Necessary. But hard. Necessary because he needed her to know that he was content to spend time with her that didn't involve sex. Of course, he'd kind of blown that. The whole thing had been specifically *not* about him and all about her, but it would definitely be considered sexual by—okay, pretty much anyone. But there wasn't a heterosexual man on the planet who could have touched Amanda the way he had and *not* taken it further.

He wasn't a professional masseuse, but his mother was—among other things—and she'd taught him everything she knew. He'd given plenty of massages to people for everything from stress reduction to a strained calf muscle. And even with the hottest girls, he was able to keep that separate from any attraction. But he couldn't have kept his mouth off of Amanda for all the money, beer or touchdowns in the world.

"Oh, we definitely saw Amanda," Mac said with a grin. "Just as she was leaving."

"You guys can't say—" Ryan focused. "She was leaving?"

"Yep."

Well, fuck. Somehow he'd known she'd leave. He wasn't surprised. He was, however, inordinately disappointed. He'd hoped… Well, it didn't matter now.

"I was… It was… We didn't sleep together."

"You must have done *something* right, judging by the blush I got from her."

Ryan couldn't help a small grin at that. "Yeah, thanks. I guess. But we didn't sleep together," he felt it necessary to repeat.

"Well, maybe that's why she left," Mac said with a shrug.

"Why not?" Dooley asked at the same time.

"It wasn't…the right time." Ryan knew that sounded stupid, but it was true.

"Did you tell her that?" Dooley asked, his expression showing that he thought it sounded stupid too.

"No. I…" Ryan trailed off and ran his hand through his hair again. "I told her that I had to get to practice."

Dooley shook his head, almost with sympathy. "And it looks like the right time isn't going to happen at all now."

Ryan frowned. Had Amanda said something? Okay, so he'd told her that he'd leave it alone if she decided not to stay. They could still be friends, blah, blah, blah.

But he didn't want to leave it alone.

The thought hit him and he had to think about it harder. That never happened. He always wanted to leave it alone. If the other person wasn't into it—whatever "it" was—Ryan was good with that. He didn't want people doing things they didn't want to do—whether it was seeing a movie or having sex in the shower. And he wasn't really into convincing people that they should feel or think something they didn't.

"The right time's gonna happen," Ryan told Dooley. How, he wasn't sure. He wasn't exactly the on-his-knees-begging type of guy.

Dooley looked thoughtful. "Good luck, brother."

Mac slapped him on the back. "Ah, you might be better off

than you think. Like I said, the look on her face was... Well, you definitely have a chance."

"The thing is," Dooley said, "women are like fine steaks."

Mac gave a little groan and Ryan smiled. Dooley had all kinds of analogies for women and relationships. They were surprisingly insightful. Sometimes.

"How so?" Ryan asked.

"Don't encourage him," Mac said.

"The outcome is about heat and time," Dooley went ahead, ignoring Mac. "Without heat, you get nowhere. Things stay cold and raw. Not good. Too much heat and things end up burned and ruined. But with the right amount of heat, for the right amount of time, you get pink, moist and warm in the middle."

Ryan looked from Dooley to Mac. Mac was staring at Dooley.

Mac wrinkled his nose. "Seriously?"

"What's pink, moist and warm in the middle?" Conner asked from behind Ryan.

Ryan jumped and said, "Steak," as Dooley calmly replied, "Women."

Conner looked at Dooley with the same combination of wonder and confusion that Ryan felt.

"That's...interesting," Conner said. "Why are you talking about women and steak and holding up practice?"

Unconcerned about the Hawks' practice schedule, Dooley said, "I was explaining about the proper application of heat and time to women."

"And steaks," Mac added.

Conner grinned at Mac. "Well, you do know something about the prime cuts."

Ryan covered his laugh with a fake cough. Conner was getting more brazen in his comments about Sara Gordon. It came from the fact that Conner had firmly established himself as one of the best paramedics in Omaha and the fact that Mac had never acted on any of the threats he made when Conner spouted off.

Everyone, including Conner, knew that Mac had absolutely no reason to worry about his wife running off with another man.

Ryan knew Conner really did have a thing for Sara, but he also had a thing for giving Mac a hard time. Ryan wasn't sure which was a stronger factor. It was entertaining either way.

"Don't," Mac said simply to Conner.

"And I think I get what you mean," Conner said to Dooley. "Like, if you apply too little heat, even over a long period, it never gets quite *done*, you know?" Conner grinned at Mac. "Like if your heating element is too old to do the job or something."

Mac pointed a finger at Conner's nose, reacting exactly as Conner had hoped. "If I'm the old heating unit in this analogy, I'm gonna put you on your ass."

Conner chuckled. "Now why would you assume I was talking about you when I mentioned something being old? You worried about something?"

The fact that Mac was twelve years older than his wife—and that Conner was only three years older than Sara—was a common jab.

Mac sighed, then shoved Conner. It wasn't quite hard enough to put him on his ass, but it wasn't a friendly nudge either.

Conner laughed and rubbed his shoulder. "Okay, let's go, Kaye. We've got practice."

"Yeah, right behind you."

Conner jogged back to their waiting teammates.

Ryan wasn't sure that he should exactly thank Mac and Dooley for their advice, but he felt the need to wrap up the conversation. Maybe with another warning not to say anything about Amanda to her big brother.

"Remember," Dooley said before Ryan could speak, "don't keep things simmering too long. Turn up the heat a little and get things done."

Yeah—"pink, moist and warm" were not exactly the words Ryan needed in his head as he joined his team on the field. But the words wouldn't leave him, and as his hunger grew, it definitely wasn't steak he was craving.

"What the *fuck*, Dixon?" Shane Kelley demanded forty minutes later.

Ryan turned to see Shane getting up from the ground—and Conner walking back to the line of scrimmage. Shane was an offensive lineman, in place to protect the quarterback and the ball. In the drills they were running, the only defensive players were the ones downfield covering the receivers. There was no reason for Shane to be on the ground.

Shane got up and stormed after Conner. "We're on the same goddamned team," he said. "And you're the fucking quarterback in case you forgot."

QBs didn't make tackles, or even do much blocking, unless maybe they threw an interception and were the last line of defense.

"What's going on?" Nate asked, getting between the guys before the coach could hit the field.

"I hit him," Conner said simply.

"From behind on an *offensive* drill," Shane added.

"Why?" Nate asked Conner.

"He got Isabelle in trouble at work."

Ryan sighed, along with everyone else.

Conner generally preferred to ignore the fact that a friend and teammate was dating—and sleeping with—one of his sisters. But there were times he couldn't. Like when Isabelle got hurt.

"So is one hit enough?" Cody asked, looking between the men. "It's over now?"

"I don't know," Conner said, frowning at Shane. "This shit is getting old."

"I agree," Shane said, stepping forward. "You getting involved in stuff that's between me and Iz is definitely getting old."

"You messed up a business deal for her," Conner said.

"The guy hitting on her was being an ass."

"The guy 'hitting on her'," Conner said, "was the head of pediatric cardiology at St. A's."

"He's married," Shane said.

"He was talking to her about a new medication her company just introduced, you jackass," Conner said. "You embarrassed her and probably ruined her chances of ever getting another meeting with him."

"What did you do?" Cody interrupted to ask Shane.

"I didn't do anything. I *threatened* to do something."

Nate frowned. "Shane, you're a cop. You can't threaten people and you definitely can't actually hit anyone just because they're talking to your girlfriend."

"He was talking about her tits."

Conner rolled her eyes. "They were talking about—"

"I was sitting right there," Shane interrupted. "When she went to the bathroom he looked right at me and said, 'Tits that nice can't be real, can they?'"

All the guys held their breaths and looked at Conner.

Conner scowled as he processed that. Then he pulled in a long breath through his nose, then let it out.

"*You* pissed her off."

"Yeah. Because by the time she got back I'd told the guy to get lost."

"You deal with criminals all the time who don't understand consequences. How do you not get that what you do can affect Isabelle?" Conner asked with clear frustration.

Shane frowned. "I do get that, Dixon. The consequence to my action was getting Isabelle away from that slimeball."

"And messing up a work situation *and* upsetting her, which is what landed you on your ass a little bit ago," Conner snapped. "Consequences."

Shane stepped forward. "I'll do it again if it ever comes up.

Your sister deserves respect and part of my job as her *boyfriend* is to protect her."

"Then I'll put you on your ass again," Conner said.

For God's sake. "Let him hit him," Ryan said. He stepped forward, too. "In fact, why don't you take a couple swings at me too, Dixon?"

Conner scowled at him. "I'll hit you for messing with Emma. What do I need the other swing for?"

"How about just in case? Then if I do something in the future, we're even."

"You have a plan you want to share?"

"Nope." He had a plan, but he definitely didn't want to share how he was going to do things to Amanda that would make even Shane blush.

"Then I'd prefer to beat your ass as you deserve it." Conner looked around at all the guys. "That goes for all of you."

Shane snorted.

Conner looked over. "What?"

"I might have hit the ground, but it didn't even hurt my ego."

Conner grabbed the football from Nate. "How 'bout we run another play?"

Shane shrugged and moved to the line. "If I know you're coming, you're never gettin' me off my feet."

"Uh-huh," was Conner's response.

"You do realize that he's one of the guys who will be keeping the big, mean guys on the other team from getting through to you next week, right?" Cody asked Conner.

"This is about right now," Conner said.

Which was true. On game night they were a team, no matter what else happened. None of the big, mean guys on the other team would be getting to Conner through Shane. No matter how much of a prick Conner was being.

Ryan took off downfield on Conner's call, following the pattern of the play. He caught the ball and was brought up short on the ten-yard line. When he got up and looked back, he saw Conner climbing to his feet. And Shane walking away.

An offensive lineman tackling the QB? Sure, Coach would love that.

Coach Henry shouted some expletives and an order to pull their heads out of their asses from the sidelines, Conner raised a hand, signaling he was fine, and the team huddled up.

The next play Conner got Shane down again.

Then Conner called another play that sent Ryan down the field. It was a play designed to pull two defensive players to Ryan, leaving Cody open. But Conner threw to Ryan. Into double coverage. And Ryan caught the ball. But he got slammed into from both sides. Hard.

He got up slower than usual and headed straight for Conner.

"What the hell?"

"I was thinking about that 'just in case' thing," Dixon said.

"And?" Ryan demanded.

"Thought maybe it was a good idea to be safe."

"You can be a real asshole, you know that?"

"Keep that in mind," Conner said, turning away. "Burgers or pizza?"

Ryan watched the best quarterback in the league walk away. Yes, he could be an asshole, but he was also a really good guy.

Ryan rubbed his ribs where he'd been hit by Parker on that last play. The play that had given him a "just in case" to spend. And after that intentional double hit, he was going to make it count.

"I'm gonna pass on dinner," Ryan said as the guys all gathered their bags and gear.

"You never pass on dinner," Cody said. "What's up?"

It was true. He didn't have better stuff to do generally. Women would typically be a higher priority than beer or pizza, but he never scheduled dates on Sunday nights.

Which made this whole thing with Amanda even more unusual.

"Not in the mood."

"For pizza and beer? Isn't that a perpetual mood?" Shane asked.

True again.

"Perpetual? What's with the fancy words?" Cody asked, elbowing Shane.

Shane flipped him off.

They all laughed, and it occurred to Ryan that Amanda was pretty much the only thing that promised to be more fun than these guys.

"Yeah, it's unusual for me to pass up beer and pizza with you charmers," he said. "But I got something to do."

He ignored the questions about what he had to do and if the *something* was actually a *someone*. He made a big deal about packing up his equipment—slowly—as he waited until the guys had mostly moved off. Then he grabbed Shane's arm and pulled him to the side.

"Hey, you think Conner's ever gonna get past you dating his sister?"

The tension between two guys on the team was bad enough, but there was no way he and Conner could survive if Conner wanted to constantly hit Ryan while they were on duty. And if he knew even a third of the things Ryan wanted to do with Amanda, Conner would want to hit him. Hard. Constantly.

Shane shrugged. "Hope so."

"Why do you keep rubbing it in his face?"

"Because I'm not going anywhere and he needs to figure that out. He doesn't have to like it, but he does have to deal with it. I'm not going to walk away from Isabelle, and I'm not going to walk on eggshells around my friend just because he's her brother."

Okay, Ryan could respect that. "But you can't blame him for wanting to hit you when you upset Isabelle."

"If she was upset because I was being mean or hurting her, I'd be fine with him hitting me. But Conner's always been the big hero to those girls, fixing everything, taking care of everything. Now I'm here and she doesn't need him as much and it's bugging him. He's just picking fights."

Ryan thought about that. It made sense.

What didn't make sense was how much he liked the idea of being the one Amanda depended on to fix things for her.

"You think Conner will eventually come around to the idea that another guy can love one of his sisters as much or more than he does?"

Conner was looking out for his sisters, and Ryan—and he suspected Shane too—understood and respected that.

But Conner didn't know everything.

Like the side of his sisters that he never got to see—the sexy, sweet, passionate and vulnerable side that had Ryan in knots.

Shane raised an eyebrow. "Emma?"

Ryan shook his head.

"Ah." Shane nodded. "Amanda."

Ryan stared at Shane. He didn't look a bit surprised. "You're not shocked?"

Shane shrugged. "Amanda's amazing and you're a smart guy."

Ryan smiled. He couldn't argue with that. "Will I survive?"

Shane chuckled and clapped Ryan on the shoulder. "Well, I've got a couple extra ice packs you can borrow."

He hoped that was all he'd need to heal things after Conner found out about him and Amanda. Because he would. Because Ryan didn't have a chance of staying away from her.

He pulled his cell from his pocket as he headed for his car. He dialed Emma's number. He was going to need some help.

"Hey," she answered on the third ring.

"Any chance you could get Olivia away from her condo for a while tonight?" Amanda and Olivia lived together and, while he didn't know the youngest sister well, he had the impression she was a stay-at-home-on-a-Sunday-night kind of girl. Like Amanda.

"Uh." There was a long pause. "Hang on."

The sound on her end of the phone was suddenly muffled—he assumed by her hand. A minute later she was back. "I'm at their place now."

"Amanda there?"

"Yep."

"Olivia?"

"Yep."

"So you and Olivia need to get lost."

He knew Emma well enough to know that she was smiling.

"I'm making dinner."

"Stop."

"It's gonna be good."

"Em… I'll…" He thought fast. What would definitely get Emma on his side? "…buy you new shoes."

She chuckled. "Wow. You know my taste in shoes, so that's pretty big."

"Yeah." Emma didn't do anything the simple way if there was a harder way, or the cheap way if there was a more expensive way.

"But this is my chance to impress my sisters."

He couldn't help but grin. Emma would do this for him even without the promise of new shoes, but she was testing him. She knew him. She would know what this meant.

Was he ready for someone to know what this meant? Did *he* really know what this meant?

He was going after a girl for the first time in practically forever. It meant something. Something big.

"What do you want?" he asked.

"Ooh, gee, let's see. I have a feeling I could really push this."

He sighed. "Yeah."

"But I'm thinking that *you* are off the list of options."

He frowned. "What's that mean?"

"It means, if I wanted a long, hot weekend with you in exchange for getting Olivia out of here for a while, I'm guessing that's a no-go."

"Is that what you want?" It didn't matter. She couldn't have it...or him.

"I'm just asking."

"Fine. No. I'm not an option."

"Because..." she prompted.

"Because I don't think Amanda would be into sharing me. Especially with her sister."

He wasn't sure how he knew exactly, but he had the feeling that once Amanda decided to be with someone, she would be the possessive type. Just like she was protective of the people she cared about and who depended on her, she wouldn't want someone else messing with someone she was intimate with.

He liked the idea of her feeling he belonged to her somehow. Even if it was for a short time.

Besides, having any other woman in his bed didn't sound good, or right, now. Considering Amanda hadn't even been in his bed yet, that was also...something.

"Okay, you're totally right and I'm glad you realize that. So, I'll help you. But I need about forty-five minutes to make it convincing."

"That's too long." Five minutes was too long.

"Fine. I'll tell Amanda what's going on and to meet you on her bed wearing nothing but a big red bow and a smile."

The image of Amanda like that hit him hard.

Except Amanda wouldn't do that. In fact, he knew that he couldn't give her a chance to think about any of this for too long. He'd already asked her to stay and she'd left. Giving her a chance to mentally review the pros and cons here was not going to work in his favor.

"Okay, I'll be there in forty-six minutes."

"Don't push me, Kaye. I said I need forty-five minutes. Which for me means more like sixty."

"Make it fifty and I'll throw in dessert at dinner."

"You're paying for dessert *and* drinks *and* the cab home anyway," Emma informed him.

Ryan grinned. He really did like Emma.

But he'd never given up pizza and beer for her, and he'd never gone so far as to get someone else involved in getting her alone.

If he had asked her to stay and she had left anyway, he would have let it go.

As he probably should with Amanda.

"I'll be there in sixty."

"I'll be out in sixty-one."

He sighed. Emma Dixon was one hot, fun, huge pain in the ass.

"I burned the lasagna."

Amanda looked up from the research article she was pretending to read. She pulled her reading glasses from her nose to focus on her sister. "You what?"

"Burned the lasagna," Emma repeated, pulling a cute little white linen jacket on over her bright purple tank top. "So, we're going to the Olive Garden. Want to come? My treat."

"You *burned* the lasagna?"

Emma sighed. "Yes. Okay? But I'm taking Olivia out so she can still have it tonight."

How did someone burn lasagna? "You're a good cook," Amanda pointed out the fact that would likely surprise most people who knew Emma. She didn't seem the domestic type. At all.

Emma rolled her eyes. "I was doing my nails and forgot to set the time." She wiggled her fingertips.

Amanda frowned. "They look the same."

"I used the same color." Emma tucked her hands into her pockets. "You coming or not?"

Amanda had already taken her makeup off and changed into her yoga pants. Emma knew she didn't like to go out after she'd changed at the end of the day. She'd go to the hospital or police department to pick up one of her sisters like this if necessary, but no way was she going out to dinner dressed like this. She could, of course, change, but Emma was already swinging her purse up onto her shoulder.

"No, I'm good," Amanda told her.

Emma shrugged and started to turn.

"Hey, bring me cake though, 'kay?" Not that cake was a substitute for Ryan, but she was going to give filling the void with sugar a valiant effort.

Emma gave her a thumbs-up.

Interrupted from the article about gait analysis in geriatric patients with big toe amputations, Amanda followed her sister into the kitchen.

It definitely smelled like burned lasagna. Damn. She really liked lasagna and Emma really was a good cook.

But she also really took her nails seriously.

Amanda glanced at the stove where the ruined pasta sat, still covered with aluminum foil with the oven under it still on. "Five hundred degrees?" She swung to face her sister, mouth open. "You set it for five hundred degrees?"

Emma shrugged again. "Must have bumped it up accidentally."

She was eating PB&J because Emma had accidentally cooked their lasagna at one hundred and fifty degrees hotter than the directions called for? Dammit.

"Ready," Olivia said, coming into the kitchen. She looked at Amanda. "You're going like that?"

"No, she's not coming," Emma said quickly, grabbing Olivia's arm. "Let's go. I'm starving."

"Oh, come on, Amanda, come with us," Olivia said. "It'll be

fun."

"She's fine," Emma said, waving a hand in Amanda's direction. "Already took her makeup off." She started for the door, trying to tug Olivia with her.

"We can wait," Olivia protested.

"No, we have a reservation," Emma said, pulling the door to the garage open.

"The Olive Garden takes reservations for two?" was the last thing Amanda heard as Emma pulled Olivia into the garage and slammed the door.

Wow, Emma was really excited about the Olive Garden.

Amanda crossed to the oven and lifted the corner of the foil. This was really too bad. The edges were definitely black and crisp. She pulled the foil back a little further. The rest didn't look so bad though. Maybe the middle was salvageable. When it came to lasagna, she wasn't too proud to eat straight from the pan. She grabbed a fork and was about to dig in when there was a knock at the door.

She looked back at the lasagna. She could pretend she wasn't here. Or didn't hear the knock.

But the next knock was accompanied by several presses of the doorbell.

Fine. She cast a longing glance at the lasagna and put the fork down—for the two minutes it would take her to get rid of whoever was bugging her on a Sunday night.

But all thoughts of noodles, sauce, and even cheese—and that was saying something—vanished when she opened the door to Ryan.

"Here's the thing," he said, stepping over the threshold before she could say a word. "As soon as you stop wanting me around, I'll stop being around."

She backed up as he came forward, surprised by how glad she was to see him.

"You say the word and I'm out," he promised. "But for right now—" He pushed the door shut behind him. "—let me stay."

He cupped her face and leaned in to kiss her.

Yes, was all that Amanda could think. He'd come after her.

This kiss was far sweeter than she'd expected. She wanted hot and wet and deep.

This was sweet. And still hot and deep.

Ryan lifted his head long, delicious seconds later. "Let me stay. Let's have some fun. I promise not to complicate things."

Wow.

"What's the word?" she asked softly.

"The word?"

"You said all I have to do is say the word. What's the word?" She was teasing him. She couldn't imagine actually using a word that would make Ryan go away. Which was a problem.

But when he looked at her like he was now, she had a really hard time remembering why.

"Huckleberry."

She blinked up at him. "Huh?"

He gave her a sexy half smile. "The word is *huckleberry.*"

Ah. Okay. "That's…"

"Not a word that would come up accidentally," he pointed out. "Like if we used *kiss,* that could get confusing when you're begging me to kiss you."

He bent and did it again, a hot, open-mouthed kiss that almost went as deep as she needed it to. Almost.

"I'd never suggest we use a word that we're going to be saying as often as *kiss,*" she said, pulling back. "Or a word like *fuck.*"

She yanked his shirt up and over his head. "Or *cock.*" She ran her hands over his chest. "Or *suck,* or *harder* or—"

He cut her off with another hot kiss that was finally, exactly the deep, wet, hot kiss she'd been longing for. He ran his hand up under her T-shirt, his middle finger trailing over the bumps of her spine. "Sorry," he muttered against her lips, "Couldn't hold back anymore. But please feel free to keep going with those words."

She smiled up at him. "Words? Like what?"

"*Clit, pussy, wet, hot—*"

Yep, that worked. She kissed him this time.

Pulling back several seconds later, she took a deep breath and remembered to say, "But you have to promise to use the word too if you want to get rid of *me*."

He chuckled. "Okay, babe. Deal." He kissed her again. "Just please don't use it for the next hour or so."

She went up on tiptoe and wrapped her arms around his neck. "Deal," she whispered. Then she kissed him the way she'd been aching to.

Their tongues met in long, bold strokes as his big hands gripped her hips and backed her up against the nearest wall.

Her shirt and bra landed on the floor on top of his shirt a moment later, and his fingers were at work on the front tie of her yoga pants when she pulled back to look at him.

She'd seen him without a shirt a time or two at practice, but up close and under her hands was much preferred to from a distance and while he was talking to other women.

"Bedroom is the second door on the left. Feel free to leave your pants here," she told him.

She was almost to the bedroom door when she felt him move in behind her. The next thing she knew she was in his arms and he was striding toward her bed. He dumped her onto the mattress and tossed a condom onto the comforter beside her. Amanda realized he'd taken her seriously about the pants. And underwear.

Ryan wore naked very well though. He had dark hair, neither too thick nor too sparse, that covered his chest and trailed down his nicely defined abs to his cock. Which was fully erect...and fully magnificent.

As someone who made a living appreciating what the human body could do at its peak, she was at a loss for any words other than *mine*.

For tonight he was hers.

"I'm going to be very tired tomorrow," she told him. She lay back and started to shimmy her pants and panties off, but Ryan took over, whipping both off and throwing them over his shoulder.

His eyes darkened as he looked at her. "You know how earlier we were working on relaxing and being mellow?"

"Yeah."

"Now I want you revved up. *Really* revved up." He climbed up on the mattress, covering her body with his.

The soft hair on his chest rubbed over her nipples, and she arched closer. "So far, so good."

He kissed her hungrily, then moved his mouth down her throat to her collarbones. "I haven't spent enough time here," he said, kissing down her chest and over the upper curve of her left breast. He lifted his head as his hand cupped her breast, and he studied the nipple. "How do you feel about talking during sex?" he asked. "Because I feel the need to tell you how gorgeous you are and how lucky I feel to be here with you and then go into detail about all the things I want to do to you."

His hot gaze on her body had been enough to make her wiggle with the need to move, to get closer, to do *more*, but now she felt like every inch of her was jumping and squirming for him.

"You can do whatever you want," she said sincerely.

"Oh, babe, be careful saying that to a man when you're lying there naked like that."

"Come on, Ryan. Try to shock me."

He groaned. "You got it." He bent his head to her nipple and took a long lick.

She gripped the back of his head and let her breath out on a long hiss.

"I want to suck right here until you feel the pulses in your clit," he said gruffly.

She held back the little whimper that threatened and

pressed her legs together.

"Oh, no," he said, shifting to his side and running his hand down her torso to her mound. "Open up."

"Ryan," she moaned.

"I love how easy it is to get you going," he said.

Yeah, well, that was more because of him than anything, but she didn't say it out loud. She parted her legs though.

"There we go." His hand still rested on her mound, not moving lower. "Now let's see how bad we can make you ache."

"I want you to ache too," she said, lifting her hips, her body seeking his hand.

Ryan pressed his hips closer, his erection firm against her thigh. "Babe, I've been aching for you since I heard about our one night together."

She smiled. "That was just a story."

"In my imagination it was the hottest night I've ever had."

That took her breath for a moment. Then with all seriousness she said, "Show me."

Chapter Six

Ryan felt like she'd set him on fire. He burned for her everywhere.

He lowered his head and took her nipple into his mouth, sucking lightly at first, then harder as she moaned.

He felt his entire body being pulled toward her. For just a second, he resisted. The strength of his need for her was new and a little frightening, frankly. But then he dove right in. He wasn't much for regrets and tomorrow was a long way off.

"You feel it?" he asked, moving to her other nipple. He played with the wet one, rolling and pinching slightly.

"Yes," she breathed.

"Where?"

"All over."

He smiled. "Your toes tingling?"

She nodded.

"Your scalp tingling?"

She smiled and nodded again.

"And your clit?"

She licked her lips. "Definitely."

"I want you to the point that all I have to do is stroke one finger over you and you'll come apart."

"Let's find out." She spread her legs further and Ryan groaned.

She was beautiful. She was bare except for a small triangle of blond hair and he could see how wet she was.

He sucked on her other nipple hard, making her cry out, before lifting his head and sliding down her body. He took a thigh in each hand and spread her wide.

"I want to taste you," he said, looking up at her. "But I don't want you to come yet."

She was breathing fast and her cheeks, throat and chest were flushed. She nodded.

"Do you think you can wait? Hold off?"

She shook her head no.

He chuckled. "Promise to try?"

"Yes."

"Anything I want to do, right?"

Her eyes got bigger, but she nodded.

Then he flipped her onto her stomach.

She gave a surprised gasp, but couldn't say anything before he pulled up on her hips. "Hands and knees, Mandi."

She pushed up, straightening her elbows without pause.

Ryan groaned in appreciation. He loved this position.

"This is one of my favorites," she said, wiggling her delectable ass.

Ryan felt his eyebrows rise. "Is that right? Why is that?" He ran a palm over her sweet, smooth skin.

"It just feels dirty or something," she said. "And it's deeper this way."

Ryan breathed out a long breath. "Deep and dirty. You're my kind of girl."

She wiggled again. "Good."

Oh, it sure was. He could see all her wet pinkness and he ran a finger along her cleft. Her butt and thighs clenched at his touch.

"Remember, you can't come yet," he told her, leaning in to lick her.

She gasped and her hands tightened on the bedspread. "I'll...try," she managed.

Her breasts swayed as he stroked her again with a single finger and reached up to cup one, then pinched her nipple.

She pressed back against his hand. "Definitely tingling all over," she told him.

He grinned, aching to drive into her, but loving playing with her more at the moment. He slid his finger partway into her heat.

Her heartfelt *yes* made him press further, but then he retreated as he felt her inner walls clench, trying to hold on to him.

"*Deep* and dirty," she protested.

He took a deep breath. "I've got more dirty for you before we go deep," he said.

He wanted—needed—to see how far she'd let him go, how he could push her. He couldn't even come up with something that would be adequately dirty and satisfying. He wanted to do it all with and to her and still knew he wouldn't feel *done*.

"Bring it on," she said sassily, looking over her shoulder at him.

"You sure?" he asked, moving around to her head.

"Yeah."

She tried to rise onto her knees but he put a hand on each shoulder, keeping her on all fours.

"I want you right there while you suck me."

Her attention was already on his cock. Her eyes flew to his, then back to his throbbing erection.

"Oh, yay," she said with feeling.

He almost lost it right then.

Thankfully, he kept his cool because he would not have wanted to miss the experience of Amanda Dixon shifting forward and licking the head of his cock.

He swore and cupped the back of her head. She started to lift a hand to his shaft, but he stopped her. "I'll do it." For one thing, the touch of her hand on him might very well set him off. For another, he liked having bossy Dr. Dixon a little submissive.

She looked up at him and simply licked her lips.

Holding his breath, Ryan took his heavy shaft in hand and put the head to her mouth.

She opened willingly and he pressed forward, feeding her an inch at a time.

Then she sucked. And he swore and gripped her hair. And she sucked harder.

She pulled her head back, her lips firm against him as he slid from her mouth. When he moved again she took him fully, her tongue and lips and suction heaven on earth. He slid in and out of her mouth for several strokes, feeling the pressure building.

She was good—no doubt about it—and with her hands involved too, she might have killed him. But more it was *her*. She hummed with pleasure, she sucked greedily, she took it all.

Amanda Dixon was amazing. And that was before he knew she gave a mind-melting blow job.

Ryan jerked his hips back suddenly. It was not going to end like this. "Turn around."

She did, further firing his blood.

He slid two fingers into her, gratified to find her wet and hot and ready. He drew the pad of his thumb over her clit, and her whole body shuddered. He wanted to make a quip about *deep* now but all he could say was, "God, Amanda."

Her arousal for him was enough to make him want to howl with satisfaction.

"Ryan," was all she said in return, but he couldn't have wanted her more.

He slipped on the condom with shaking hands—his hands never shook—then he gripped her hips and thrust forward, sliding deep, every inch of him pulsing with pleasure as he filled her.

She moaned and pressed back, ensuring he was as deep as he could go.

He paused, absorbing the feel of her, of them together. But Amanda wasn't shy. She pulled forward and pressed back, taking him deep again and again until finally he had to take over—and increase—the rhythm.

He pumped into her, their groans and gasps mingling.

She felt amazing, perfect, unbelievable, and soon he could tell she was close.

"I want to see you when you come," he said, pulling out and flipping her to her back.

Before she could even take a breath, he pulled one of her knees over his shoulder, keeping her leg high and wide, and plunged deep again.

She gasped and he felt her muscles begin milking him, her orgasm building.

"Ryan."

His gaze focused on her face, the way her eyes slid shut, the way she pulled her bottom lip between her teeth and the way her brow furrowed as her climax built and then finally crashed over her.

Her muscles clamped down hard and she cried out.

Only then did Ryan let his own orgasm go. It ripped through him, tearing a shout from his chest that sounded a lot like a roar of an animal.

He loved that five minutes later, Amanda was still breathing hard. He finally rolled to one side, resting his hand on her belly. "So, now that we're warmed up..." he said.

She laughed and rolled toward him. "You shouldn't tease. I've got plenty of ideas to keep you here."

Ryan shifted to lean on his elbow. "Do you now? I'd love to hear some of these. Feel free to go into detail."

"Really?"

She looked excited by the idea.

"Of course. A gorgeous woman with fantasies? Fantasies that she wants to play out with me? Hell yeah, really."

She propped up on both elbows, distracting him with her beautiful breasts. His tongue remembered the feel of the hard tips, the taste of her skin perfectly.

"Have you ever done any role-playing?"

His gaze bounced from her breasts to her face. "Seriously?"

He'd had one girlfriend who'd liked it and they'd done it a couple of times. Mostly she just liked him to talk her through the fantasy—things like *your husband will be home soon and I don't have the plumbing fixed yet* or *if you want an A in my class you better give an A+ blow job*. But once or twice she'd dressed up too. He'd enjoyed it. A lot.

"I've done a little," he finally said, once he unglued his tongue from the roof of his mouth and ignored the image of Amanda in that pirate slave outfit he'd conjured.

"So you'd do that with me?" she asked, her eyes bright.

"I'll do *anything* with you," he told her. And he was afraid that really was true.

"We should go to that cool costume place," she said, sitting up and swinging her legs over the side of the bed.

"Now?" He sat up too, but with the intention of pulling her back underneath him.

She grabbed for her yoga pants and grinned at him. "Yeah. It's still Sunday night. Or we could go to a bar and you could pretend to pick me up. Or I could pick you up—and we could have sex in the storeroom."

"Who *are* you?" he asked, climbing from the bed. "Never mind. I don't care. Let's go."

Just then he heard the loud rumble of her stomach.

"Maybe we should eat first," she said with a cute eye roll. She took a new bra and shirt out of her dresser and pulled them on. "Ooh, maybe we could pretend that you're a food critic and I have to have sex with you so you'll give me a good review."

She was really into this. He grinned, suddenly gung ho. "Let's get something quick and head for the costumes. I have a pirate fantasy gaining steam here."

She twirled to face him as he pulled the sheet from the bed to use while he retrieved his pants from the first floor.

"Really?" She looked like a kid who'd been promised a trip to the circus. "A pirate? Like Johnny Depp?"

Not exactly. But he did appreciate what Depp had done for

women's interest in pirates. He'd always wanted to be a pirate. "Really. An eye patch and everything."

"Ooh, let's go." She was still holding her socks as she started for the steps.

He followed and dressed quickly, already picturing the skimpy dress that his pirate slave would need to have. And maybe one of those iron rings for around her ankle to help keep her in place.

"Let's get something there," Amanda said from his front seat a few minutes later as they drove down the main street toward downtown.

"The convenience store? Really?" He would not have pegged Amanda for the gas-station-burrito-and-slushie type of girl.

"If they've got dill pickle chips, I'm good."

"You need your calories, girl. You have an upcoming workout. With those chips, I'd recommend Gatorade, some cookies and some Twizzlers to start."

She laughed. "Well, I wouldn't say no to a king-size Snickers."

He pulled into the lot. The sooner he fed her, the sooner he could get her into the outfit...and then out of it.

She headed for the chips while he went for the drinks. But he couldn't keep his eyes from wandering over to her repeatedly. She was watching him too. She lifted a Snickers bar to her mouth, pulled the wrapper back with her teeth, then licked the end before sliding it into her mouth, closing her lips around it and closing her eyes as she sucked the chocolate off the end.

Just like that he had a brilliant idea.

He crossed to the registers and handed the clerk a twenty. "Hold these for me? And put the chips and candy bar on my tab too."

The clerk knew exactly which chips and candy bar he was talking about. All four of the other men in the store did. They were all watching Amanda make love to the Snickers.

She was also swaying her hips to some unheard music, oblivious to the attention she was drawing as she checked the labels on multiple chip bags and sucked on the candy.

Amanda didn't see him slip down the aisle with the pain relievers, nail files and diapers and come up behind her. "You're in danger. I've been sent to protect you," he said quietly.

She straightened quickly and glanced around. The other patrons—except for the older woman checking out the beer selection and the two teenage girls choosing from the DVD display—were watching them. But Ryan made sure it looked like he was simply whispering in her ear. They couldn't hear what he was saying.

"What do I need to do?" she whispered back, playing along.

He smiled and put a hand on her waist, moving her down the aisle. "We need to get out of here without clueing them in that we know who they are."

"Someone in here is a threat?" she asked.

"Yes. One of these men has been sent to find you and..." He faltered, spinning the tale as he went and running into writer's block already.

"Is this about me discovering that one of my students is actually a spy?" she supplied. "He begged me to keep his secret."

"Exactly," Ryan replied easily, fighting a smile. "There are some nefarious groups that feel they need to know what you know. They're not above kidnapping you to find out what you can tell them about your student. I'm here to keep you safe."

He felt a little shiver go through her and felt an equal surge of adrenaline. It was silly—two mature adults playing a game of pretend. And the story wasn't without holes. But who cared? Amanda was clearly into it. Anything she was into, he was into.

He put her behind him, blocking her from the other people in the store. One of the guys gave him a funny look and Ryan resisted the urge to laugh. He walked backward, moving them both toward the door. "Okay, you're going to turn and walk out the door. Then I'll give you the next instructions."

She spun quickly and pushed the glass door open.

He was right on her heels.

"Take a left," he said gruffly in her ear.

The sparks of desire raced through her bloodstream as they stepped into the small alley that ran along the side of the building. They'd barely moved into the shadows before Ryan turned her to face the brick wall and moved in behind her, his big hands on her hips.

"I have to frisk you, you know," he said.

She tingled and nodded. "I understand." She braced her hands on the wall and spread her feet. This was awesome. Ryan was awesome.

His hands settled on her shoulders and skimmed over her arms, then down her sides. He took it slower over the outer curves of her breasts and actually went over that area three times. She smiled, since he couldn't see her. Then his hands continued down the outside of her legs to her ankles before coming back up on the inner seam of her yoga pants.

Amanda caught her breath and held it as one hand cupped her through the black cotton.

"I've been warned to check you out completely," he said against her neck, his big body heating the few millimeters of space that separated them.

"What does that mean?" she managed.

"I have to be sure that you're really a civilian in danger and not a rogue spy."

She didn't know why, but she liked the sound of that. "How can I prove it?"

"A trained spy will be able to mask all their emotions and reactions. A typical civilian won't."

"I promise you I'm just a regular girl," she said breathlessly. "I have nothing to hide."

"I need to know for sure."

His hands slipped under the front hem of her shirt,

continuing up until he cupped both breasts. His thumbs brushed over her nipples and she sighed. Then he dipped inside one of her bra cups and took the tip between thumb and finger. She gasped.

"Now we're getting somewhere," he said. He pressed closer, his hard cock evident against her butt. "What about when I kiss you here?"

He kissed the side of her neck, still tugging on her aching nipple. Amanda arched closer to his hand and turned her head, seeking his mouth. He kissed her hot and hard and she heard the whimper come from the back of her throat.

"Ah, yes, like that," he said.

"Do you believe that I'm who I say I am?" she asked.

"I'm not quite done with your test."

She'd been hoping he'd say that.

He kept one hand on her breast and brought the other to her stomach, pressing his palm against the quivering flesh. Then, thankfully, he slid it lower, his fingers diving behind the waistband of her pants and into her panties. He didn't even pause before slipping the pad of his middle finger over her clit, then sliding lower and into her wet heat.

She moaned his name.

"Oh, yeah, now that's an honest reaction," he praised her huskily.

"I couldn't hide what you do to me even if I wanted to," she told him softly.

He thrust his finger in and out. "The ultimate test is if you'll let me make you come like this. A seasoned spy would never let herself be that vulnerable."

"Yes," she whispered, pressing closer to his hand.

He rolled her nipple and put his mouth against her neck again. "Yes what?" he asked.

"Make me come. Let me come."

The man was good. That was the bottom line. They were playing around but her reactions to him were as real and serious as any she'd ever had. But she preferred the playing. Pretending to be someone else—or at least that *he* was someone else—gave her some distance, a buffer. Which was maybe the only thing that was going to save her from begging him to stay. Forever.

Stupid.

It was sex.

It was *awesome* sex. And it was fun. More fun that she'd had in a really long time. But it was stupid to want more. She knew all the reasons it was stupid. She did. And there were several. And they made a lot of sense.

And she'd review them—over and over—after he left.

But she couldn't think of even one of them at the moment.

She felt her entire body winding tighter and tighter as his fingers continued to move and stroke and pull and thrust. Her fingers curled into the bricks, the rough wall the only thing grounding her. Ryan made her forget everything else. Everyone else.

That was a problem...at least she thought it was...or maybe not. What did she care? As long as he kept on...

"Ma'am? Everything okay?"

Amanda's body jerked, but Ryan moved in closer and turned slightly, blocking her from the other man. He did pull his hands from her clothes though.

"We're good. No problems," he said.

"The people in the store said... *Ryan*?"

Ryan pivoted. "*Shane*? Shit."

Shane? No. It couldn't be.

"What the hell are you doing?"

But of course it was. Another interrupted orgasm and it was because of Shane Kelley. A cop. Another of her brother's closest friends. And the man sleeping with her sister Isabelle.

Amanda leaned her head onto the bricks in front of her, resisting the urge to bang it instead. Her body was still humming from the almost-orgasm and part of her—an alarmingly big part of her—wanted to turn to Ryan and bury her head against his chest. She wanted to *feel* him, breathe in the smell of him, run her hands all over him. No matter who was standing ten feet away.

And *that* was not good. Not good at all.

"Just...fuck," Ryan said. "Give us a second."

"Dude, if you're having sex in this alley, I'm gonna ticket you. Seriously. I let you go last time but—"

"We're not... give us a fuckin' minute," Ryan ground out. He leaned in to Amanda's ear. "You okay?"

"Definitely not." And not necessarily for the reason he thought. She wanted him. Badly. Not because she had been interrupted on the brink of satisfaction *again*, but because she wanted *him*. Like she'd taken a taste of crème brûlée and knew that she'd never stop craving it.

She was definitely not okay as she stood in that alley and struggled to control herself.

She should be upset. She should be embarrassed. She should be mortified, actually. And she probably would be later. But with Ryan so close, his heat and his smell surrounding her, his big hand that could do such magical things to her braced on the wall, his husky voice still aroused, but also concerned... Yeah, she couldn't come up with any emotion but *need*.

"I'll get rid of him—" Ryan started.

"No, you won't," Shane said from behind him. "You guys need to get out of here. As soon as the lady assures me she's fine."

Ryan spun on his friend. "Seriously? What do you think is wrong with her?"

Shane sighed. "I don't think anything's wrong with her. I'm not accusing you of anything. But I'm doing my job here. The store owner said you came in to the shop together, that you left suddenly without any of your food, that you hadn't come back in and that your car was still here. I have to check things out."

"I'm fine," Amanda called to him. "Totally fine."

"I'm going to have to ask you both to step out here." Shane didn't sound happy about it.

"Fuck," Ryan muttered, sounding even less happy. "I'm sorry," he whispered.

"It's fine." And it was. It was good in fact. If they were in the lit parking lot, other people around, the real world present, she could shake this off. It was just a product of having gone without sex for so long and the rush of doing something that she'd *never* let herself do with anyone else. Ryan was special for that reason. She could let it all go and not worry. That made him someone unique in her life.

That's all this weird obsession was. Probably.

"You sure?" Ryan asked.

"Yep." She straightened her shirt, licked her lips, smoothed her hair and then stepped around Ryan. "Hi, Shane."

Shane's eyes grew to three times their usual size. "*Amanda*?"

Exactly the reaction she'd been expecting. "Yes. It's me. I'm fine. Everything is fine. We'll...leave."

Shane stepped back, giving her plenty of space to walk past him. She somehow managed to walk the ten feet of alley, pass her brother's friend, the *cop*, and not die of humiliation.

As Ryan passed him, she heard Shane hiss, "In a dark alley? I kinda wanna hit you for that myself."

"In fact," she said as she turned to Shane. "If you could give me a ride home, that would be great."

What she meant was, *If you could give me a ride home that would keep me from throwing myself at Ryan again.*

Shane looked from her to Ryan. "Uh."

"That's not necessary. I'll take you home," Ryan said firmly, coming to her.

She moved away from him, but caught Shane's frown. Damn, she didn't want Ryan to be in trouble. She turned back and went to Ryan, giving him a kiss on the cheek. "It would be better if Shane takes me. Olivia and Emma will be back soon."

"I can fix that," Ryan said, catching her hand and keeping her from getting away.

"No." She met his gaze. "Really. I need to go back alone."

She'd never let him leave. She might even steal Shane's handcuffs to make sure Ryan didn't go anywhere.

Some space was a good idea. *Not* hanging out with the guy who made her not care about anything else or what anyone thought was also a good idea.

Ryan stared at her for another long second. Then he looked at Shane. "You'll take her?"

"Of course."

"I'll call you later," Ryan said to her.

She nodded. She wouldn't answer, but it would be nice of him to call.

Ryan didn't chase women. He just didn't.

So why was he in the hallway outside the offices for the faculty of the physical therapy program at Creighton University?

Because Amanda had gotten a ride home with Shane last night. And because she wasn't answering his calls.

Why wasn't she answering his calls?

Typically he wouldn't care. If a woman didn't call him back, she didn't call him back.

Of course, that didn't really happen either.

He let himself into the suite of administrative offices and the receptionist looked up with a bright smile. When she really focused on him, her smile got a little brighter.

That he was used to. The instant flirt that women put on when they met him. His female friends said it was because he didn't smile at women, he *smiled* at women. All women.

Well, he didn't do it on purpose, but he did like the result.

He smiled at the receptionist. "Hi."

"Hi," she answered back, her smile warming. "Can I help

you?"

"I'm looking for Aman—Dr. Dixon." Ryan put the paper sack he held behind his back. He also didn't bring or send gifts to women. Not that he wasn't willing. He just hadn't needed to. Until now. And suddenly his gift seemed silly.

"She's in her office. Is she expecting you?"

Ryan sighed. "You know, I really think she is." If Amanda *wasn't* expecting him, she wasn't as smart as everyone thought she was.

The receptionist glanced at the phone in front of her, then over her shoulder. "She must have finished her call. Let me check with her."

Ryan nodded. If Amanda refused to see him here, he had other ways. Lots of them. He might not have a lot of experience in pursuing a woman, but he was stubborn. And creative.

"Dr. Dixon? There's someone here to see you." The woman glanced at Ryan. "Your name?"

"The Best Night of Her Life."

The receptionist's eyes widened and she grinned, but she simply said, "He says you're expecting him—" She paused, then nodded. "I'll send him right in."

Obviously Amanda had overheard his answer.

Ryan gave her a wink. "Thanks."

"You bet. Third door on the right."

He knocked and turned the knob at the same time.

"Seriously?" Amanda asked as he stepped into her office.

She was standing behind her desk, looking so different from the girl who had been dancing at Frigid the other night he had to blink a few times.

She definitely wasn't smiling at him. Women always smiled at him.

"You can try to deny that I'm the best night of your life," Ryan said, stepping farther into the room and nudging the door shut. "But I won't believe it."

She rolled her eyes. And did not try to deny it. "What are

you doing here?"

Her hair was pulled back and clipped at the base of her head, she had glasses on and she was wearing gray slacks and a black, silky, button-up shirt.

"You didn't expect to see me?"

She sighed. "You mean after the six phone calls and four texts from you today?"

"And the five shots at Frigid, the tea, the Snickers, the pickle chips. That's more than I've spent on a woman in a long time. I'm invested here."

"I never got the pickle chips," she pointed out.

He tossed the paper bag he held onto her desk.

She almost smiled as she reached for it, opened it and looked inside. Then she did smile. Finally. She pulled out a bag of pickle chips and another Snickers.

"*Two* Snickers," he said. "Very invested here."

"That's really sad," she told him.

"That I'm invested in you?" He didn't invest in relationships. This was something. Something he still couldn't quite define.

"That this is the most you've spent on a woman in a long time."

"I..." He trailed off. Okay, maybe it was. Yeah, it probably was. He sighed. This was usually easier. A lot easier. Women really being into him and wanting to be with him was definitely easier. But Amanda wanted to be with him...didn't she? If she didn't, why didn't she?

He frowned and stepped to her desk. "I didn't like that Shane took you home last night. What's going on?"

"It's an easier break," she said.

Yeah. No way. He rounded her desk, but she scooted around the corner away from him. "What the *hell* is going on?"

"We had a fantastic weekend," she told him from the other side of the desk. "We did. I'm so glad we did...everything we did." Her cheeks got a little pink at that. "But it was just the weekend. I'm back to my real life now and—" She swallowed. "I can't do *this*."

"What is *this* anyway?" He'd really like to know.

"I don't—" She swallowed again, but met his gaze directly. "I don't know."

He grinned. That actually helped.

"But it's messing with me." She took a deep breath. "It makes me want to be reckless and not get up in the morning in spite of an early class, and eat potato chips for dinner and..."

"Make out with a spy in a dark alley?" he supplied.

She nodded. "And not care who knows."

There was something in those few words, a deeper meaning that Ryan really wanted to know more about. That was also unusual. Getting deep and personal was a sure way to make things complicated.

But he wanted things complicated with Amanda.

He moved around the edge of the desk toward her again, but slower this time, hoping she'd stay put. "So you're having some fun."

She didn't move. She watched him approach with big eyes. "Too much."

"Do you really think that's a problem?" He stopped right in front of her. He lifted his hand and took a piece of her hair between his finger and thumb, rubbing his thumb over the silky strand.

She stared up at him. "You make me want to do things that I shouldn't."

"I don't think pickle chips are a good idea any time, especially for dinner. That one's not on me."

"Yeah, but wanting to give you a blow job in my office in the middle of the workday is totally on you."

Heat licked through him and he leaned in. "Yeah, okay, I'll take the blame for that."

She took a deep breath in through her nose. "This is exactly what I'm talking about. I have to have self-control. I have responsibilities. I have people who look up to me."

"I promise not to tell anyone about the blow job."

She licked her bottom lip. But she still said, "If *anyone* asked me if they should give someone a blow job in the middle of their office during a workday, I would say it's a bad idea."

"And if Conner or Cody or Shane wanted to give someone a blow job in the middle of their office during the workday, it would *be* a bad idea," Ryan said.

"Ryan—"

"I promise not to make you a slacker or a jerk or a criminal. And I promise not to be offended that you think hanging out with me will make you any of those things."

"I—"

He leaned in. "Kiss me, Amanda."

Her phone started ringing. She hesitated. She stared at his mouth.

The phone rang again.

Ryan held his breath. And bit his tongue. He wanted to tell her to ignore it. He wanted to kiss her and know that he could distract her from everything else.

But that would just prove to her that all the things she already believed—and was afraid of—about being with him were true.

He really, really liked that he could make her do things she shouldn't.

"Son of a bitch," she said on the third ring. "I have to answer that."

He knew she was going to say that.

He leaned back and let her reach for the phone. The motion drew her pants tighter across her ass and her shirt away from her waistband. And he kept his hands to himself. See, she didn't have to worry about his bad influence. He could control himself.

Then he remembered her saying that she wanted to give him a blow job and his hands went to her waist, stroking over the smooth skin exposed.

She pushed his hands away. "Yes, this is Dr. Dixon."

He ran a hand over the curve of her right buttock. She slapped it and moved to put the corner of the desk between them.

"Damn." She paused with a frown. "Okay, I appreciate that." Another pause and a deeper frown. "I will. Thank you."

She replaced the receiver and Ryan could tell that his chances of a blow job were completely gone.

"You okay?" he asked.

She looked up and shook her head. "No. And I can't believe that you made me forget that."

He smiled. "Isn't that a good thing? I can make your day better. I can—"

"No, it's not good," Amanda interrupted. "It's bad. It's very bad. I've spent the morning trying to keep one of the best and brightest students to come through our program from quitting. And then you walk in here and all I can think about is…" She trailed off and Ryan knew better than to fill in the blank. Even if he had been tempted to fill it in with pickle chips. Which had not been the first thing to come to mind.

"What's going on?"

"Jill didn't show up at her clinical today," Amanda said.

"The girl from laser tag?"

"Yes. Her clinical instructor called me first thing this morning. Then I had a text message from Jill saying that she was withdrawing from the program."

"The program?" Ryan asked, not really following. But Amanda was upset. And he hated it. He also hated that he had nothing to offer other than tea and another massage—and he didn't think that offer would go over very well at the moment.

"The entire program. She's quitting, dropping out."

"Does she want to transfer to another program?"

"No. She says she's just done. That everyone was right and how can a deaf girl be a good therapist." Amanda's expression changed from worried to pissed in a blink of an eye. "Which is, of course, ridiculous. She's going to be a fantastic therapist. She's academically one of the best and her people skills are amazing. She's loved everything up to this point. Or at least, I thought she did."

"Maybe she was hiding it from you," Ryan suggested. "Maybe this was the final straw."

"It doesn't matter." Now Amanda looked determined. Her quick mood shifts were impressive. "Nobody quits my program because things get a little tough. She *needs* to be a physical therapist. The world needs her to be a physical therapist."

Ryan's eyes widened. "Wow. That's kind of..." But he didn't finish with *over the top*. Or anything else.

Amanda had already yanked a file drawer open and picked up her phone. She dialed, then settled the headset against her shoulder as she rummaged for a folder. As she pulled it from the drawer, she looked up at him. "I can't...do anything right now. But thanks for the chips."

Ryan plopped down in one of the two chairs on the other side of her desk. "I'll wait."

She frowned at him. "This could take a while."

"That's okay." He had a strong sense that if he left that office without a kiss, he wouldn't be getting any future kisses either. This was a turning point. Or something. The way they parted right now, today, would set the tone for what happened—or didn't happen—between them after this.

"Ryan, I really—" She paused, listening to something on the other end of the phone. "Dammit." She smacked the headset back onto the cradle.

"No answer?"

"Voice mail." She sighed. "I have to *work*."

But she wasn't upset about Jill and determined to talk to the girl because it was her job. Ryan knew that it was because of the stuff Amanda had said, and obviously believed, about Jill needing to stay in the program for a greater good.

"Is she sick or something?" he asked.

"No."

"Is someone in her family sick?"

Amanda shook her head. "No. I spoke with her mother an hour ago. There's nothing going on with the family."

"Is she homesick? Maybe she has a boyfriend back home or something."

"She's from here in Omaha."

Ryan shrugged and sat back in his chair. "Then maybe she just wants to quit."

Amanda frowned. "You don't just quit something like this. This is a career. A major commitment long before you ever get to the point Jill's at."

Amanda propped her hands on her hips and gave him a stern look Ryan was sure more than one student had received from across that stretch of mahogany.

"Getting into a program like this isn't easy," she went on. "Jill was one of forty students chosen out of a pool of three hundred and sixty-seven applicants. She had to have impeccable grades and a history of service and letters of recommendation to even get to the interview process. Then she had to go through three levels of interviews. Even getting here is a lot of work. And now she's in her second year. The first year is the hardest academically and she got through that with flying colors. She's put so much into this. I can't let her give up on it."

The passion in Amanda's voice was impressive. She believed every word she was saying, and only a person with equally strong beliefs could not get completely sucked in.

"What's different about this clinical rotation than the others she's been on?" Ryan asked.

"It's the longest one so far. This one is twelve weeks."

"Maybe she's finally realized that this isn't really what she wants to do."

Amanda scowled at him. "She loves it. She's told me that herself."

"Sure, so far. Things are getting tougher, I assume. More is expected of the students at this level, right? Maybe it finally clicked that this isn't what she wants to do for the rest of her life."

Amanda smacked her hand down on her desk. "No. It doesn't work like that."

"Sometimes it does." He leaned in. "No matter how passionate you are, you can't *make* other people feel and act and think the way you want them to, Amanda. And Jill's choices aren't about *you*. It doesn't mean that she doesn't respect you or that you've somehow failed."

Amanda sat up straight, her breathing becoming ragged. "But it does."

He frowned. "What do you mean?"

"The choices we make *are* about the people who've influenced us. The choices I make are about my mom and my brother and everything they taught me and modeled for me and sacrificed for me and...and..." She seemed to be searching for words. "And *prayed* about for me," she finally finished. "My mom and my brother both worried and worked so that all of us girls would turn out well. My mom prayed every single night that we would be okay. My brother lectured and checked up on us to be sure we would be okay. And every choice I make reflects that."

Ryan was staring at her, he knew. But this was...a lot. Certainly more than he'd expected to learn when he'd come to her office today.

"And everything that those kids go out and do, both while they're in school and after they graduate, reflects on the program. And our profession. And on me. At least in part. I'm part of teaching them and mentoring and counseling them. I believe in what this university does and what our profession does. I work my ass off to make sure this program turns out the best PTs in the country. Our whole faculty puts their hearts and passion into this program. So, yeah, I do think that you can influence the choices people make, and I do think their bad choices, and the good—thank God—are a little about me."

Ryan shook his head. He admired her passion. He really did. He hadn't felt that way about something...ever. He loved his job and he was damned good at it, but he didn't feel like he was changing the world. He helped save lives. Literally. That was something. That was big. He knew that. But he also knew that if he wasn't doing it, someone else would. He had just never felt the way Amanda felt about something.

"That's a lot of pressure and stress to put on yourself," he said. He didn't like that she was feeling directly responsible for Jill's decision, or feeling like she'd failed somehow. Amanda was amazing and if this girl didn't realize that—and realize that she wanted to be like Amanda—then it was her loss.

"Yes. And it needs to be on me. I'm in charge of the students' success at these clinical assignments."

"But Jill's her own person. She's an individual with her own life to live. You can't beat yourself up about this."

"So I should let her quit?" Amanda asked. "I should let her walk away?"

"If that's what she wants."

Amanda studied him for a several seconds. Then she nodded. "Live and let live, right?"

"Right." But he shifted on his chair, suddenly uncomfortable.

"And that's the real reason why you and I should only be a one-weekend thing." She sounded depressed as she said it.

He frowned. "Why?"

"Because I think your mom was wrong—people are worth sticking with, and walking away when things change or get hard isn't always the right thing to do."

Ryan felt his gut clench and his heart thump. Dammit.

"Amanda, I—"

"Huckleberry."

She said it softly. She looked sad as she said it. But he felt like she'd punched him in the face. Hard. He opened his mouth, trying to come up with some words, but too stunned to think any word but *huckleberry*.

He'd promised to leave her alone if she ever said the word.

Fuck.

Fine.

He took a deep breath, then pushed himself up out of the chair. But instead of going to the door, he stomped around her desk, spun her chair, leaned in and kissed her.

It was only a few seconds but he poured his feelings into it—desire, affection, respect, frustration. Then he pulled back, straightened, stared into her eyes for three heartbeats, nodded and walked out of her office.

Because walking away when feelings changed and things got hard was what he knew how to do.

Chapter Seven

"I think you have to consider the chips," Emma said.

Olivia nodded thoughtfully. "I was wondering about that. What do you think?"

"I think it's a big gesture," Emma said. "I think it deserves some attention."

Amanda took another drink of her mojito and tried to ignore her sisters. Of course, ignoring any one of the Dixon girls was hard, but when they had her cornered in a booth at Trudy's it was impossible. Especially when they were talking about her. Blatantly.

"Okay, so you know Ryan pretty well," Isabelle said. "What do you think it means?"

For some reason it didn't bother Amanda that her younger sisters knew that she'd had a not-even-quite-a-one-night stand with Ryan Kaye. That was strange. Typically she wouldn't have wanted them to know she'd been reckless and wild, even if it had only been for a few hours. Typically she wouldn't have *been* reckless and wild, even for a few hours.

It did bother her that they refused to talk about anything else though.

But her sisters had been there after she'd gotten home from work and demanded to know what was going on. So she'd told them everything. Including that Ryan had visited her office the day before.

They'd promptly dragged her to Trudy's and plied her with mojitos.

This one was her second. Or maybe it was the third. She sipped. She didn't care—they were tasting better and better.

"They're chips," she finally said. "Potato chips. It wasn't even a big bag. It doesn't mean anything." For God's sake. Emma was acting like Ryan had brought her a diamond ring.

She laughed at that and her sisters looked at her quizzically. Ryan Kaye was not a diamond ring kind of guy. At all.

"But he came to your office," Emma said.

"So?" He'd interrupted her day. He'd made her forget about the fact that one of her students—one of her at-risk students—had decided to quit the program.

"So, Ryan doesn't do that," Emma told her. "He doesn't go after girls."

"He doesn't really have to," Isabelle commented, gesturing toward the bar where Ryan was, as always, surrounded by women.

Amanda was also trying to ignore that.

She'd said *huckleberry*. It had been her choice to end things. And she knew—had heard it from Ryan's own mouth—that he let people walk if that was what they wanted. That was how he thought it should be.

But she was surprised by how much it bothered her seeing him with other women. Not that she thought he'd be serious about any of them either. Ryan didn't do serious. He didn't do long-term. He didn't do complicated.

And relationships were, if nothing else, complicated.

She looked around the table at her sisters. Boy, were they.

"Exactly," Emma said to Isabelle's observation. "He doesn't have to. And when someone's ready to move on, he lets them move on. He's not into angst or arguing."

He'd argued with her. Amanda frowned. Kind of, anyway. He'd argued with her about Jill. And he'd shown up on her doorstep and asked her to let him stay. He'd said he wouldn't complicate things, that he'd leave her alone if that was really what she wanted, but he'd asked to stay. He'd even said *please*.

And then he'd come to her office yesterday.

"He never showed up at your house or work unannounced?" she asked Emma.

Emma shrugged. "Well, we just messed around that one night. When we decided it wasn't going to be anything more than that, it was over."

"But maybe that was you. You're pretty laid-back about relationships too. Surely he's *dated* other women," Olivia said before Amanda did. "Surely he's called a woman up and asked her out on a date."

Emma shrugged. "Maybe. But if he has, I don't know any of them."

"You know *all* the women Ryan's gone out with?" Amanda asked.

Emma looked around Trudy's. "A lot of them."

Amanda looked around too. Trudy's was a local place. It wasn't a chain or in a location where people would necessarily find it if they weren't looking for it. In truth, it looked a bit like a dive from outside. But inside it was clean, had good food, a large selection of liquor, wine and beer, and everyone knew everyone. The patrons were mostly employees of St. Anthony's since it was right across the street, along with their family and friends, so it was hard to find a stranger in the place. Most of the women were nurses, paramedics, physicians, lab techs and such from the hospital, or their sisters and friends who had gotten dragged in at some point.

Trudy's easily won them over though. The margaritas and mojitos were awesome and the men were...even more awesome. They were hot doctors, paramedics and their hot friends, after all.

It was true that there was a lot of intrahospital dating. And why not? St. A's was a huge place with lots of options.

So it stood to reason that a lot of the women Ryan had dated were here in Trudy's.

Amanda looked around. It also stood to reason that she would know a lot of them.

"You're telling me that Ryan Kaye just waits to bump into women?" Olivia said. "He never actually calls them or shows up at the door with flowers and takes them out to dinner? Seriously?"

Emma laughed. "Why would I lie about that? As far as I know, Ryan runs into women everywhere he goes. If he gets to talking to one he's interested in, they make plans and meet up somewhere. He doesn't have to work very hard."

Olivia shook her head and sat back in the booth. "Wow. Poor guy."

Isabelle laughed. "Yeah, everyone feels really sorry for Ryan Kaye. I know that Shane's always saying what a rough life Ryan has."

They all chuckled, but Amanda couldn't stop thinking about all of it. Ryan never had to work for relationships? It made sense. The guy drew women like honey drew bees and then when things weren't fun anymore, he walked.

"Is it always just sex?" Olivia asked.

Amanda raised her hand to signal the waitress. She was going to need another drink here and she owed her little sis one for asking all the pertinent questions.

"Not *always*," Emma said. "He takes them out too."

"Where?" Olivia asked.

"Movies, games, concerts." Emma shrugged again. "Regular stuff, I guess."

Amanda didn't know how to feel about any of this. Ryan was fine. He was happy. This was how he liked things. So why did she feel like there should be more for him? Like he was missing out?

The waitress set two mojitos down and Amanda smiled up at her, truly grateful.

She slid one to Olivia, then sipped from hers. "Ryan stays friends with the women after they stop seeing each other too, huh?"

Emma nodded. "Ryan's awesome. It's really easy to be

friends with him. I know a lot of the girls wish they could keep seeing him, but no one ever gets mad or hates him or anything."

Amanda nodded and sipped. Then she asked, "What's his favorite color?"

Emma blinked at her. "I have no idea."

"Favorite sport?"

"Football?" But it was obvious Emma was simply guessing.

"Favorite movie?"

"What are you doing?" Emma asked.

Amanda sighed. "I don't know if any of these women really are his friends. I mean, sure, they *like* him. Ryan's very likeable and lord knows they have a good time when they're with him, but do they really know him?"

Emma leaned in to look at her closer. "Do *you* know his favorite color or sport or movie?"

"Nope." She sipped from her drink. But she wanted to. She wanted to know that stuff about him. Even more, she wanted him to know that she wanted to know it.

It was easy for Ryan to walk away, but maybe that was because there was nothing to really walk away from.

"I'll be back." She slid from the booth before her sisters could say anything more—and before she could think any harder about what she was doing.

Yes, she'd said *huckleberry* and she'd been relieved that he'd kept his word and left her alone after. But she'd also been missing him. It had been just yesterday afternoon when he'd last kissed her. She should have barely had time to miss him, or even to think about him. Between finally getting a hold of Jill and counseling her and convincing her to give things another try, on top of all her usual daily responsibilities, she'd been swamped. But she had missed him and thought about him more than she should have.

And when she thought about going to Trudy's and seeing him but not talking to him or flirting with him or touching him...it had made her stomach hurt. Ryan was distracting her.

And tempting her. And—whether she liked it or had time or the energy for it—making her feel good. At least he did when she could talk to him and flirt with him and touch him.

And now there was something more. Now she was feeling protective. Of course, that was what she did. She protected the people she cared about.

She had the suspicion that Emma wasn't the only one of Ryan's ex-girlfriends who didn't really know a damned thing about him.

That kind of pissed her off.

He was a good guy. He deserved to be with people who cared enough to know what his favorite color was.

She took an empty spot at the bar before someone else could slide onto the stool. It was not a coincidence that the seat put her right in the midst of three women she knew Ryan had dated at one time or another. Not that it was hard to find women Ryan had dated. She couldn't spit in here without hitting one.

"Hi, girls."

"Hi, Amanda," Melanie greeted her. Mel was a nurse in the ER and knew Conner and Ryan well.

Amanda made small talk with the women for a few minutes, then casually confirmed that they'd all gone out with Ryan at one point. Of course. Then she asked if they knew when his birthday was. She lied about Conner not being able to remember and being too embarrassed to ask Ryan. None of them would confirm that story with her brother anyway.

None of them knew Ryan's birthday.

Melanie asked a couple other women who were standing nearby and who, of course, had also dated Ryan.

They didn't know either. They asked yet another woman. Who also didn't know.

Amanda was ticked.

It only took her fifteen minutes to ascertain that none of the women really knew anything of substance about Ryan. One did know that his favorite pizza topping was sausage. One knew that he liked ham mixed into his scrambled eggs. One knew that he'd once won a burger-eating contest. But beyond miscellaneous facts about Ryan and meat, they didn't know much.

Oh, they all liked him, thought he was great, were so glad they'd stayed friends, blah, blah, blah.

But none of them knew him.

And that made her mad.

She excused herself when talk turned to the new, hot doctor in general surgery at St. A's. She headed straight for Ryan.

Or straight for where Ryan had been.

She did a quick scan of the room and still couldn't find him. But she did see her sister Emma near the dartboards. When Emma caught her eye, she waved and gestured for Amanda to come over. Emma wasn't smiling. What the hell?

Amanda started in that direction.

As she got close she heard Emma say, "Knock it off, Brent," to the beefy guy blocking her from stepping around him.

"What's going on?" Amanda asked.

"I was wondering if you speak asshole," Emma said, regarding Brent with clear irritation. "Because I don't seem to be getting through."

Amanda frowned at the man. "What don't you understand?"

"She said winner gets a kiss." Brent was the brother, or something, of one of the doctors who hung out at Trudy's. He reached out and grabbed Emma's wrist. "I won the last game so I'm collecting my prize."

Emma tugged against his hold. "I gave you your kiss."

"A peck on the cheek? I don't think so." Brent tugged hard and brought her up against his chest, his other hand going straight to her ass. "I want a little bit of what I hear Matt Dawson's getting from you."

Amanda started to reply, but Emma picked up one foot and brought the heel of her shoe down hard on Brent's foot. "I said no."

Unfortunately, Brent was wearing boots and it barely registered.

In fact, he sneered as he said, "You didn't say where the kiss would be. And I have a request."

"She said no." Amanda put her hand on top of Brent's hand on Emma's arm.

Brent scowled at her and pulled away. "It's none of your business."

Amanda sighed. "Well, see, that's a stupid thing to say. She's my sister and you're harassing her. And that's not only my business, but it also really pisses me off."

She wanted to punch him, but instead kept her cool and reached for where Brent was holding Emma again. Instead of his hand, though, she took her sister's, turned it and pulled against the weak point of Brent's hold, like she'd been taught in her self-defense class. With Emma's help, he lost his grip, and Amanda spun to move Emma out of his reach and put herself between them. Predictably, he grabbed for her as soon as she was loose, but instead of contact with Emma, somehow his elbow smacked into Amanda's nose.

The pain was instantaneous and intense.

Her eyes started to water as her hands flew to her face. They came away wet and red.

Dammit, her nose was bleeding.

She tipped her head back, trying to ease the flow, but that made her dizzy and the pain in her face shot to the top of her head. She brought her head upright again but couldn't focus on anything.

She heard a *son of a bitch*, a few gasps and a couple of *dammit*s, but other than Emma's voice asking if she was okay, she couldn't place any voices. Until one came through loud and clear.

"You're a dead man."

The voice was not laid-back, fun-loving, or joking. Ryan was completely serious when he addressed Brent.

She turned quickly, then wobbled as the motion made her dizzy again. Ryan had Brent's shirt in both fists, the shorter man up on his tiptoes.

"I didn't mean for it happen!" Brent was shouting, his hands on Ryan's wrists.

But Ryan was moving him toward the door with little effort. That didn't stop Shane from grabbing one of the man's arms and helping Ryan haul him out of Trudy's.

"Amanda? Amanda?"

She heard her brother's voice but didn't look at him, leaning to look around him to where Nate and another guy had the door to Trudy's open for Ryan and Shane.

"Are you okay?" Conner grabbed her arms and shook her slightly.

"Ow." She frowned at him. "My head's killing me."

"Jesus," Conner said. "Sit down."

Someone pushed a chair up behind her on the dance floor, someone else pushed wads of napkins into her hands and Conner knelt in front of her. Emma leaned in behind him and Isabelle and Olivia were gathered behind that.

Amanda held the napkins to her nose.

"Focus on my finger." Conner held up a finger and moved it back and forth in front of her face.

"It's my nose, not my eyes." She pushed his hand out of the way.

"He hit you hard."

"It was an accident. It's not like he swung."

Conner frowned. "Still..."

"I'm fine. My head hurts, my face feels like—someone hit me with his elbow."

Conner didn't smile.

Emma did, slightly. Then she opened her mouth, but before

she could say anything, she was spun away from them.

Ryan had come back in and grabbed Emma. He barely spared Amanda a look.

"Come here." He started away from the little crowd around Amanda.

He was worried about *Emma*? That really made Amanda frown. What the hell?

"I'm good," she said firmly to her brother. "Get me some ice or something."

"Here." Shane handed her a homemade ice pack—a plastic sandwich bag with crushed ice in it. "Put in on the bridge of your nose. It'll constrict the vessels and—"

"Yeah, fine." She did what he said, peering over his shoulder to find Ryan and Emma. But Shane's big body was in her way. She pushed Conner back and stood, leaning around Shane. "Then get me another mojito. A large."

"You need to stay sitting and put pressure on the bridge of your nose," Conner said. "Stay leaning forward or you might swallow some blood and—"

"*Conner.*" When he looked at her instead of her nose, she said, "I'm fine. I'm going to the bathroom to wash my face."

He didn't look happy but he stepped back. "If you're not back out in five minutes I'm coming in after you."

"Or you could, you know, send one of the *girls* in," she said.

He rolled his eyes.

Everyone stepped back as she started for the restroom, except for Shane. "You sure you're okay?" he asked. "Maybe you should take Isabelle with you."

"I just need a minute," she said. His concern was nice, but she couldn't deal with anyone distracting her while she was trying to figure out what was going on with Ryan.

On her way to the ladies' room, napkins still against her nose, Amanda scanned the room. Ryan had Emma to one side. He had one hand on her upper arm and they were standing close. Really close.

Thankfully, though, they were on the way to the bathroom.

As she drew near she heard Emma say, "I didn't mean anything. It was a stupid dart game. And Brent sucks at darts. I had no idea he would win."

Ryan frowned down at her. "But you're always messing around. You push. All the time."

"I don't mean to."

"Yes, you do," he shot back. "You're cocky. You think you can handle anything and usually you get lucky, but you also know that when your luck runs out, you'll be fine because someone will be there for you. But this time your sister got *hurt*."

So he had noticed that. Amanda tucked herself behind a guy so Ryan wouldn't see her—though he seemed intent on Emma at the moment.

"And I feel terrible about that," Emma said.

"She'd do anything for you, you know," Ryan told her. "Amanda won't even care that he almost broke her nose as long as you're okay."

Amanda drew up taller. He was championing *her*? She hadn't been expecting that.

"I know." Emma pulled her arm out of Ryan's hold. "You don't have to tell me that."

"Someone does. Someone needs to remind you that when you're screwing around, it *does* affect someone else—Amanda. Every time."

"She doesn't need to worry about me all the time. But I can't change that she does."

"You can quit pushing." Ryan shoved his hand through his hair, clearly frustrated. With Emma. His good-time gal, his pal, his swimming buddy.

Amanda felt a little lighter suddenly. Maybe he did get it. At least a little.

"It's like you're always pushing the limits, seeing how far you can go, testing," he said to Emma. "Do you really need to constantly reassure yourself that people will be there for you? Because she will be. This is Amanda. She'll be there, even if you don't deserve it." He finally sighed. "She's got this mama-bear protective thing going and...it's one of the things I like best about her. Don't mess it up."

Amanda felt her heart turn over in her chest.

Ryan was standing up for her to Emma. He knew the things already, somehow, that she hoped and prayed that her sisters would know—she would always be there for them.

And he liked it about her.

Emma looked stunned. "Okay. Yeah. I got it."

"You sure?" he asked. "No more fucking around?"

Emma raised her hands in surrender. "Not if I have to start answering to you too."

He nodded. "You do."

Amanda's eyes widened. *Wow* was right.

"Can I go now?" Emma asked, the sarcasm clear.

"I guess. But I'm watching you. *I'll* be the one in the way of the flying elbow next time, not Amanda. And if it happens again, I'm throwing your ass out on the curb too."

Emma had the audacity to grin. "Thanks for the warning."

She turned and headed for the booth with her sisters, no doubt to fill them in on every detail of Ryan's lecture.

Ryan's lecture. Ryan Kaye had lectured someone.

Wow.

The guy Amanda was hiding behind suddenly moved, nearly stomping on her toes, and she was left standing there staring at Ryan.

He looked surprised to see her for about two seconds, then he moved toward her.

And she moved toward the bathroom.

She needed a minute to collect her thoughts. And to wash the snotty blood from her face.

Of course, her being in the women's bathroom wasn't something that would slow Ryan Kaye down. He walked in right behind her.

She bent over the sink and wet a paper towel without a word.

"You okay?"

She nodded. No, she wasn't okay. He'd just amazed her. And made her want him even more.

"Let me look."

"It's blood. You've seen gallons of this stuff." She wiped at her face with towel, surprised that the damage wasn't worse. The pain in her head had centered in her forehead now and the blood had definitely stopped.

"It's your blood. That makes it different."

She looked up at him in the mirror behind her. "I'm okay."

"Let me be sure."

She took a deep breath, then swiped at her nose again, removing the rest of the blood, and turned to face him.

He cradled her face in his hands, his gaze on everything but her eyes. His thumbs brushed over her cheekbones, pressing gently. "Pain?"

"Not really. The whole thing is a little sore but nothing bad."

He rested the pads of his thumbs on either side of her nose and pressed gently. "Okay?"

"Yes." It was also sore, of course, but she knew he was checking to see if anything was broken. It didn't hurt that bad.

"You should get some ibuprofen."

"Okay."

"It'll be sore tomorrow too."

"Probably."

Finally his eyes focused on hers. "I really wanted to break *his* nose."

"Me too."

Ryan smiled slightly. "Not because of Emma. Because of you."

"You weren't concerned about Emma?"

"I didn't see what was going on with Emma. I would have probably shoved him a little bit for that. But I don't punch people. Typically."

Yeah, she knew that. Ryan could get physical if needed. She'd heard stories from Conner about them having to break up bar fights and such. Ryan could do it, if motivated, but it took a lot to get him to that point.

"You wouldn't have punched him because of Emma, but you would have because of me?"

He nodded. His hands were still on her face, but he wasn't pushing and prodding anymore.

"Well, I guess he did actually hurt me, even if it was an accident."

"Yeah." Ryan gritted his teeth for a moment. "But I wanted to punch him even before that. Because he was hassling you."

"You saw that?"

"Yeah. I was on my way over when you got Emma loose and then stepped between them."

She opened her mouth, but had no words. No one really ever stood up or protected her. She was the protector. Like he'd said to Emma, *she* was the mama bear.

"Shane kept me from beating that guy's ass."

She smiled. "If you punch everyone who hassles me, you're going to have a sore hand."

He didn't look happy about it, but he nodded. "I know. Being the protector is hard work, isn't it?"

She knew he meant her. "It doesn't feel like work," she said softly. "It feels...natural."

He looked at her for a long time. Then he said, "Take it back."

"What?"

"*Huckleberry.* Take it back. I know I was pushing in your office, I know I should have gotten out of the way. Give me another chance."

A lump formed in her throat. God, she liked him. She

knew, from what she'd heard and observed since Ryan and Conner had worked together, and from what Emma had said and what Ryan himself had told her, he didn't go after women, he didn't say please, and he didn't ask for another chance.

She wanted to wrap her arms and legs around him and never let go. Especially if she got him out of his clothes first.

But the thing was, lots of women had done that. Lots of women had appreciated his body. Not many had appreciated him.

"I have a proposition for you," she finally said after swallowing twice and clearing her throat.

"Anything."

She smiled. That was a nice, immediate, no-questions-asked response.

"Let's be friends."

He blinked four times then asked, "What?"

"Let's be friends."

"I have enough friends."

She shook her head. "You have male friends. Good ones. But you don't have female friends, Ryan."

"I do. Your sister for one—"

"No, you don't. You think you do. You like her, you get along, you don't fight. But I mean a real friendship. Someone who knows you and appreciates you and that you can have fun with that doesn't include sex."

"Yeah, see, you lost me on the 'doesn't include sex' part."

She smiled. "I know. That's the most important part too."

"I'll find a different friend. Olivia and I can be friends," he said. "Then you and I can still get naked." He pressed close and she had a hard time taking a deep breath. "Because I still want that one night that we supposedly had. We still haven't made it overnight, you know."

She wanted that too. Badly.

But she wanted Ryan to know that someone could want him and like him at the same time.

She assumed that women never got to know him well enough or for long enough to know he had any flaws. So no one had ever shown him that he could be loved in spite of those flaws. As far as he knew, when flaws showed up—or at least when they got to be too much—that was when things were over.

She wasn't an expert in many things, but sticking with someone even when they showed their flaws, even if it was over and over again, was something she definitely knew a lot about.

She looped her arms around his neck and said sincerely, "I want you. The idea of you being naked with another woman makes me nuts. But, believe it or not, it makes me even more jealous to think of you getting close to and having a true friendship with another woman. That's what I want."

He stared at her. His gaze shifted to her lips, then back to her eyes. "I'm not going to stop trying to get you naked."

"Okay." She wasn't worried. There was no one more manipulative and stubborn than Isabelle and Emma. She'd resisted those two for years. She could resist one Ryan Kaye. "And I'm not going to stop being your friend, wanting to hang out with you and wanting to know all about you."

"How about this." His hands moved down to her waist, then her hips, then her butt. "I'll tell you anything you want if you dress up in that pirate slave outfit and let me tie you to my bed like we talked about."

Her body flooded with heat and she had to take a couple of seconds to calm her pulse. "Um." She cleared her throat. "Did we talk about me being tied to your bed?"

"Well, what else would a pirate do with a slave girl?"

"Hmm. You might have a point." And her whole body was now shouting *do it, do it, do it!* "I was thinking more like we'd order food and rent a movie."

He looked suspicious. "What kind of movie?"

She smiled. He was expecting the words *Sandra Bullock* or *Reese Witherspoon*, no doubt. "Whatever you want."

"Military action thriller? Lots of shooting and blood and

swearing?"

"Okay."

"Raunchy frat-boy party movie? Lots of beer drinking and jokes about farting?"

"Okay."

"Girl-on-girl-on-girl porn?"

"Wow, three, huh?"

"The more the merrier."

"That's what they say."

"So, yes? Any of those?" he asked, his smile growing.

Could she sit through blood flying, farts flying and...bras flying? Probably.

"Sure. Any of those. I just want to spend time with you."

"Uh-huh." He looked at her again for a long moment. Then he leaned in and kissed her.

For several long, delicious, hot, wet seconds Amanda forgot all about wanting to do anything with Ryan but *that*. She would be content just to kiss him for hours.

Ryan eventually ended the kiss, but kept his lips against hers. "I'm not going to stop doing that either."

Amanda pressed her lips to his for another few seconds, then said, "Okay." She could resist doing more. This was for Ryan. Not that it would be easy, she conceded, looking up into his blue eyes.

"I get to pick the movie and order the food," he said, straightening and stepping back so suddenly that she wobbled forward a bit before catching her balance.

"That's fair."

"I'll see you at my place tomorrow at seven." He started toward the door to the ladies' room.

Amanda wondered what he was up to. He'd suddenly given in way too easily.

"I'll be there."

"Oh, and I generally sit around without my shirt on. So wear something that comes off easily."

The door bumped shut behind him and she grinned even as she shook her head. This was going to be interesting.

She wanted to be his friend.

Ryan kept thinking about that over and over the rest of the night and all through the next day at work. His friends—the ones he already had—noticed. He'd left Trudy's unusually early, right after kissing Amanda in the ladies' room, and he'd been distracted at work throughout the shift.

He was never distracted. He never had anything to be distracted about.

Being distracted as a paramedic wasn't a good thing.

Gabrielle Evans pulled the door to the fridge open and grabbed a soda. "What is going on with you?"

Gabby and Sierra were the only female paramedics on the entire team for St. Anthony's and they both worked on the crew with Ryan and Conner. He wasn't sure how they'd gotten so lucky, but Gabby and Sierra were some of the best paramedics he'd ever worked with. Sierra was the sweeter of the two. She was amazing at calming people down in the midst of a trauma and was the one they always assigned to any victims under the age of twelve if possible. Gabby was spunkier. She was always right in the thick of things with Conner and Ryan and she never hesitated because something or someone was too big or too tough or too dangerous. Gabby was the most dedicated, driven person he'd ever met, and she'd push him and Conner if she thought they could do more or do it harder or better.

"I'm...distracted."

Gabby brought the can of cola to her lips, studying him over the top. "You want to talk about it?"

"Not really."

"Then knock it off."

He chuckled. "Sorry to bother you."

Gabby shrugged and took a seat in the armchair across the

coffee table from him. "It's weird to see you so quiet and thoughtful. Makes me nervous."

They sat without talking for about three minutes. Then Ryan said, "I have a girl question for you."

Gabby swallowed her mouthful of soda. "A question about girls or a question because I'm a girl?"

"Both."

"Okay, shoot."

"If you said you wanted to just be friends with a guy, what would that mean exactly?"

Gabby gave him a funny look. "What makes you think it would mean anything other than what it sounds like it means?"

"Well, that's what I want to know. Could it mean more?" He felt tight through his gut and he hated it. Gabby's answer mattered more than he wanted it to.

"Has someone said this to you?"

"Yes."

"A woman?"

"Yes, a woman."

"It means she doesn't want to sleep with you." Gabby tipped her soda can back again.

Ryan waited for her to swallow so she could add to her statement. When she didn't he said, "Uh, no, I don't think that's what it means."

"Why not?" she wanted to know.

"Because we already...did that."

Gabby's eyes got wide. "Oh. Well, then it means that she doesn't want to sleep with you *again*."

He scowled at her. "No way. That is *not* what it means."

"Dude, if she wanted to keep sleeping with you, she'd be saying things like 'I made a trip to Tease and need you to help me try some new things out'," Gabby told him, referring to the sex toy and lingerie shop downtown.

He sighed. "Seriously. I don't think that wanting to be friends is about not sleeping together."

"So what do *you* think it's about?"

He knew exactly what it was about. And he wasn't sure how to feel about it. "She thinks she's taking care of me."

Gabby looked intrigued by that. "You're the happiest, most satisfied guy I know. You have this Zen thing going on."

He nodded. He really did feel Zen most of the time. At least until Amanda Dixon had come along.

"So you don't want to be just friends, but that's what she wants?" Gabby said. "Sounds like it's time to make a break."

Yeah, it did. And usually he wouldn't need someone else telling him that. But this was Amanda.

"Would it sound stupid if I said that I think being just friends would help *her*? She has this thing about taking care of the people who matter to her. It's who she is. She thinks I need this, so it would be like I'm doing something for her."

Gabby smiled slowly. "And you like the idea of her taking care of you because you want to be someone who matters to her."

"I..." He sighed again. "Really like her."

"Are you fricking *kidding* me?" Dooley Miller's voice came from the break room doorway.

Ryan groaned, then turned to find Dooley Miller, Mac Gordon and Sam Bradford coming into the room. They had the late shift. And if Ryan hadn't been so distracted, he would have thought of that and would have gotten out long before they showed up. He hadn't seen any of them since the day they'd tracked him down at practice and discovered his secret about Amanda.

Dooley was pulling out his wallet and Mac was grinning. Dooley started to hand a twenty to Mac. "We are talking about Amanda Dixon, right?" Dooley asked.

Ryan shot up off the couch. "Keep it down." He looked toward the door to the locker room. "Conner's still around."

"Yep, guess we are," Dooley said, handing the money to Mac.

Ryan frowned at them, then Sam. "What's that for?"

Sam shrugged. "Mac told Dooley you'd be head over heels the next time they saw you. Dooley thought you were a bigger player than that."

Ryan stomped over to toss his soda can in the trash. "I said I *like* her."

Sam took an apple from the bowl on the counter and took a big bite as he nodded. "That's how I went down," he said after he'd chewed. "Wanted her first, then liked her. That's the point of no return."

"Me too," Dooley added. "If you just want to sleep with her, that's one thing. Or if you *just* like her. But once you combine them, you're in trouble."

Ryan glanced at Gabby, who was taking it all in. "Well, we're going to be friends."

"Uh-huh," Mac said. "Been there, tried that."

"Seriously. That's what *she* wants."

"You haven't slept with her yet?" Dooley asked. "Come on, man."

Ryan coughed and averted his eyes.

Mac laughed. "Guess you already took care of that part."

"Oh, boy," Dooley said. "You mean she wants to be just friends *after* the sex? Ouch. Sorry, man."

"Shut up," Ryan said. "It's not about the sex."

"Yeah, this means even more than the sex," Gabby said.

Dooley shook his head. "That's stupid."

Gabby threw a pencil at him.

"What do *you* want?" Sam asked Ryan. "The sex, the friendship or both?"

"For her to have what she wants," Ryan admitted.

Sam rolled his eyes. "Oh, yeah, you're in trouble."

"We're going to be *friends*. She wants to show me that I deserve to be more than a lay," Ryan said. "I think that's...nice."

"That is nice," Mac agreed. "She's worried about your self-worth and shit. Kind of something a mom or an older sister worries about, you know?"

Ryan flipped him off. "It's how Amanda's wired. It means that I matter to her."

"And you want her to feel good about making you feel good," Dooley said. "Got it." He pocketed his wallet. "No more betting against Mac. He's got you pegged."

Mac looked pleased as he tucked the twenty in his front pocket and reached for the bag of chips on top of the fridge.

Ryan knew he should keep his mouth shut. Instead he said, "So, Mac and Sam, you probably could give some good advice about a guy dating a friend's sister, huh?"

"Thought you were just gonna be friends?" Dooley asked.

"Well—" Yeah, they were. He did mean it when he said it was important to Amanda and so important to him.

"Hypothetically?" Sam suggested.

"Sure. Hypothetically," Ryan agreed.

Gabby snorted from where she was still parked in the armchair, blatantly eavesdropping.

"Well, hypothetically I'd say proceed with caution," Sam said. "It's a big deal to a guy like Conner—I mean a big brother."

Mac shoved him.

Dammit. Ryan knew that, but, yeah, okay, so he'd been hoping to hear Sam say they were all overemphasizing how much Conner would care.

"But," Sam went on, shoving Mac back, "never underestimate the power of making her happy."

Mac gave his friend a grin at that and Sam rolled his eyes.

Ryan took a deep breath. Okay, so he and Conner had that in common—making Amanda happy was a big deal to them both.

He turned to Mac. "Anything else?"

Mac lifted a big shoulder. "Don't let her brother convince you that he knows everything about his sister. Every woman has secrets and needs that her big brother doesn't know about."

Ryan would have typically laughed at the dirty look Sam

gave Mac, but the man's words had hit Ryan hard.

Did Conner know how much Amanda needed to be needed?

Maybe. But Conner had three other sisters to worry about too. Amanda deserved someone's full attention.

"Thanks, guys." His mind still spinning, Ryan started for the break room door.

As he pulled it open, Mac called out, "Kaye!"

"Yeah?"

"It's not cool to mess with a friend's sister. So...don't just mess around."

Ryan swallowed hard. That was it right there. He wasn't messing around with Amanda.

And if she needed to just be his friend, then, by God, he'd be the best friend she'd ever had.

Chapter Eight

He'd picked the least sexy or romantic movies he could come up with. *Mission Impossible* and *The Dark Knight*. He'd ordered very unromantic food—hot wings and nachos. No one wanted to kiss and get sexy with buffalo sauce on their breath. He'd dressed in running pants and a T-shirt, like he would with any of his buddies. And he left all the lights on and sat in the recliner instead of beside her on the couch.

But even sitting several feet away from her with the lights on made him want her.

In spite of all the precautions, he still found himself shifting restlessly, not catching any of the major plot points of the movie and barely tasting the nachos—even the jalapenos.

It didn't matter how many things Tom Cruise blew up— Amanda Dixon was in his house, she smelled amazing and she looked...cute.

He knew she'd been trying for casual and comfortable, just like he had. But it didn't matter. Jeans or skimpy party dress, he wanted her.

In fact, at the moment, he wanted her more than he had the night at Frigid. Her being here like this, trying to be his friend, liking him, the wing sauce and hot peppers the spiciest things that would occur that night... It all made him feel...like writing her a love note. Something sappy and cheesy just to make her smile and to be sure she was thinking of him. He never did sappy and cheesy with the women he hooked up with.

Ryan rubbed a hand over his face and tried to concentrate on the movie again.

But two minutes later, he was thinking about Amanda again.

The jeans reminded him of the night she'd dropped everything and met him and Emma at the hospital. She'd been disheveled that night, but still took charge and made sure Emma had everything she needed and that everyone was doing their jobs one hundred percent—just like she did.

That wasn't the first time he'd seen her protective instincts toward her family. He distinctly remembered the time Conner had gotten burned on a call. It had been a house fire and he'd been treating an unconscious victim too close to the house. A burning shingle had come down, and he'd reacted to protect his patient. The shingle had landed on his arm, giving him second-degree burns.

Amanda had been there almost immediately after hearing the news and demanded to know every detail, going so far as to chew Cody's ass because he'd been one of the firemen on the scene and hadn't dragged Conner away from any threats. She and Cody had gotten into a shouting match that had landed them in front of the then-chief the next morning. Amanda hadn't backed down even for the chief.

What Ryan remembered even more than her standing up to the big fireman was when she'd left Cody to come yell at *Ryan* because, as Conner's partner, he should have been watching out for him. When he mentioned that he'd been busy with his own patients, she'd jabbed him in the chest. And when he said that if this was how she reacted when he got a second-degree burn on his arm, Ryan didn't want to see her if Conner ever *really* got hurt, she'd gotten right up in his face and said, "You're right. You don't want to see me then."

"What?" she asked, looking over at him.

Ryan realized he'd been watching her instead of the movie. But it was cute how she picked the tomatoes and peppers off her chips, but was sure to choose the ones with lots of cheese.

He never thought women were cute.

He shook his head and turned back to the TV. "Sorry. I didn't know you didn't like tomatoes."

He never noticed that much detail about how women ate.

Good God.

"I like cold tomatoes," she said. "But not hot. But I like tomato sauce and tomato soup," she added.

He kept his eyes on the action on the screen. Tomatoes were not cute. Tomato soup was not cute.

At least they never had been before.

"I'll remember that," he said.

Amanda shifted to tuck her feet up underneath her on the couch. He noticed that her toenails were painted a pink a few shades darker than her shirt. The color reminded him of the color of her nipples.

He shifted on his chair cushion. *That* was not a we're-just-friends kind of thing to think about.

She lifted her glass to her lips and drank, and Ryan faked an itch on his face to block the sight of her licking her lips after she swallowed.

It didn't matter if he saw it or not. He'd had those lips around his cock. He could conjure that image and the feel of it in a millisecond.

He shifted again and gave a real effort to concentrating on the dialogue.

Then she reached for the remote on the arm of his chair to turn the volume up. That simple motion shouldn't have stirred the air enough that he could smell her body spray.

But it did.

He worked on not groaning.

He was going to be her friend. He was.

But having her over here like this was not a good idea. They were alone, there were lots of sturdy horizontal surfaces, there was whipped cream in the fridge, and they were sitting in the same room, not three feet from where he'd laid her back, spread her legs and made her come just a few days ago.

His erection throbbed, his gut tightened and he shifted again.

Being friends with her might just kill him.

Amanda used the remote to pause the movie. "Be right back." She headed for the bathroom.

This was torture.

Every time Ryan stretched his long legs out or shifted in his chair or cracked his knuckles, she was aware of him, his body, how he filled up the room.

Heck, every time he breathed or blinked she felt like she refocused on him. She had no idea what was happening in the movie. She had no idea if the wings or...whatever else they were eating...were any good. She frowned and thought hard. There was something else out there on the coffee table other than the wings. What the hell was the other food he'd ordered? She lifted her head and stared into the mirror. Holy crap. She was in trouble.

She knew nothing except that sitting in the living room where Ryan had given her tea, the best massage of her life and an amazing, fast, delicious orgasm was not a good way to keep from wanting sex from him.

Oh, and that she was in *trouble*.

Her cheeks were even flushed when she looked in the bathroom mirror.

"You want him for more than that," she told her reflection. "He deserves more than that."

She splashed water on her face and took several deep breaths.

She had to pull it together.

This was all her idea in the first place, and it was important. Ryan was a great guy and she was determined to prove that to him.

A minute later, she stepped into the living room and immediately focused on Ryan. He had one foot propped on the corner of the coffee table, his hands linked behind his head, his eyes on the frozen television image. The position pulled his T-shirt tight across his chest, and the soft cotton of the running pants molded against his crotch.

She pasted on a smile and said the only thing that made any sense.

"I think I'm going to get going."

He turned and blinked at her. Clearly he'd been lost in thought.

She'd love to know what he'd been thinking about. Frankly, everything about Ryan made her curious.

He stretched to his feet and nodded. "Okay."

So he wasn't going to try to talk her into staying? She didn't frown. Going home was a really good idea. It would keep her from ruining this being-friends thing on the very first night.

But he could *act* like he wanted her to stay. Or fake it.

"So, I'll see you—"

"How about we try this again Saturday night? And I'll invite some other people. We'll barbecue or something."

She liked that idea. She could see him, be his friend, but with others around there wouldn't be this constant sexual tension. Or, she amended, looking into Ryan's eyes and feeling the heat curl through her even from several feet away, at least they wouldn't be able to *act* on the sexual tension that would be there.

"The girls too?" she asked.

"Yep, invite them all. I'll tell Gabby and Sierra."

"We can do a potluck. We'll all bring something," she said, definitely liking this idea.

"Maybe we'll play some cheesy party games or something."

She grinned. "That would be perfect."

He grinned back. "Then it's a date."

She knew he'd said that on purpose. The friends-only thing was her idea, not his. But she did appreciate that he'd resisted any sexual innuendos and more blatant comments—or touches—tonight. He was going along with her request to be friends only. For some reason.

She was choosing not to think about the fact that it might

be because he could quite easily get the sexy stuff from just about any female in the greater metropolitan area.

"Sounds like fun," she told him.

"It does."

They stood just looking at each other for a really long time. Long enough for her to imagine crossing the floor, pushing those loose-fitting pants to the floor and wrapping her legs around his waist.

She cleared her throat and made her feet move in the opposite direction, toward the door.

"'Night," she said. "Thanks for the wings and the..." She still couldn't frickin' think of what else they'd had.

"Nachos," he supplied.

Right. Nachos. She frowned. Nachos? There had been nachos? She really liked nachos.

"Thanks for all of it," she said.

"No problem."

He stayed right where he was, not making even an attempt to walk her to the door.

Which was a good thing. Being walked to the door might tempt her to kiss him good night. Friends didn't kiss good night. They didn't kiss any other time either.

Which, now that she thought about it, was one of her least favorite things about this plan.

It wasn't like Emma wouldn't have volunteered to be in charge of the party games at Ryan's the next night, but Amanda knew for a fact that Ryan had *asked* her sister to be in charge.

The rat.

Emma didn't play Monopoly or even charades. Oh, no. Emma played things like Suck and Blow, truth or dare and this new one called Balls.

"It's easy," Emma told the group that was gathered in Ryan's living room.

Conner, Nate, Cody and Shane stood to one side, all with beer bottles in their hands. Gabby was there, perched on the arm of the chair where Olivia sat, though Sierra had been unable to make it. Ryan was leaning against the wall next to the bookcase and Amanda stood next to Isabelle near the sliding glass doors.

"I need someone to help me show everyone." Emma looked around. Olivia started to get up but Emma shook her head. "No, a guy." She reached and grabbed the closest male and tugged him up in front of the group.

Nate didn't look happy.

Of all the guys, Nate was the most serious, certainly the least silly. He could have a good time and had a great sense of humor, but he didn't get as rowdy as the other guys did and he definitely had more decorum. It didn't surprise Amanda that his teeth were usually gritted when Emma was around. It did make her smile though. As it did everyone else.

"You take a ball." Emma held up a little pink rubber ball that was about three inches in diameter. "Then you put it between you, like this." She rested the ball against her stomach with one hand as she grabbed the front of Nate's shirt and pulled him around to face her...close enough that his stomach was against the ball as well.

Everyone's eyebrows went up. Except Nate's. His eyebrows definitely pulled down.

"Then the object is to be the first couple to roll the ball up to the chin of the shortest person. Without using your hands."

Nate took a huge step back the minute Emma started wiggling, trying to move the ball between her body and his.

The ball fell to the floor and bounced under the coffee table.

She frowned at him. "Not like that. Obviously."

"I'm not doing that," Nate said calmly. But firmly. He tipped back his beer bottle.

Emma ran a hand through her hair, then put her hands on her hips. "So, is it just hives or is it like full anaphylactic shock?" she asked Nate.

"What are you talking about?"

"You know, if you have fun. Is the allergic reaction mild or something we need an EpiPen for?"

Nate turned to the guys. "I'm an intelligent man. Why do I encourage her by asking things like 'what are you talking about' when I know she's physically incapable of being anything less than a smartass?"

The guys chuckled and Conner slapped him on the back. "Gee, Em, maybe he just doesn't want to rub up against you," Conner said to his sister.

"Uh, I don't think that's it," Cody said.

Conner swung to face him and the fire chief held up his hands. "I'm just sayin'."

"Don't."

"Hey, Nate," Emma said, not quite ready to let the doctor just walk away. "Tell you what—you play this game as my partner and I won't talk for...thirty whole minutes."

Nate snorted. "You'll explode."

"A risk I'm willing to take," Em told him.

Nate stepped toward her, clearly suspicious. "What's the catch?"

"Nothing. No talking. Thirty minutes. All you have to do is play a two-minute game with me and you'll have peace and quiet for half an hour."

Amanda watched the exchange with interest. She was kind of on Nate's side. Thirty minutes of no talking would be tough for Emma, no doubt about it.

She couldn't help it. She glanced at Ryan. He was watching *her*. He was clearly amused, but he was standing with his back against the wall, his arms crossed, obviously content just to watch. And his subject of interest seemed to be her.

She felt warm and gave him a smile, but dutifully turned back to the game and their friends and family. They were just hanging out. It didn't matter to her where his attention was.

Except that she could have sworn she felt his eyes drop to the butt of her jeans. The fitted ones. With the pink rhinestones on the back pockets. That she might have paired with a silky pink top and pink heels tonight, hoping he'd think she looked nice.

Amanda groaned inwardly. This wasn't how this was supposed to be. She hadn't been thinking about what Cody or Nate would think of her outfit. Dammit.

"Why do you want to be his partner?" Cody asked Emma, stepping forward. "I'll gladly roll the ball with you." He gave Emma a little wink.

She grinned. "'Cause we'd definitely win," she told Cody. "You and I could shimmy and wiggle together just fine. It's more fair to everyone else if I'm paired with Nate."

Cody laughed and elbowed Nate. "You don't think Nate can shimmy and wiggle when he needs to?"

Emma shrugged and looked at Nate. "It's gotta be hard to move when you've got such a huge stick up your ass."

Nate's expression didn't change as he met Emma's gaze evenly. He continued to watch her as he tipped his bottle back again and finished his beer. Then he handed the empty to Shane. "Honey, I know you're just goading me to get me to partner with you because you want to make sure that you don't have any competition from whoever *does* pair up with me."

"Sure, that must be it," Emma said dryly, watching him step forward again.

"But if you want to be up against me that bad, I can hardly say no. I don't want you to have to beg or cry in front of all your friends."

"You're a prince," she told him, patting his cheek.

"Uh-huh. Where's the ball?"

Conner sighed.

Gabby rose from her seat. "Come here, Dixon," she said to Conner. "There's a considerable lack of females you can wiggle against in here without it being gross."

Conner looked around the room, realized she was right and went to stand next to her.

Shane, of course, made a beeline for Isabelle, leaving Olivia, Amanda, Cody and Ryan not paired up.

"Well, darn, guess I have to go front-to-front with Amanda or Olivia," Cody said, giving Amanda a grin.

She smiled back and told herself that she would *not* be disappointed not to be paired with Ryan. It was most definitely for the best. Which meant that she also would *not* be jealous of her sister.

She did, however, notice that Emma was trying to catch Olivia's eye over Nate's shoulder. Then Nate said something that claimed Emma's attention.

Ryan stepped up to Amanda's side. "I'm thinking maybe—"

"Come on, Cody, you're with me," Olivia said, grabbing his sleeve and tugging. "We're better matched for height."

Cody was maybe an inch shorter than Ryan, but Olivia was a good three inches shorter than Amanda, so maybe that made sense.

Amanda turned to face Ryan. She saw the look in his eyes. The same combination of "this is gonna be great" and "oh crap" that she was feeling. Yeah, this was going to make something, but she didn't really think it was sense.

"I kind of thought the group thing would *keep* me from being up against you tonight," Ryan said quietly, as Emma tossed rubber balls to everyone.

Amanda nodded and tried to swallow. "I can switch with Iz or even Olivia," she offered.

Ryan caught the ball with one hand, never taking his eyes off of her. "See, now that would make this being friends thing even harder."

"How?" How could it get harder to ignore their attraction and forget about the awesome sex than it would be rubbing up against each other?

He reached up to run his thumb over her jaw. "I'd be

feeling way more possessive and jealous than a guy who's just a friend should."

Oh. And she was liking that a lot more than a girl who's just a friend should.

"We could refuse to play," she suggested, really hoping he'd shoot that down too.

He gave her a slow, sexy grin and held the ball up. "Babe, I can act chivalrous and chaste, but I can't act stupid. No straight guy in his right mind would sit this out."

She grinned and felt a combination of relief and desire hit her.

"Remember, you have to roll the ball all the way up to the shortest person's chin," Emma called out as everyone positioned themselves and the balls at bellybutton level. "No hands. First couple to get there wins."

Amanda became immediately aware of only Ryan. His big body moved in against hers and his scent and heat surrounded her.

"What do we win?" she vaguely heard Shane ask.

"You get to go first for Seven Minutes in Heaven," Emma called back. "With your choice of partner."

Conner and Nate groaned.

Cody asked, "Did I hit my head and suddenly wake up back in seventh grade?"

"Love that," Shane said.

Emma just laughed. Likely she'd just pulled that one off the top of her head. Then again, Amanda could totally see Emma playing and loving all these games. She just hoped the night ended before Emma decided it was time for strip poker.

"Ready. Set. Go!" Emma started the game and the race was on.

Amanda was out, mentally anyway, within three seconds. They couldn't use their hands on the ball, but nobody said they couldn't use them on each other. Ryan's hands rested on her hips and he guided her motions with touch and soft coaching.

"Okay, dip your knees a little."

She grabbed a handful of denim on each of his hips to keep from falling over and squatted down. That brought the ball up a few inches. He shifted and rotated his hips a little, trying to move it up.

"Come up slowly," he said.

She followed the command, very aware of the heat and hardness on the other side of the insignificant distance created by the ball.

Then Ryan took a little pressure off the ball, bent his knees a bit and—

"We won!"

Everyone groaned and all the other couples stepped apart, balls bouncing to the floor as Shane shouted out their victory.

Ryan stood, slowly, the ball still rolling between them, their bodies sliding against each other. Neither of them stepped back. Neither of them let go of the other. Neither of them broke eye contact.

She could see, clearly, that he was remembering the other night when they'd been this close but with no clothes between them—and no friends around them. The desire in his eyes made every nerve in her body feel like it had been stretched tight and she was waiting for something to let go, knowing she'd feel it all over.

"Of course you did," Emma groused.

"Well, we're pretty good at wiggling against each other," Shane said.

"God, just shut up, Shane," Isabelle said.

Her sharp tone pulled Amanda and Ryan away from each other—physically and mentally. Their ball bounced away as Amanda turned to look at her sister.

Shane was loud and boisterous and funny and didn't at all mind being center stage. He was essentially a six-foot-four, two-hundred-and-sixty-pound, goatee-wearing Emma Dixon. Which meant that his filter wasn't always on and he didn't have a mute button.

He often exasperated and sometimes embarrassed Isabelle. But Amanda had never heard her sister actually get mad at him.

She sounded mad now.

Everyone else had quieted and turned to face Isabelle and Shane.

Conner's eyes narrowed and he stepped forward. "What's going on?"

He'd obviously noticed the rigid way Isabelle was holding herself, the pink of her cheeks and the way she wasn't looking at Shane.

And then there was the frustrated look on Shane's face.

They had clearly been fighting.

"What's going on is between me and your sister," Shane said tightly.

So something *was* going on.

"Okay, let's go again!" Emma said brightly.

"No," Conner told her firmly. "This was a terrible idea."

"Really?" Emma, always one to push past the point of someone's temper or comfort zone, turned to Nate. "Was this a terrible idea, Doc?"

Normally, Amanda would have expected Nate to sigh and give her some sarcastic comment. Instead he frowned at her. "Shut up, Emma You're not helping."

Amanda's eyes widened. She was the first to agree that her sister needed more people telling her when she was over the line, but she was a little surprised that Nate was the one doing it. Nate was usually more...*calm*, she supposed was one way to put it. He was composed. He didn't typically get riled up unless they were on the football field. Of course, Emma had a way of doing that to people too.

"I think it's time for Seven Minutes in Heaven, right?" Shane asked, his eyes on Conner. "I pick Isabelle."

Emma rolled her eyes and shook her head.

Cody muttered "dumbass" under his breath.

Isabelle swung to face him. "There is no way I'm going in any room with you alone. I can't believe you're even here today."

Amanda sucked in a breath. *What* was going on? And why hadn't Isabelle said anything before this?

"I'm here today because you're here today," Shane said firmly.

"Funny, that rule didn't apply Thursday night when you went to Vegas to see your ex instead of staying here with me," Isabelle said.

Everyone sucked in a breath at that.

"What the *hell*?" Conner demanded.

Nate moved closer to Conner. "Easy, buddy."

Shane's jaw was tight when he said, "I told you nothing happened. She needed my help. End of story."

Amanda watched Shane with fascination. The guy was one of the toughest players in the entire amateur football league, and she knew he'd taken down bad guys and broken up bar fights. There was no way that he was *always* the jovial, good-time, everyone's-best-buddy guy that they all knew. But she had never seen him as anything else. Until now.

He was quite clearly furious.

But he wasn't the only one who was furious. Isabelle's eyes narrowed and she poked a finger into his chest. "Well, I'm not going to pretend that everything's fine and that we're madly in love when you've just waltzed back in from an all-nighter in Vegas with your ex-stripper-girlfriend."

There was total silence in the condo for ten seconds. Then Shane said, "She's not an ex-stripper."

"Ah!" Isabelle yelled, then grabbed her purse and stomped toward the bathroom.

"You're such an idiot," Cody told Shane.

"So she's a *current* stripper?" Nate asked. "But she's your ex-girlfriend."

Shane's only response was, "Fuck."

"I'm going to murder you."

Everyone turned to look at Conner. Furious seemed to be contagious. Nate grabbed Conner's arm.

"It's fine, Dix," Shane said. "Nothing happened."

"Isabelle's upset."

"Isabelle will be fine," Shane said firmly. "I'll take care of it."

"I think you've done enough."

Ryan stepped forward as Conner did. "Okay, enough."

There were still several feet separating the two men, but it felt like someone was about to throw a punch. Ryan was the calming influence in the group. And it was his house. They'd listen to him.

"How about everyone take a deep breath. Shane, you move into the kitchen and we'll have a talk; Conner, you head out with Nate and take a little walk."

Several seconds ticked by. Neither man moved. No one said anything.

Ryan looked back and forth between his friends. "Guys? What do you think?"

Okay, so the calming influence might need to include some of his mother's tea. Or something stronger. Maybe he had some other calming herbs. Was marijuana an herb?

Amanda rubbed her forehead. She looked at Olivia. Olivia nodded and went after Isabelle.

Well, at least no crying would happen in front of Conner. That might help. Even though he'd probably assume that Isabelle was crying—even if she wasn't. Isabelle never cried.

Then again, her boyfriends never spent the night in Vegas with their stripper ex-girlfriends.

"Let's go outside," Nate said to Conner.

"No way," Conner said. "I want to know what the fuck is going on."

"Listen, guys," Ryan said. "Just cool it."

"I'm not messing around," Shane said, directly to Conner. "I love her."

"Well, she deserves better," Conner told him.

"She deserves a guy who will give her exactly what she wants and needs in every way...and that's me," Shane said.

Both men stepped forward again, and Amanda's heart thumped hard in her chest.

Ryan held up his hands, keeping both men at arm's length. Opposite arms. "Dix," he said to Conner, "you gotta know there are things about your sisters that you don't know."

Conner—and everyone else—looked at him in surprise. "What's that mean?" Conner demanded.

Amanda crossed her arms and waited for the answer.

"You're their brother," Ryan said, "They don't confide everything in you. You don't automatically know everything they're thinking and feeling just because you're their big brother."

Amanda and Emma looked at each other with expressions that were a cross between stunned and amused. No, of course Conner didn't know everything about them. But he thought he did, and they let him think that. It made him happy and made their lives easier.

"And there are things *you* know about them that I don't?" Conner asked Ryan.

"There are things *I* know," Shane said.

Amanda wanted to smack him. *Why* did he insist on rubbing this in?

Ryan swung his gaze to Shane. "And *you*," he said, pointing at Shane. "You need to just concentrate on Isabelle. Conner wants her happy. If you think you can pull that off, then *do* it. If not, leave her alone. But it's about *her*. Stop mouthing off to Dixon."

Amanda was a little impressed at that. It was true. Shane needed to be concentrating on making Isabelle okay. It wasn't about Conner being okay.

She looked from Ryan to her brother, then around the room.

Huh.

It wasn't about Conner.

And all the people in that room that she was related to—including the man whom she'd spent so much time trying to impress, whom she'd tried to help by reducing his burdens and worries, the man who had been her solid ground for so long—were really pissing her off.

"Conner, I think you need to go with Nate," she said, stepping forward.

Her brother looked at her, clearly surprised. "What?"

"I think Ryan's right. You need to cool off."

Conner crossed his arms and glared at Shane. "I'm not leaving until Isabelle leaves."

"Me either," Shane said.

"Maybe Isabelle's not coming out of the bathroom until you both leave," Emma said.

"Maybe you should go try to talk to your sister and see how she's doing," Nate said to Emma.

She shrugged. "It's way more interesting out here."

"Maybe I should have brought more beer," Cody muttered.

"Maybe I should run and get some," Gabby volunteered, getting to her feet.

Amanda didn't blame her for wanting to get out of here.

"For God's sake," Ryan muttered and headed for the hallway that led to the bathroom.

He was actually stomping. Ryan never stomped. Or muttered.

Everyone's eyes got wide a moment later when they heard him pound on the bathroom door and shout, "Isabelle, get your butt out here."

Conner's stunned look quickly changed to a frown, and as Ryan came back into the living room, he said, "What the hell, Kaye?"

Isabelle and Olivia were right behind him.

"Everybody out," Ryan announced, pointing at the front

door. "Now."

Everyone stared at him. Emma asked, "You're throwing us out?"

"Yes."

"And you're yelling," she pointed out.

"I know," he yelled.

"You don't yell," Emma said.

"And you don't throw your friends out of your house," Cody mentioned.

"I don't care," Ryan told him. "You can all be stupid and hard-headed outside as well as in. And if you're out, I don't have to listen to it. Out. Now." His tone was firm, his gaze was steady and his finger pointing at the door left no room for confusion.

Everyone decided that he was serious, and the women grabbed their purses while the men set their beer bottles and cups down on the nearest surfaces and headed for the door.

Amanda wasn't as amazed at Ryan's outburst as the rest of them seemed to be. Ryan didn't do drama or chaos. He'd tried to be the peacekeeper, but when that hadn't worked, he'd decided the next best course of action to remove the stress was to throw it out.

Amanda tried to get next to Isabelle, who was trying to avoid being next to Conner or Shane. Which was difficult because both of them were waiting for her and both of them were annoyed that the other was waiting for her. Amanda reached out to grab Isabelle's arm, intent on keeping her away from *both* men, when she suddenly felt a tug at the back of her jeans.

She glanced over her shoulder to find Ryan hanging on to her. "Not you," he said simply.

"But, I..." She glanced at her sisters, then her brother.

"You're staying."

Since it was what she wanted to do deep down anyway, and because she felt as bad about Ryan's irritation as she did about her siblings being at odds, she stopped struggling immediately.

The door shut behind Cody without anyone really noticing that she wasn't in the pack. They were all talking, arguing, chastising each other and wondering about Ryan suddenly getting loud and firm, and Amanda figured it would be awhile before anyone realized she wasn't with them.

"Are you okay?" she asked Ryan, who was still holding on to her jeans even though she'd turned to face him. It brought her up closer to him than friends should probably stand, but she couldn't quite bring herself to protest.

He looked into her eyes as he chuckled softly. "Seriously? You're asking *me* if I'm okay? I'm fine. What about you?"

"But you yelled. At your friends."

"Yeah."

"You don't do that."

"I don't need to do that. Usually."

"Why now then? The fight with Conner and Shane isn't brand new. You've been there when they've argued before and you've never yelled."

Ryan sighed. "It's because of you."

Amanda felt her eyebrows rise. "Me?"

"They were upsetting you. All of them. Isabelle running out of there and the guys squaring off. I knew it was stressing you and I didn't like it."

Something funny and warm and indescribable swirled through her chest to her belly. "You yelled at your friends because they were upsetting me?"

He gave her a little smile. "Does it feel that weird to be on the receiving end of the mama-bear thing?"

She thought about that. "Yes," she finally said. "Does it feel weird to be doing the mama bear thing?"

He nodded. "Yes."

"I don't hate it though," she said honestly. Having someone looking out for her and wanting her to be okay was nice.

It wasn't that she thought her siblings wanted her to *not* be okay, but really, none of them went out of their way to make sure she was. Because she was. As far as they knew.

"So you're going to worry about me all the time now?" she asked. She kind of liked that idea. And that was stupid. Not only was she not used to people worrying about her...she specifically worked to *not* make people worry about her. Plus, Ryan didn't worry about people. Live and let live and all that.

He brought her up a little closer and his voice dropped lower. "Maybe."

Her attention went to his mouth. This felt good. Too good. Not just being up against him, but the idea of him taking care of her.

And that was a really bad idea.

She could not fall into this—whatever it was—with Ryan thinking that it could last.

She finally managed to pull back from him. "You know, these attempts at friendship are not working so well."

"You mean because whenever we're together we want to rip each other's clothes off no matter what else we're trying to do?"

She couldn't help a little smile. "Yeah, something like that."

"Maybe we should just give in to it."

Uh-huh. That would be easier. For a guy who didn't really like to fight and try and stick, giving in to lust would be easier than working on something harder, like a real relationship. Even friendship took some effort.

He'd told her that he didn't think the people he cared about should cause him stress. But the people she cared about caused it daily. And she'd brought it right into his living room.

She should just let him off the hook. But that wasn't really her style.

"Maybe we should try it in public," she said.

"Ripping each other's clothes off in public?" he asked. "I could get into that. When and where?"

"Ha-ha." She stepped back even farther and took a deep breath. "I mean, we should hang out somewhere more public together. As friends. That might work better."

Ryan studied her as he tucked his hands into his back pockets. "You don't give up easily, huh?"

She shook her head. "Nope."

She definitely didn't. She could have left Emma to find her own ride a thousand times, she could have told Isabelle to shut the hell up about Shane on a daily basis over the past several months, she could have told her students at the college that she was available eight to five, Monday through Friday *only*. But she never did. She didn't give up on people. No matter how much it drove her crazy or how inconvenient it was for her.

This friendship thing with Ryan was a good idea. No one could have too many friends, and nothing else was really going to work between them. Yes, the sex was amazing, but she could already feel that she was turning it into more than that. She didn't have time to nurse a broken heart of her own when he figured out that the anti-Zen display her family had put on tonight was a four-times-per-week show.

However, she couldn't quite bring herself to just leave him alone completely. Or to have him leave her alone.

She loved the sexy flirting, she loved his sense of humor, she loved his ability to make things calmer and easier, and she loved that, for whatever reason, *she* could get him to shed that calmness and really react.

"When and where?" he finally asked.

She had no idea. "Anything that's not sexual."

"And I was going to suggest the strip club. Darn."

She smiled. "Right. And we can't go for ice cream."

"Why's that?"

"I always get whipped cream on my sundaes, and there is no way you could survive watching me lick whipped cream off a spoon."

His gaze heated slightly as he clearly imagined her doing just that. "We could go to a movie."

"In the dark, sitting so close together for almost two hours?

It would be too tempting to hold hands. Or hold something else," she teased.

She shouldn't tease. It was true that being that close to him would be far too tempting. Hell, she hadn't been able to sit in the same *room* with him and watch a movie without wanting to kneel down between his knees and open his fly and...

She breathed in nice and slow and long like he'd taught her.

"Or something?" he repeated. "I've never gotten a hand job in a movie theater."

She felt her whole body flush with heat hearing him say "hand job". She wanted to do that to him. Right now, in fact.

Dang, this wasn't working at all. She shouldn't flirt. He'd respected the boundaries she put up, he'd gone along with the idea of being friends only, he'd said a few sexy sweet things earlier playing the dumb ball game, but for the most part he'd been a gentleman about all of this. Last night in his condo when she hadn't even been able to make it through an entire DVD, all he would have had to do was say "come here" and she'd have been all over him.

But he hadn't. He'd let her leave, hadn't even tried to stop her or kiss her goodnight.

But if she was going to start with the innuendos and sexy talk, he wasn't about to let it go by.

She blew out a quick breath and decided to move on—mentally and conversationally—from the hand job. "Maybe the hockey team's in town." She knew lots of women found the hockey players sexy, but with Ryan next to her she doubted she'd even be able to keep track of the score.

"I don't know--there are a lot of sexual terms in sports," Ryan said. "*Scoring. Putting it in. Slamming it home.*"

She swallowed hard. *Slamming it home* sounded a little violent, yet...she wanted it. "That's—" She had to clear her throat. "That's more of a basketball term, isn't it?"

He grinned a slow sexy grin. "Let's go see some basketball

then. 'Cause I like the look it puts on your face."

She put her hands to her face. "I'm thinking the zoo."

"You want to go to the zoo together?"

"It's pretty nonsexual," she said. Then she thought about it. "Isn't it?"

"Sure, as long as no one mentions breeding or mating."

Right. With her luck the zebras would be going at it front and center.

"Well, I don't have a better idea."

He shrugged. "I think we might just have to accept that everything we do together is going to seem sexual."

He was probably right.

"Okay, we're going to risk the zoo. I'm going to take the afternoon off. I'll pick you up at two."

"I'll be ready."

She started for the door, but at the last minute she turned back. "Thanks for trying to do this with me." The friendship thing seemed silly considering they'd already had sex, she knew. And Ryan certainly didn't need to do anything to impress her or try to get her into bed. He wouldn't be lonely at night unless he wanted to be.

Ryan pulled in a deep breath. "Sure. As long as you don't figure out that I'd do anything for you, I'm probably okay."

And then he said stuff like that and she really wanted...more. More of...everything. Being with him, talking to him, kissing him, touching him.

Dammit.

She stepped close and stretched to press her lips against his.

He couldn't have been expecting it, but he reacted as if he'd been waiting and planning on this moment. He cupped her face in both his hands and walked her back until she was against the wall next to the door.

Then he *kissed* her.

His lips and tongue tasted every inch of hers, taking over

and demanding her surrender. Which she willingly gave. Heat filled her and she felt like she could completely melt into him. He held her right where he wanted her, though she wouldn't have dreamed of moving. Well, except maybe to get closer.

She arched her back, pressing her hips to his, and he groaned.

He was holding on to her, but her hands were free and she put them to good use. She stroked up and down his back, loving the firm heat under the cotton of his shirt. Then she slipped her hands underneath the shirt, needing to be skin on skin. She dug her fingernails in lightly, and he made a soft growling noise in the back of his throat.

Oh, she really liked that.

Her hand swept down to his firm ass, squeezing him and pressing him more fully into her. With the wall behind her, she felt every delicious bit of his arousal against her belly. And she needed more.

Bringing her hands around to the front, she ran her hand up and down the hard-as-steel flesh behind his zipper. He was so big and so hard and so... Everything in her felt like it was winding tighter and tighter and she was only touching him. And through denim at that. But she wanted every hot, hard inch, and she wanted him groaning and panting. She wanted his fingers tangled in her hair as she took him into her mouth. She wanted to feel him pulsing against her tongue and the salty taste of him on her lips.

She squeezed him and he pulled his mouth from hers.

"Damn, Mandi."

She quickly unbuttoned and unzipped him. For some reason, she feared he would stop her and she had to get him naked before he realized what was happening and—

"Oh, no, you don't." He caught her under the arms as she attempted to go to her knees in front of him.

"Ryan," she moaned. "Please."

He stared down at her, his gaze hot. His breathing was

ragged. Finally he asked, his voice rough, "Please what?"

"Please let me."

"Let you what?" he pressed.

She licked her lips. His hand slid to the base of her skull, his fingers deep in her hair.

"What do you want, Mandi?" he asked softly, rubbing the pads of his fingers against her skull.

"You. In my mouth."

His jaw tightened and he tipped her head back slightly. "That's a lot more *friendly* than I expected us to be tonight."

"I want you," she said softly. "I can't help it. We can be friends, but I need this too."

His eyes darkened and he clenched his jaw again, as if he was fighting for control. She knew the feeling. She felt *hungry*, hot, like she was on the verge of begging.

"*You* need this?" he repeated. "You need to get on your knees and put that pretty mouth on my cock?"

She nodded as far as his hold on her head would allow. "Yes."

He shook his head. "Holy hell."

"Please," she said again. She loved how it made his eyes narrow slightly. His need was clear in his eyes, and she knew that even though she would be the one on her knees, she was in control here.

"I'm not going to come in your mouth," he finally said. "I'm going to put you up against the wall and bury myself deep before that happens. Got it?"

Oh, yeah, she got it. "Definitely," she breathed.

He kept his hold on her, but dropped one hand to his fly and finished unzipping his jeans, then pushed the denim and cotton encasing his huge erection out of the way, his gaze locked on hers the entire time.

She couldn't tip her head to see, but she knew he was stroking himself with his hand and she felt her knees soften with want.

"Say 'please' one more time," he said, his gaze dropping to her mouth.

She licked her lips again, then said, "Please, Ryan."

He groaned and pushed gently, encouraging her to her knees. She went quickly, finally able to look at him. He was so big and hard and delicious. He still had his hand wrapped around his cock, and she found the sight incredibly erotic. She was hot and wet and ready for him too, but she needed to taste him, to give him this pleasure first.

She leaned in and he held his cock for her. Her lips closed around the tip as she put both hands on his ass, pulling him closer. She could tell he was holding his breath as he slowly pressed past her lips, his length sliding over her tongue, his girth stretching her open. She concentrated on relaxing, wanting as much of him as she could get. She took a moment to revel in the hot, pulsating feel of him. Then she sucked.

His hand on her head flexed and he muttered a curse under his breath. He put the hand not holding her flat on the wall, bracing his arm and leaning forward slightly.

She lifted her head, her lips tight around him as she slid to the tip, then sucked again.

Then her phone rang.

She looked up. Ryan was staring down at her, breathing hard. He looked...amazing. His cheeks were flushed, his eyes dark, his mouth set in a firm line that she knew indicated he was barely holding on to his control.

And she wanted him to lose it. To lose all of it. With her. Because of her.

Her phone rang again.

Her purse, phone and car keys were on the floor next to his foot. She must have dropped them there when she'd kissed him.

He looked down. "It's Emma."

She'd known by the ringtone, but knew he would see Emma's name displayed on the screen as the phone rang as well.

"I don't care." It was true. She didn't. There wasn't a thing that her sister needed right now that was more important than Ryan.

Somewhere in the back of her mind, she realized that that should scare the crap out of her, but it didn't. She wasn't leaving him. And not just because she was in the midst of the best blow job she'd ever given, but because he'd sent them away for her. She wasn't going to go running after them the minute they needed her. They could figure things out for themselves for a change.

"Maybe they're just wondering where you are since you didn't leave with them."

"I don't care," she repeated. "There's a limited number of places I could possibly be. And she'll think of that."

Her phone stopped ringing. And Ryan's started.

"See?" she asked, grinning. She moved a hand to stroke up and down the length of the gorgeous erection right in front of her.

Ryan's breath hissed out between his teeth. "Maybe they're worried," he managed, though his voice sounded choked.

"Don't care." She leaned in and licked the tip of his cock.

Maybe worrying a little would be good for them. God knew they spent very little time on it and never for her.

Ryan's phone stopped ringing too.

"I'll call her back later," Amanda promised. "I don't think this is going to take real long."

She squeezed lightly and stroked him again.

He groaned, then said, "I should be offended by that." He pressed close and tightened his hand in her hair. "But I think you might be right."

She licked up and down his length, loving the feel and the taste of him. Then she sucked him into her mouth, swirling her tongue over his tip before taking him deep. He pulled out and pumped in again several times before finally hauling her to her feet.

"For the record—and for future reference—skirts work really well in these scenarios," he said, unsnapping the snap on her capris.

"Noted," she said breathlessly as she fumbled with the condom she'd pulled from his pocket. "The no-underwear thing will help though."

He paused with his thumbs hooked in her waistband. "No-underwear thing?"

"I don't have any on."

He quickly pushed her pants to the floor and stared. "Thank you," he said sincerely. "But why?"

She laughed and rolled the condom down his length. "Just in case."

He pushed her up against the wall, put a big hand on each thigh and lifted her, spread her open and then thrust.

She gasped, then moaned. She was more than ready and he hit *exactly* the right spot.

She gripped his shoulders hard, but could do nothing else to help. She had no leverage and, frankly, everything in her seemed to have liquefied anyway.

But Ryan didn't need any help.

He held her up against the wall like it was nothing. He thrust deep and true, stroking every deep nerve ending, sending sensations she'd never experienced before skittering all over her body. The tingles spread out, running to the top of her head, the tips of her fingers and toes, but then came back and centered right where they were joined, where the friction and heat and pressure teased and swelled and built.

Ryan moved, somehow spreading her legs even wider, and pumped harder, burying his thick length deep just as he'd promised.

"God, Amanda, you feel amazing," he told her. "You look amazing, you sound amazing."

She did feel pretty damned amazing. "Ditto," she managed,

somehow.

"I want to feel you come around me," he rasped. "You were so fucking good with your mouth, but I want this hot body around me when it happens. I want to feel you clamping down on me, milking me."

His fingers spread on her ass and lifted her slightly, then brought her down on him again, fast and hard. How the hell he managed that she didn't know. Or care. It was awesome.

"Ryan," she moaned.

"That's right, babe. I'm right here. Barely holding on. Come for me, Mandi."

She was pretty sure it was the "barely holding on" that got to her. She loved making him crazy. But it might have been the "Mandi" thing. Or maybe it was pure and simple that this was Ryan, and she couldn't have held her orgasm back if she tried.

And really, why would she possibly do that?

The heat and tension pulled tight and then suddenly burst free. She went over the edge, her inner muscles contracting hard, determined to take Ryan with her.

And she did.

He came with a loud roar right on the heels of her orgasm. The orgasm that she felt even in her earlobes and that went on and on and on.

She was *so* glad he went to the gym on a regular basis. He was able to hold her up against the wall for another few minutes after the muscles and nerves started to quiet, and when he did let go and let her feet back down on the floor, it was slow and gave her time to make sure her legs were going to hold her up.

Ryan didn't really let go of her though. He leaned in to rest his forehead on the wall next to her ear, keeping her pinned—happily—between his big, hot body and the wall.

"I'm pretty sure," Ryan said after taking a huge, deep breath, "that this is the *best* friendship I've ever had."

She snorted before she could tamp it down. Her hand flew

up to cover her mouth, but he leaned back with a grin, having heard the not-very-ladylike sound.

"Seriously. I mean, I like movies and hot wings just fine, but girl, there isn't a damned thing in this city I'd rather do than *that* with *you*."

And somehow, in spite of the fact that he'd been with a number of women in a number of places—probably several more exciting and unique than the wall in his front hallway—she believed him when he said he'd rather be with her.

That was...awesome. That word was certainly getting used a lot between the two of them.

"So, it occurs to me," she said, looping her arms around his neck. "We *still* haven't had that one night that initially started this whole thing. How do you feel about a sleepover?"

He stared at her, then a huge grin spread his mouth wide. "Oh, thank God."

"Really?" That was a great reaction.

"Well, yeah, really. As long as you understand that *friends* don't spend the night. You wake up here in the morning and, well, let's put it this way—your brother is going to find out."

She arched an eyebrow. "How will he find out?"

"I'll tell him."

She arched her other eyebrow. "You will?"

"I want the world to know we're together, and I think he should hear it from me."

"We're *together*?"

He lifted a hand to her cheek and gave her the sweetest smile she'd ever seen. "I can help you take care of your crazy sisters, I can definitely let you take care of me and I can make sure you have all the calming tea, massages and games of laser tag that you need to be okay yourself."

Her heart felt like it was swelling in her chest and she felt tears stinging in her eyes.

"And nachos," she added. "I love nachos."

"Yeah, I noticed. You ate more than half of them the other

night."

She'd eaten more than half of the nachos she didn't even remember seeing? Wow. "And pickle chips," she said.

"Of course. And Snickers bars. And *lots* of role-playing," he said with a sexy wink.

She wiggled against him. "And orgasms. That's right up there with tea for stress, isn't it?"

"It's right up there with lots of things for lots of things," he said, squeezing her hips.

Her phone beeped just then with a new text message. She sighed. "I'm feeling a little stress building right now."

He laughed. "Why don't you go get in the shower? I'll check the message on my phone and take care of whatever it is, then join you in there."

She stared at him for a moment. Someone else to lean on? Someone else to return messages and make decisions? Wow.

"What's wrong?" he asked, frowning.

"Nothing," she said honestly. "Absolutely nothing." Which was an absolutely wonderful feeling. Ryan was there. He'd help her take care of whatever came up. And he'd take care of *her*.

Absolutely wonderful.

"Meet you in there," she said, starting for the bathroom. "I'll be the naked blond singing Lady Gaga at the top of my lungs."

Chapter Nine

He was falling in love.

It hit him hard and without a doubt as he watched Amanda sashay down the hallway, where she would be getting into *his* shower, rubbing *his* soap all over her, and then wrapping up in *his* towel. After she had another couple of orgasms from *him*.

And he was ready to go again just like that.

It had to be the love thing that was making everything feel stronger and more amazing than it ever had. He wasn't sure why anyone ever fell *out* of love if it felt like this.

He had really never seen this coming. And he wasn't sure what to do with it. Except wallow in it for as long as it lasted.

That he could do.

He headed across the living room for his phone. He knew the caller had been Emma and that she'd left a message. Probably called him a couple of names for not picking up too.

Two minutes later, he let himself into the bathroom. "Amanda?"

"Yeah?"

He could see the silhouette of her body through the thin curtain and his body urged him forward. But he kept his hands on the doorframe. "Hey, Emma, Isabelle and Olivia need a ride home from Trudy's."

Amanda poked her head out. "What happened?"

She looked adorable and sexy at the same time. Her wet hair hung against her shoulder, water droplets ran down her face and he could quite easily imagine what the rest of her looked like—wet and soft and warm…

He cleared his throat and gripped the doorframe. "Shane

and Conner happened," he said. "They continued to be assholes and Nate and Cody finally took them home—separately. The girls refused to go with either of them, so they're down at Trudy's."

"Dammit. Okay, just give me a—"

"You know what I'd love?" he interrupted.

She looked at him. "What?"

"For you to stay here. Finish your shower, curl up in bed—preferably naked—and wait for me to get back."

She looked surprised—and tempted. "You're going to go?"

"Yeah. I can take the girls home, no problem."

She seemed to not know what exactly to do with that. Finally, though, she nodded. "That would be...great."

"And if I stop on the way home, do you want pickle chips or nachos or something else?"

"I want you to not stop on your way home. To just get back here as fast as you can."

He felt something that was just as hot as desire, but seemed softer and sweeter at the same time, spread through him. He could call the girls a cab. Or call Nelson or someone else from the team to go get them. It wasn't like it required him or Amanda to actually be the driver.

But he immediately realized that doing this for Amanda would be worth it. He wanted to be the one who helped her with everything. From here on out.

And that was definitely a scary thought.

Sure, the love thing felt really good, fun, exciting. But it wasn't all about that, he knew. There would be tough stuff too, and he didn't really know how to do that. He hadn't had much for role models there, that was for sure. He loved his mother. He knew that she was happy, content, had no regrets. But he really wanted to try this with Amanda, and that would require being able to stick through the not-so-good-fun-and-exciting times too.

"I'll be back soon." Maybe some time to think things

through was exactly what he needed.

Or maybe he'd just figure it out later.

Either way, he needed to get in his car so he could get back here to the sexiest, sweetest, strongest woman he'd ever met.

After her shower, Amanda wrapped up in Ryan's bathrobe and did as instructed—got in bed. It felt decadent. Not just being in Ryan Kaye's bed after amazing sex against the wall, but knowing that there was a minicrisis that *she* was not attending to. Yet it was being handled.

It was really nice.

It was nice to be able to trust someone else to take care of the people she loved. It was nice to know that someone else could care about them in spite of their craziness. It was nice to be able to truly relax, knowing everything was fine.

She stretched and sighed and flipped Ryan's bedroom television on. And started thinking about all of the things she wanted to do to him when he got back.

After it had been a half an hour, she mentally calculated how long the whole thing should take. It was easily fifteen minutes to Trudy's and another fifteen to the closest apartment, then probably twenty to get back here. So there was no way he'd be back already.

At an hour, she wondered if her sisters had made Ryan drop each of them off separately rather than letting them all out at Emma's, the closest address, and having her drive Isabelle and Olivia home. But maybe Emma had been drinking.

Okay, it was likely Emma had been drinking.

She tried to call, but Ryan didn't pick up. And neither did any of her sisters.

That pissed her off. Had they talked him into staying at Trudy's for a few drinks? Had he run into other friends? Did they have the music too loud in the car to hear their phones?

At an hour and a half she was solidly into worry.

She called Conner's phone, but it wasn't her brother who answered. It was Cody.

"What the hell is going on?" she demanded. Had those dumbasses pulled Ryan into another of their fights?

"Amanda, Jesus, I just... They're on their way over. They should be there—"

She heard the pounding on the front door and hung up on Cody. Why was Ryan bringing the girls back here? And why had it taken so damned long to do it?

But it wasn't Ryan or her sisters standing on the condo's front step. It was Dooley Miller, Mac Gordon and Kevin Campbell.

"Hey, Amanda." Kevin stepped forward and took hold of her elbow, almost as if he was trying to keep her from falling.

"Hi, guys."

She didn't want to know why they were there. She could feel it.

"We need to take you to the hospital," Kevin said gently.

"I'm sorry it has to be us," Mac added. "But we thought it was better that it was someone you know. The other guys shouldn't be driving right now."

"The other guys?" she asked, not really processing anything.

"Shane and Cody and Conner."

She almost wilted right then. "They're okay? Conner's okay?"

"Yes." Kevin said it firmly, meeting her eyes directly. "They're all fine."

"What about Nate?" Maybe something had happened with the guys when they were all together. That would make sense why Shane and Cody and Conner were at the hospital.

"Nate's in surgery," Mac said. "He's okay."

She took a deep breath, her stomach pitching before she even knew why. "What's he having surgery for?"

"He's *performing* the surgery," Mac clarified.

That was what she'd been afraid he was going to say. "And I'm going to the hospital because..."

"There's been an accident," Kevin said calmly.

A sob swelled in her chest, tight and painful. She knew who was involved.

"Are they...okay?" she choked out.

"They're..." Kevin took a deep breath and looked at Mac.

"They're all alive," Mac said.

She was glad for Kevin's strong hold as she felt her knees give out. The big ex-football player swept her up in his arms and stepped into Ryan's condo. They all headed for the couch, and he deposited her in the middle.

"Here's the deal," Dooley said, crouching in front of her. Kevin sat right beside her and Mac stood behind Dooley.

Together they definitely exuded strength and confidence.

"There was a car accident. They were hit by a truck on the passenger side, where Emma and Olivia were sitting. Ryan and Isabelle are also banged up but they're stable. Nate's working on Emma. She's got a fractured pelvis. Olivia's...okay." He stopped and watched her, likely seeing if she was going to faint or puke.

Both seemed very possible.

"What about Olivia?" she asked, gripping Kevin's hand hard.

"She was unconscious and they took her in to do brain scans and tests to see what was going on."

The urge to puke overtook the feeling of faintness, and Mac thrust a bowl into her lap just in time. After she'd emptied her stomach, Amanda breathed deep. Then noticed that the bowl had held chips or popcorn earlier during the party. The party where everything had been fine and then, in an instant, things had gotten tense and ugly.

In an instant everything could change.

Like a car accident.

"Let me get dressed," she said, handing the bowl back to

Mac who, thankfully, was a paramedic and therefore had a strong stomach.

Kevin helped her up, but she felt amazingly steady. She had to get to the hospital. Her sisters needed her, Conner needed her, Ryan needed her. She would be steady, dammit, as always.

"I don't typically take cases where the guy's parts are all still attached and functioning." Ben Torres slid Ryan's X-rays back into their sleeve. "But I love to work on St. A's paramedics because the stories that put you guys in here are always entertaining."

Ryan shook his head. "Wasn't a work thing tonight, Doc."

Ben tossed the X-rays onto the counter and crossed his arms. "Yeah, I'm aware. I'm actually here because Mac and Kevin asked me to check up on you." He gave Ryan a serious look. "So what happened?"

"I fucked up."

"Also aware of that. Pretty common story among patrons of the ER."

"I don't have a better explanation." Ryan felt his chest tighten and he shifted on the bed, trying to ease the discomfort.

Ben just stood looking at him. "Aren't you going to ask me?"

"Ask you what?"

"How the girls are?"

Ryan blew out a slow breath, the discomfort in his chest immediately turning to pain. He knew how they were. At least for the most part. They were hurt. Because of him. That's really all he needed to know.

He'd been fully conscious through the whole thing. He knew Olivia hadn't been. He'd made sure she was breathing, he knew her heart had been beating, but he couldn't rouse her. He also knew Isabelle had a concussion and Emma had broken her leg—at least. As a paramedic, he'd seen a lot. Broken bones were common and many times the least of their concerns. But seeing Emma's leg bent up under the dash of his car...he had to swallow hard even now.

He and Emma had danced together, gotten drunk together, laughed together...it had never been serious. Seeing her hurt like that was as serious as it got.

"How are they?" he asked dutifully.

"They're going to be okay," Ben said.

Ryan nodded. "I'm glad."

"So what really happened in that car, Ryan?"

He took a deep breath. "Told you. I fucked up."

"Sure. But there was more to it."

Ryan looked at Ben. "Why do you think that?"

Ben raised an eyebrow. "I know a lot of the St. A's paramedics, Ryan. I know what kind of guy it takes. You pull people out of smashed-up cars in intersections all the time. No way you would have run a red."

Ben Torres was married to Sam Bradford's sister, Jessica. Sam and his crew—including Dooley Miller and Mac Gordon—were widely known as the best in the city.

Ryan sighed. "Physician-patient confidentiality?"

Ben shrugged. "I'm better than a priest."

"I was trying to break up a catfight. I had a green but I didn't even see that guy coming." A drunk had hit them. That wasn't Ryan's fault. But he could have reacted defensively, maybe, if he hadn't been distracted by the girls.

Ben's eyes got wide. "A catfight?"

"Kind of." Ryan rubbed a hand over his face. "The girls were wound up over Conner and Shane's argument. By the time I got there to pick them up, the girls were bickering about Isabelle leading Shane on. That led into several other topics even after we were in the car. As I was approaching 72nd Street, Emma threw a shoe at Isabelle—apparently it was Isabelle's and she wanted it back—then Isabelle made a grab for Emma's earrings which were also, apparently, hers. I was reaching to try to keep Emma's ear from being torn off."

Ben didn't respond for several seconds. Then he shook his head. "Wow."

"Yeah." It was a damned mess. The girls had been mad. And loud. But he should have known better—exactly as Ben had said. Being a paramedic made a guy careful. Or it should anyway.

"All your friends are here," Ben finally said.

Yeah, he figured they would be. "I don't want to see anyone."

"I kind of thought you might say that. But you can't avoid them forever."

Ryan knew that. But he was going to avoid them for now. "I can't tell them about what happened."

"You're going to let them think that you're completely at fault?"

"I am."

"Ryan—"

"Look, Ben, it's complicated."

"Okay." Ben leaned back against the counter and crossed his arms.

"You want to hear this?"

"Have you met my family? I'm an expert at complicated. And chaotic."

Ryan shrugged. Okay, fine. He could admit that it might be nice to say some of this to someone else. "I don't want Amanda to know that her sisters were fighting again, on top of everything else. Things are tense enough with Conner, with Isabelle's relationship with Shane, with everything. I don't want her to know that they were screwing around in the car. It's going to be killing her that she didn't go pick the girls up. If she finds out they were part of the problem, she'll go crazy."

"She's going to be mad at you, isn't she?"

"Probably." It was his fault after all.

"You're okay with this messing things up between you?"

No. Not at all. "How did you know there was something between us?"

Ben chuckled. "Because I've fallen in love myself. You're protecting her feelings—not wanting her to feel guilty about what happened—and her relationship with her sisters. For *her* sake. That goes a little beyond an acquaintance or even a friend."

Ryan sighed. "Yeah, okay. She just doesn't need any more stress right now."

Ben pushed off of the countertop and reached for Ryan's X-rays. "Okay. I'll give her the message. But I can't guarantee she'll believe that you don't want to see her."

"You're not a good liar?"

"*You're* not good at hiding your feelings for her."

The first thing Amanda saw upon entering the waiting room of the St. Anthony's emergency room was her brother sitting, his elbows propped on his knees, his head in his hands, with Shane right beside him looking equally like shit.

Thank God, they could figure out that there were more important things than their stupid fight.

Shane saw her first. "You okay?" he asked, coming forward.

She shook her head and hugged her arms tightly across her stomach. She was in a jacket that one of the other paramedics had found for her. It was huge on her, but it was keeping her from shaking. Kind of. "How are they?"

"We don't really know much," Shane told her. "Come on." He put his arm around her and started for Conner.

She wanted to cling to her brother, cry, beg him to tell her everything would be okay. But that wasn't fair to him. He couldn't tell her that for sure, and he needed comforting as much as she did.

Conner looked up as she approached.

He looked horrible.

She took a seat next to him, slid her arm around him and rested her head on his shoulder. They sat like that for a few minutes, no one talking.

Amanda noted that not only were Shane and Cody there, but Mac, Dooley and Kevin also settled into the chairs in the waiting area. She understood. Ryan was one of them, a paramedic at St. Anthony's, and they were like a family. So was Conner, and he needed support right now.

"Hey."

They all looked up toward the doorway as Gabby and Sierra came into the room.

"Hey, girls," Cody greeted them, his voice not-quite-normal-but-close.

"Heard there was a party going on here," Gabby said. She crossed to Conner and held out a cup of coffee.

He accepted it without a word, but gave her a little nod. That must have been good enough for Gabby, because she gave him a smile and moved to sit next to Dooley.

Sierra stood next to Cody.

No one said anything else. Gabby sat back and crossed her legs. She lifted her cup to drink. Three times. She uncrossed her legs. She leaned forward to rest her arms on her thighs, mimicking Conner's posture. Then she sighed. Finally she looked around the room. "So, what happened exactly?"

Amanda squeezed her brother. She wasn't sure she wanted to hear this. Yet she had to hear it.

Conner shook his head. He either didn't know or he wasn't willing to tell the story.

Dooley cleared his throat. "Um, we took the call."

Amanda looked at him with surprise. Mac and Dooley and Kevin had been the crew called out?

"You have details?" Gabby asked.

Dooley nodded. "Yeah."

"What happened?" Amanda asked.

Dooley shifted in his chair as if a little uncomfortable, but he met her gaze. "They were on Dodge, going through the 72nd Street intersection. Ryan, um…"

Amanda straightened. "Ryan what?"

"He…ran the red."

She stared at him. Her whole body went cold. No. That couldn't be right. Ryan wouldn't do something like that. Of course, people made mistakes, but surely Ryan would very specifically *not* do something like that if he had other people in the car.

"He *what?*" Conner demanded, straightening.

Amanda could feel the tension emanating from him. She tightened her arm around him, but wasn't sure if it was for his sake or hers.

Dooley nodded. "That's what the witnesses said. The truck that hit them didn't have time to stop."

"No fucking way," Shane said firmly. "No way. Ryan wouldn't mess up like that. No way."

Dooley looked at his buddies. Kevin and Mac both nodded, supporting Dooley's story.

"They're looking at traffic cams and stuff, but it could take a while," Mac added.

"Fuck that." Shane pulled his phone from his pocket and dialed. No doubt calling the station or a buddy who could find out what those traffic cams showed.

"Conner?"

They all swung toward the door where a physician in a long lab coat had stepped into the waiting room.

Conner got to his feet and Amanda stood with him, not willing to let go of him for a moment.

"Ben Torres," he said to Amanda, offering his hand. "I'm one of the trauma surgeons here."

She nodded, not able to speak. She really hated the word *trauma*.

"What's going on, Ben?" Conner asked.

"Emma's still in surgery. They tell me things are going well, but a little slower than expected. But that's likely more of an issue with Nate than it is anything to do with Emma."

Amanda breathed deep. Yes, Nate was in with Emma. He'd take a lot of time, go over everything thoroughly, be sure everything was okay.

"Olivia is still unconscious," Dr. Torres told them. "Which isn't great, but they haven't found any bleeding. They're monitoring for swelling."

Amanda dug her fingers into Conner's arm. She knew she was holding her breath. But she really wished Ben Torres weren't quite so calm and cool. She wanted the information fast.

"Isabelle is banged up and sore, but she's conscious and stable. She wants to see you."

"And Ryan?" Conner asked.

"Also bruised and sore. But he's okay."

"Can we see him?" Amanda asked.

Dr. Torres cleared his throat. "He's asked not to have anyone in right now."

Amanda frowned. "He said that?"

"He asked me to convey the message." Torres looked directly at Amanda. "To *all* of you."

Everything in Amanda protested at that. First of all, Ryan wasn't the type to close himself off from his friends. Except that maybe he was. Being supported after a car accident where he'd been injured and felt at fault was, after all, more complicated than what these guys typically did for one another. More complicated than Ryan liked things.

But she *wanted* to see him. As much as she wanted to see her sisters. Which rocked her world more than a little bit. Ryan had quickly moved up her list of priorities, that was for sure. And not being able to see for herself that he was fine was not acceptable.

She did things for people for their own good, whether they

liked it or not, all the time.

Why should Ryan be any different?

"That's bullshit," Cody said. "If he wants to be left alone, he'll have to throw us out himself."

Shane returned to the group, having just hung up his phone. "Ryan had a green," he told the group. "He was swerving but the truck blew the red. Apparently that's very clear on the camera."

"So that just leaves us to find out why he was swerving and not paying attention," Gabby said.

Everyone turned to look at her. She looked right back.

"What?" she asked. "We all know Ryan. There's no way he was driving crazy unless there was a good reason."

Amanda really liked Gabby.

"I'll take Conner and Amanda up to see Isabelle," Ben said. "We want to observe her overnight, so she's up on third floor."

Amanda looked at Cody and Shane as Conner started after Ben. They'd go and see Ryan and snap him out of this I-don't-want-to-talk-to-anyone funk "Um."

Conner glanced back. "What?"

"I'm...going to go see Ryan."

Conner stopped and turned fully to face her. "What?"

"I'm going to go see Ryan. I'll come to Isabelle's room in a little bit."

Conner crossed his arms. "You're going to see Ryan instead of Isabelle."

Amanda crossed her arms too. "Yes."

"You're going to see my friend Ryan—the guy who put three of my sisters in the hospital—instead of seeing your sister who was just in a car accident?"

Conner was looking at her like she had announced she needed to get a pedicure before she could see Isabelle—like it was the stupidest thing he'd ever heard.

But she wanted to see for herself that Ryan was okay—and being ornery. She wanted to hear him argue with her and try to throw her out of his room. She wanted to touch him, run her hands over the body that made her feel more comforted and more alive than anything ever had.

She needed the smile that he gave her when she was riled up about something.

Because she was keeping it together pretty well at the moment, but there was no doubt that she was riled up.

If he thought she'd been a mama bear before, he hadn't seen anything yet.

She was about to go mama-bear for the man she loved.

Amanda lifted her chin and met Conner's gaze. "Yes."

"I don't even know what to say to that," he said. Clearly he meant for his expression or his tone of voice to be enough to convey his displeasure without saying it word for word.

Well, it did. She got it. She knew he didn't like this. But that didn't change anything.

"You don't have to say anything at all. But I'm going to see Ryan."

Conner's expression changed quickly from displeased to angry. "Fine. When you do, ask him what in the fuck he was doing with my sisters in his car."

Amanda felt *her* temper spike a few notches at Conner's tone. "He went to pick them up for me," she said calmly, in spite of the way her heart was pounding.

"What? *Why?*" Conner demanded. "How did Ryan even know they needed to be picked up? And why didn't *you* go?"

And that was it. Amanda's temper snapped. Sure, it might have been a bit of her own guilt at play or all of her own questions—what if she'd gone instead? Had he been driving distracted because of her? Was he in a hurry to get back to her, so hadn't been obeying the speed limits?—but she did not like Conner's clear accusation and suspicion.

He was suspecting that she'd been with Ryan and she most certainly had been. She wasn't even slightly embarrassed about it and she was more than happy to answer all of Conner's questions.

"Because when Em first called, I couldn't answer because I was in the middle of having hot sex up against the wall in Ryan's hallway. And because he returned the call while I was in the shower after the hot sex up against the wall in his hallway. And because he offered to go pick them up so I didn't have to get dressed again after the hot sex up against the wall in his hallway."

The look on Conner's face would have been humorous if she hadn't just given her brother a shock that would ripple between them for a very long time to come.

Then, as he processed what she'd said, his expression changed from befuddled to shocked and, finally, to disappointed. The look she'd hoped never to experience from him again. The look she'd specifically *worked* never to experience from him again. For a moment she was flung back to that night when he'd walked into Coach's office and seen her at her absolute worst.

But then Ryan's face came to mind. That low point had been a long time ago. She had nothing to be sorry for when it came to Ryan.

Ryan needed her. Isabelle didn't. Conner would be there for Isabelle. Shane would be there as soon as he thought he could get there without upsetting an already tormented Conner. Sure, the guys and girls in the room would be there for Ryan. But, while Conner and Shane loved Isabelle every bit as much as Amanda did, no one there loved Ryan as much as she did.

And he needed to know that right now.

Or maybe she needed him to know that right now.

After several long, tense moments where no one said a word or even moved to itch their noses, Conner simply nodded, then turned and started for the elevators again.

"Conner!" She ran after him and grabbed his arm. "Do *not* go up to Ryan's room. I mean it. Leave this between the two of us."

"Don't ask me that," Conner said, jerking his arm from her

hold. "It can't be just between the two of you, and you know it."

She did know it. Her brother and sisters were such a part of her life that they would be a part of anything big that happened in her life—like bringing someone else into her heart. "Don't go up there now," Amanda said, wanting to reach out again, but resisting. "He's *my* first stop. Go to Isabelle."

Shane moved in beside them and put a hand on Conner's shoulder. "It's okay, buddy," was all he said.

But it resulted in Conner actually taking a deep breath. He stared down at Amanda. "Ryan comes before Isabelle for you?"

She swallowed hard. "At this moment? Yes."

Conner wanted to say more, she could see it in his eyes, but he didn't. And she was pretty sure she was glad about that. He was stressed and hurting. He'd been fighting with Shane already today, then the accident and now her bombshell. Whatever he would have said would have probably been regrettable. She appreciated his restraint.

He turned and stalked to the elevator doors. He punched the button and then looked at Shane. "You coming or what?"

Shane gave Amanda a tiny nod. "It'll all work out," he said softly. Then he turned on his heel and joined Conner as the elevator arrived.

She watched the doors slide shut. Shane was on his way to Isabelle's room with Conner. Maybe it would all work out.

Amanda faced their friends. "I'm going up to see Ryan," she told them.

They all nodded with wide eyes.

"I'd appreciate it if you'd all give us some time before you come up."

"Of course," Dooley said quickly.

"Yeah," Cody agreed. "We'll just...wait here."

"That would be great," she told them.

She walked confidently to the elevators and pressed the up arrow firmly, absolutely positive about what she was doing. She waited for the car to arrive, not even shifting her weight foot to foot. She also didn't glance over to the tiny crowd of people whom she could feel watching her. She was sure about what she was doing. Upstairs with Ryan was where she needed to be right now, where she *wanted* to be.

She was inside the elevator with the door shut before she let herself really fill her lungs. The air went in easy, but as she let it out, it was shaky and her eyes got a little blurry.

She was in love with Ryan. She wanted to see him, needed to be sure he was okay.

But dammit, Conner was her brother, and no matter how old they got, or how responsible they were, or how much she cared about another man, it would always hurt to disappoint her big brother.

The elevator dinged, then opened, and she stepped out onto the third floor, then realized that she didn't know if Ryan was on the third floor.

Feeling distracted and restless, she turned toward the nurses' station.

The woman behind the counter looked up Ryan's name and directed Amanda back to the ER. Apparently Ryan wasn't going to be observed upstairs. Which meant that he was fine.

One of the huge knots in her gut let go with that knowledge. Her sisters were still less than fine, but at least Ryan was okay.

The door on the exam room where Ryan waited was partially open and she didn't hear any noises from the other side, so she cautiously pushed it open and peered inside.

Ryan lay, propped up in the hospital bed, his head back and eyes closed.

"I thought *I* was the one who was supposed to be waiting in bed," she said quietly.

His eyes snapped open and he sat up quickly. "I told Torres to keep you all out of here," he said crossly.

"Dr. Torres relayed your message," she said, moving farther into the room, beyond relieved to see him looking and sounding well. Irritable, but well. "I chose to ignore it."

"I'm shocked."

She went to the side of his bed. She resisted touching him, but it was incredibly hard. He was clearly fine. Bruised maybe, annoyed for sure, but fine. But she wanted to crawl right into the bed next him, wrap her arms around him and not let go.

"You knew I'd come anyway?"

"When it comes to saying what you think and letting people know where they stand, you don't let much get in your way."

He wasn't looking at her. He was staring stubbornly at the wall.

"You know what?" she asked. "You're exactly right. You definitely need to know what I think and where you stand."

She folded her arms and held herself back from touching him. For now.

"Fine," he said. "Do it."

She took a deep breath. He was beating himself up. He was hurting—inside and out. She knew he cared a lot about her sisters and felt horrible that he was the reason they were in the hospital. He felt that he'd hurt Conner—his friend, crewmate and teammate. And he'd hurt her—his whatever-she-was. She had to be careful not to dump so much on him at once that he couldn't, or wouldn't, handle it.

This was complicated.

Ryan didn't like complicated.

But that was just too bad.

"I don't think this friendship thing between us is going to work out," she said.

She saw his jaw tighten as he gritted his teeth, but he gave only a simple nod. "I think you're right."

"I mean, with the way I feel about you, I don't see how we can continue with that," she went on, pushing, wanting him to look at her. One look into her eyes and he'd know how she felt.

"I understand."

"It's too hard to be around you when I—"

"I get it, Amanda," he interrupted. He still wasn't looking at her and the hand closest to her was clenched into a fist.

She moved closer to the bed. "I wasn't done. What I was going to say is that it's too hard to be around you when I constantly want to kiss you and tell you that I'm in love with you."

That got his attention. He whipped his head around to stare at her. "What the hell did you just say?"

"I said I love you. And even though we have yet to have a whole night together, I want a lot more than that."

He was frowning deeply as he looked at her. Exactly as she expected. Before the accident, she'd imagined telling him in a romantic setting, or maybe curled up beside him in bed...and him responding with happiness and an *I love you too*.

But as soon as she'd known about the accident, she knew it was going to freak him out.

"How are Emma and Olivia?" he asked.

Definitely freaked out. But she still had to tell him.

"I'm serious, Ryan. I know this isn't the perfect setting or time, but I'm in love with you."

"How," he repeated firmly, "are your sisters?"

She sighed. "We don't know anything yet. Emma's in surgery and Liv is still unconscious."

He pressed his lips together, his fist clenching again. Then he asked tightly, "Doesn't it feel wrong to be here talking to me instead of waiting and worrying about them?"

Her heart tripped at his words. It didn't feel wrong to be here with him at all. "My sisters are in trouble. I have a huge, heavy knot in my stomach and my neck is so tight I can barely turn my head. I hate this and I'm praying for them to be okay, of course. But being with you makes me feel better. Love does that." She moved in closer, grabbed his chin and forced him to look at her. "It is very important to me that *you* know that, in spite of all of the things that happened, I love you. That doesn't change. Got it?"

He swallowed hard and she saw a million emotions in his eyes. Still he said, "You need to go."

Right. Walk away. That's how it worked. That's how they did things in Ryan's world.

This was complicated. And if things got worse for Emma or Olivia, it would be even more so.

But this wasn't just Ryan's world. It was hers too, and walking away was not how she did things. She could, however, protect him. She wanted him in her life but she knew that was asking a lot. Her life was chaotic at times. He wanted peace. Well, she'd been protecting Conner for years from the pandemonium. She'd keep the crazy away from Ryan too.

"If I go now, it's only temporary. I'll be back. But I promise—"

"No."

"Yes. Ryan, it's not—"

"This won't make it better."

She let go of him. "What do you mean?"

"Telling yourself that you're in love with me won't make it okay in your mind that you were with me when your sisters needed you. Not deep down. Not after it sinks in."

Amanda felt her mouth drop open. "Wh...what? What are you talking about?"

"Sex isn't a good enough reason for not going. You'll hate yourself later. Unless you're in love with me. Then putting me first isn't so bad."

Her heart thumped. He knew her. Very well. And that was thrilling...and terrifying.

But he was wrong.

"That isn't why—"

"Dammit, Amanda!" He glared at her. "*Huckleberry.*"

She froze. And gritted her teeth. Her frustration was partly his use of the word and partly the fact that he'd raised his voice. He didn't do that. Unless he really meant it. Like when he was throwing his friends out of his condo.

Well, fine. He could mean it all he wanted. Mama bear was here and she wasn't going anywhere for good.

Knowing his bruises and bumps would make it hard for him to move quickly, she leaned in and pressed her lips to his. Then she turned and started for the door.

As her hand touched the door handle, she heard him say gruffly, "I'm sorry."

She looked back at him. She knew he was talking about her sisters. And she knew that it was killing him that they were hurt. She wanted to help him. She *needed* to help him. And loving him and not budging was the way to do that.

"I know," she told him sincerely.

"I'm..." He broke off and took a huge breath. "I'm just...sorry."

Maybe that *sorry* was about more than the accident, but she wasn't acknowledging that. As far as she was concerned, there was nothing else to be sorry about. He couldn't be sorry about a breakup that wasn't going to happen, and he sure as hell better not be sorry about anything that had happened between them up to that point.

"See you later," she said firmly, then pulled the door open and stepped through before he could respond.

She only got five steps down the hallway before she ran into Cody and Shane.

"Did you see Isabelle?" she asked Shane.

"For a little bit. But..." He sighed. "Conner needed me to not be there right now."

Amanda was impressed. She knew that not being there with Isabelle had to be as hard on Shane as walking away from Ryan was on her. Still, Shane understood that Conner needed to be the comforter right now. He wasn't going to let Conner dictate what happened between Shane and Isabelle, but he was going to respect Conner and Isabelle's relationship with each other.

"So, you'll take Ryan home?" she asked.

Cody nodded. "We've got him."

"And call me immediately if my brother shows up at Ryan's place." And Conner would, at some point. Probably.

Cody gave her a salute. "Yes, ma'am."

She looked at Shane. "You okay?"

The big cop scrubbed his hand over his face. "Hell, no."

Amanda nodded. She really did believe he cared about her sister, but the two of them had a really hard time being reasonable adults when they were together. "I'll text you when the coast is clear. But it'll be a while." Conner was going to camp out at the hospital until all of his sisters were well out of the woods.

"I know. Tell her…" He clearly wasn't sure how to put his feelings into words.

Which could very well be a huge part of their problems.

Finally he pulled himself up straight. "Tell her I'll bring ice cream sandwiches later."

Amanda didn't know any stories about ice cream and Shane, but she had the distinct impression that ice cream sandwiches from Shane wouldn't be simple snacks to Isabelle. "I'll tell her."

"Thanks."

She started down the hall again, but couldn't help swinging around again and calling, "Hey, Shane?"

He turned back. "Yeah?"

"Do you think Ryan would like it if I brought him ice cream sandwiches?"

The question successfully got a huge grin from her favorite officer of the law. "Yeah. He definitely would."

"Tell him I'll bring them over later." She paused, then added, "And tell him why he'll like that."

Shane gave her a wink. "You got it."

Amanda was grinning as she stepped into her sister's room a few minutes later. "I'm going to need to hear all about the ice cream sandwiches," she told Isabelle as she crossed to her sister's bedside and leaned in to hug her.

Isabelle hugged her back, but then shot a glance at Conner before asking, "What about them?"

"I'm going to go see if I can get a report on the girls," Conner said, coming to his feet and exiting the room without even looking at Amanda.

She sighed. "Did he tell you where I was?"

Isabelle nodded. "Yeah. You and Ryan, huh?"

"Are you shocked?"

"Not even a little bit."

That made her smile. "No?"

"I'm not blind, Amanda. And neither is Conner. He's not surprised either."

Amanda liked that. It meant that there was something between her and Ryan that even other people could see. That made her feel more secure about her plan to show him exactly how things went when someone made her love them.

"But he's mad," she said of their brother.

Isabelle shrugged. "He's worried. It comes out as mad."

"He doesn't need to be worried."

"It doesn't matter." Isabelle gave her a small smile. "He'll always worry, Amanda. If it's not this, it'll be something else."

Amanda took the chair Conner had vacated and pulled it closer to her sister's bed. Isabelle had all of her gadgets—BlackBerry, phone, iPad—all spread out on the small rolling table that was common at hospital bedsides.

"Are you mad I went to see him before I came to see you?" Amanda asked.

Isabelle shook her head. "No. Conner was here."

Exactly. "Ryan thinks I think I'm in love with him only because it will make me feel less guilty about sending him to pick you up instead of coming myself."

Isabelle met her gaze. "Is that why you think you're in love with him?"

"Not at all."

Isabelle leaned back against her pillows, crossed her arms and regarded Amanda with a serious look. "So, why do you love him? You've only been hanging out for a few days."

Amanda leaned back in her chair, crossed her legs and thought about it. "Because he makes people feel good when he's around. Because he's sweet and sincere. Because he doesn't judge people and he lets them be who they are. He's sexy and he's fun and he makes me feel like the most interesting, beautiful woman in the world."

She paused and took a deep breath. Isabelle said nothing and, looking away from her sister's intense stare, Amanda made herself really think about the question. She let her mind go to the stuff that she hadn't let herself dwell upon in the whirlwind of the past few days, the things that tightened her throat and chest and made her ache with the need to be with him.

She cleared her throat. "Okay, it's because he gets me—he likes the things about me that are most...*me*. He admires the way I protect the people I love. He understands that I want to be someone who challenges others to be better, but I also have their backs if they fall short. He likes how I sometimes need to be crazy or silly or strange. And with Ryan I feel like I can be all of those things without apology or explanation."

Isabelle pressed her lips together and pulled a long breath in through her nose. She swallowed, then said, "Well, I suggest you go and tell him all of that."

Amanda nodded. "Yeah. If he'll listen."

Isabelle laughed lightly. "Amanda, I can't remember one single time in all the years I've known you that you let something like someone not wanting to hear what you're saying stop you from saying it."

Amanda had to admit her little sister was right. "Should I really be taking relationship advice from you?" she asked bluntly.

Isabelle's smile died, but her gaze was sincere when she said, "Yes. Because everything you described about why you love Ryan is what I *don't* have with Shane."

"So, what's going on? You love him?"

Isabelle nodded, looking miserable. "I do. But you said that Ryan loves the things about you that make you most you."

"Right."

"There are things about me that Shane doesn't even know. Shane met and fell in love with the public me, the fun party-girl persona I put on. But not the real me. At least, not *all* of me."

"But…you're so happy together."

"Sure. Because I'm giving him exactly what he wants and he's…Shane. It's really hard not to love Shane."

Amanda nodded but said nothing.

"This was supposed to be a fun, short-term thing," Isabelle went on. "I never expected to still be with him six months later and I definitely didn't expect to be in love with him."

Amanda wasn't sure what to say. "Ryan and I are very different too. He's laid-back and easygoing while I'm intense and driven."

"But if Ryan sees that in you and, even more, appreciates that about you, that's all you need. Ryan's seen the good, the bad, the ugly, the boring. You did it right. Shane and I are different and…" She sighed sadly. "I'm not someone he would choose to be with long-term, Amanda."

That, of course, couldn't be true. Isabelle was beautiful and had more than enough male attention. And she had a naughty streak that was very evident whenever she was around Emma. Or schnapps of any kind.

Isabelle and Emma had always been the troublemakers, even when they were little. But Isabelle had never gotten into anything by herself. Something Emma couldn't say. Amanda knew it was Emma who instigated it all and talked—or dared—Isabelle into it. Now that they were older and Isabelle worked in a field that required her to be more sophisticated—and without an arrest record—she had matured and found interests beyond pushing the boundaries and bending the rules.

Something Shane couldn't say.

Amanda reluctantly agreed that Shane seemed to be the type to fall hard for the girl who had won a short-shorts contest the same night she won a trophy for best naughty limerick. That had been a wild St. Patrick's Day night.

"So you're breaking up with him?" Amanda had only known Shane for a short time, but it made her strangely sad that Isabelle was going to let him go. Everything her sister said made sense. But it didn't feel right.

Isabelle nodded. "I can't keep going at this pace, and if I stay with him any longer it's going to be even more painful when I'm not enough for him."

Amanda also *hated* that Isabelle thought she might not be good enough for Shane...or for anyone. But if Shane didn't appreciate all of Isabelle, then *he* was the one who wasn't good enough for *her*. "Do you believe that nothing happened with him and his ex?"

Isabelle nodded. "That's not the reason I need to call it quits. Shane's like...a roller coaster. A ton of fun, everyone loves it, it makes your stomach flip and your heart pound. But you can only ride it so many times before it's just too much. That adrenaline rush is thrilling at first, but it starts to give you a headache and stomachache after a while."

Amanda was following her. Kind of. "Shane's giving you a stomachache?"

"When it's two a.m. and I find out that he's in Vegas with his ex? Or when the ER calls because he's been shot—again? Or he shows up with coffee and bagels for breakfast because he's on a three-day suspension? Or he pulls me up on stage on karaoke night and insists I sing 'Paradise By the Dashboard Light' with him? Yeah. He gives me a stomachache."

Amanda didn't know what to say. And that sucked. She was used to giving advice—good advice—to her sisters. "I'm sorry, sweetie."

Isabelle nodded. "It's for the best. I can catch up on my sleep, get caught up on the TV shows I've been missing, get caught up on my knitting projects." She sighed. "I've missed my boring lifestyle."

Amanda just hoped Isabelle missed all of that as much as she was going to miss Shane.

"Emma's out of surgery and Olivia's awake and Mom's on her way," Conner said, coming into the room.

At his news, Amanda felt the tension that had held her muscles tight since Mac and Dooley had shown up on Ryan's doorstep loosen enough that she could take a full, deep breath.

"Then let's go." She got to her feet and leaned over to kiss Isabelle's cheek.

"One of us should stay here with Iz until Mom gets here," Conner said. "She's in Lincoln. It'll be about an hour."

Isabelle waved her hand. "I'm fine. I'm going to try to get some sleep."

Conner looked like he was going to protest, but he glanced at Amanda. She shook her head. Isabelle needed to be alone right now, even if it went against every protective instinct in Conner's body.

Much to her surprise he simply sighed, then crossed to Isabelle's bed and kissed her on the head.

Amanda had to swallow hard at the obvious affection in his eyes and his tone when he said, "Call us if you need anything, Iz."

"You bet. Love you guys."

"Love you too," Amanda called as the door to Isabelle's room swung shut.

"Olivia's in room four twenty," Conner said, starting for the elevator.

Amanda grabbed his arm. "Conner."

He turned back, clearly reluctant. "What?"

"I'm in love with him."

Conner rolled his eyes. "I'm sure you are."

She straightened, letting go of him. "Did you just *roll your eyes* about me being in *love*?"

Conner finally met her gaze. "I'm rolling my eyes about you

telling me that you're in love with Ryan."

"Why?"

He looked like he was deciding if he should actually answer the question. "Fine. You like him, he's a good guy, and you're attracted to him. Things...happened...between you and now you're afraid that if it was just a fling, you're going to mess up my friendship with him and cause problems like Isabelle and Shane do. So you want it to be more serious because you're trying to protect him. And me."

Amanda opened her mouth to reply. Then shut it without saying anything. Because she realized that if it had been just a fling, she might have done exactly what Conner thought she had done. For exactly those reasons.

But there was one very important thing wrong with Conner's theory—she *was* in love with Ryan.

"What happens when I'm still with him in six months? Or a year? Or forever?" she asked.

"My eyes are going to get really sore from rolling forever," Conner said.

She huffed out a frustrated breath as her brother turned to the elevator again.

"You'll understand when you fall in love," she called after him.

Conner gave a short bark of laughter. "Never gonna happen. The *last* thing I need is another woman in my life making me nuts."

Amanda really hoped that he didn't mean that. She knew that he often wondered what he'd done in his past life to deserve the four women who'd been making him crazy his whole life. But she did hope that someday he would find a woman who would make him crazy in a whole different—much better—way.

Chapter Ten

His condo smelled like her.

That was the first thing that hit Ryan when he stepped through the door. Which was crazy. She'd showered here, but she'd had to use his soap and shampoo. Was it really possible that her body spray still lingered in the air?

No. But the scent would linger in his memory forever.

He missed her like hell.

That was the second thing that hit him. Hard.

He'd made love to her only a few hours ago in the very hallway where he now stood only half listening to whatever Cody was saying. Okay, maybe he wasn't listening at all. Cody was just rambling to fill the silence anyway.

Shane had stayed behind at the hospital to see Isabelle. Conner was still there too, with his sisters. They'd gotten word that Emma was out of surgery and Olivia was awake before they got to Ryan's place. His throat had tightened when he'd heard the news and he'd offered up a prayer of thanks.

Ryan stepped into the living room. It was still a mess from the party, with cans and bottles and cups sitting on various surfaces. And still what he noticed most was that Amanda wasn't there.

And he missed her like hell.

She said she was in love with him.

God, that had almost done him in. It wasn't true, of course. He knew that. But hearing her say it had felt damned good.

But he was going to have to move now. Everywhere he looked he was reminded of her. The living room was where he'd first tasted her, where they'd tried to be friends, and where—

thanks to a little rubber ball and a crazy junior high party game—they'd realized being friends wasn't going to work.

Then there was the hallway.

And he was never going to be able to take another shower here.

He threw his jacket onto the couch and shoved a hand through his hair. "This sucks."

Cody stopped midsentence. He sighed. "Yeah. It does."

"Thanks for the ride."

"Yeah." Cody glanced around. "You want to watch TV or something?"

Ryan shook his head. "I'm gonna take some ibuprofen and go to bed."

"Okay. I'll um...clean up around here," Cody said, moving into the living room.

Ryan waved him off. "Nah, man, don't worry about it."

"It's no problem. You won't have to worry about it then."

"Seriously. I just want to head to bed."

"Go ahead. I'll..."

Ryan frowned. "Cody, what the hell are you talking about?"

Cody stopped and sighed. "Amanda won't like it if I leave you alone."

"She said that?"

"She implied it."

Ryan gritted his teeth. "Ignore her."

"No way." Cody started gathering cups. "I'm not messing with Amanda. You want her to forget about you, *you* tell her."

Ryan scrubbed a hand over his face. That was the problem right there—he didn't really want her to forget about him.

"Fuck it. I'm going to bed. You do whatever you want," he told Cody.

"Sleep tight."

Ryan was hit hard by emotion and sensation when he stepped into his bedroom. The towel Amanda had used after her shower lay crumpled on the floor—likely where she'd dropped it when she'd dressed in a hurry to go to the hospital.

He kicked it toward the bathroom, stripped off his clothes and got into bed. The bed that was rumpled from where Amanda had curled up to wait for him as he'd asked. The bed where he'd planned to finally spend a full night holding the first and only woman he'd ever really fallen in love with.

Hitting the light, Ryan forced his eyes to close and his mind to quiet.

He'd miss her just as much in the morning, he knew. He'd miss her every day from here on out. But maybe he'd get lucky and have a few hours of peace while he slept.

Of course, that didn't happen either.

He dreamed of her, then the accident, then her again all night long.

He did, however, manage to stay in bed unconscious for almost ten hours.

Groggy and grumpy, he made his way into the bathroom the next morning. A hot shower worked to clear out some of the cobwebs produced from the stress of the accident, having his head smacked against his side window and throwing the woman he loved out of his life.

Or attempting to throw her out anyway.

He made his way to the kitchen, dressed in sweatpants and a T-shirt. He wasn't surprised to see Cody was still there.

And his kitchen counter was covered with dishes.

"What the hell is all of this?"

"Muffins, cinnamon rolls, a casserole, cookies, a pot of chicken soup, and more cookies," Cody informed him, gesturing to the various pans.

"You made me chicken soup and cookies?" Ryan asked dryly, lifting the lid on one of the pans. Chocolate chip. His favorite.

"Uh, no," Cody said, a muffin in hand. "These are from girls."

"Girls?" Had Amanda cooked for him? That seemed like

something she would do.

"Girls from the hospital," Cody said. "Nurses mostly, I believe. They pretty much came in pairs. Only one came by herself."

"Girls from St. A's have been showing up here with food all morning?" Ryan clarified.

"Yep. Seems that you're a pretty popular guy and this is the perfect reason to come over. I think you could have your own personal nurse twenty-four-seven if you wanted one."

But he didn't.

He didn't want any other woman in his house besides Amanda, and when she showed up here—and he knew she would—he was going to throw her beautiful butt right back out.

She would try to turn this into something more serious because she wasn't the type to have a wild fling that made her irresponsible and disappointed everyone in her life. She would need this to be a lot more than just hot sex with a friend. She would need to make this a real, solid relationship because she wouldn't want her sisters to think she would ignore an important phone call from family because she was giving a blow job to some guy who was only a weekend fling. She would want to make this more meaningful because she wouldn't want her brother to think that he needed to worry about her blowing off her responsibilities to have a little fun instead.

No matter what they'd started building, even if they'd both admitted it was more than friendship, there was no way he could keep going with this. He'd never know if she really felt something for him or if she was trying to make what they'd done acceptable to everyone—including her.

"Chicken soup for bruises?" he asked.

Cody shrugged. "It's the thought that counts. And if you'd seen what she was wearing, you wouldn't care what she was feeding you."

Except that it wouldn't have mattered a bit.

The doorbell rang and Ryan sighed. It was nice that the

girls were concerned and trying to make him feel better. Sure, he knew that they were also trying to get his attention, but it really was thoughtful.

He just didn't want to have to worry about hurt feelings when he didn't follow up on any of this.

"You can have all the muffins if you keep answering the door," he said to Cody.

"No way, man. Every time I open the door, the girl on the other side is visibly disappointed. My ego can only take so much."

Ryan sighed and went to the door. But when he pulled the door open, Amanda was on the other side.

"Hi," she said simply.

"Hi."

She looked amazing.

She also had a big paper bag with her.

"What's up?" he asked, already knowing what she was going to say.

"I told you I'd be back."

"Amanda—"

But she stepped forward and he had to move back to avoid her pressing up against him. He couldn't touch her. He'd never stop if he did.

"This doesn't have to be difficult," she said, moving past him and into the condo.

He stayed in the doorway, breathing deeply in and out, using the relaxation mantras he knew so well—to no avail.

He finally followed her inside, finding her in the kitchen with Cody.

"I'll send the casserole to Nate—he and Michael can use that for sure. You want to take the cookies to the station?"

She was putting the food from the other girls into various plastic grocery bags.

"You're getting rid of my food?" he asked.

"Yes," she said simply, sliding the pan of cinnamon rolls

into a bag.

"Why?"

"There are plenty of single guys who would really appreciate this stuff," she said. "You don't need it. You have me."

He sighed. He wanted to have her, that was certain. And he liked that she was a little jealous. But he didn't have her.

Fuck.

He watched her unpack the paper bag she'd brought with her, storing fruit, sandwich meat and a bowl of what looked like salad in his refrigerator.

Part of him loved that she was clearly trying to take care of him. But part of him realized that she simply couldn't help it. Like her sisters, like her brother, like her student Jill, Amanda couldn't rest until everyone was okay. Until she *made* them okay.

He took a deep breath. "Amanda." When she turned to face him, he said simply, "*Huckleberry.*"

She frowned. "I just got here."

He didn't respond. The rule was they just had to say the word. She knew that. And he knew she'd respect that.

She huffed out a breath. "Fine." Still she gathered up the sack with the casserole and some of the cookies in one hand and the plastic container of soup in the other. "Olivia loves chicken soup," she told him.

"Tell her I hope she's feeling better," he said seriously.

"I will." Amanda stopped in front of him, went on tiptoe and planted a kiss on his lips. "I love you."

Then she left.

Ryan had to clench his hands at his sides and breathe deep to keep from going after her. As the front door shut, he looked at Cody.

"Seriously?" his friend asked.

He shrugged. "It's complicated." That was the understatement of the year.

"Life often is," Cody said.

"It doesn't have to be." He knew how to keep things simple and tranquil.

And that was what he wanted.

He was pretty sure.

"You're an idiot," Cody said, grabbing one of the remaining cookies from the plate on the counter. "I'll see you later."

"You're leaving me now?" Ryan asked. He wouldn't hate it if his buddy stayed. It would help keep his mind off of Amanda. Maybe.

"Gotta get to work," Cody said, clapping him on the shoulder as he passed. "I'm sure Amanda will send someone else over, though."

Ryan was sure she would too.

But eventually she'd get tired of this. It would take a while, he knew, but eventually she'd figure out that he wasn't worth all the trouble.

Nate was the next one to show up.

He was able to fill Ryan in on every detail of Emma's injuries, surgery and recovery.

Unfortunately.

Ryan couldn't quite bring himself to shut his friend up though. It seemed that Nate needed to talk about it. It was clear that putting the pieces of Emma's pelvis back together had shaken the surgeon.

"But she's good now?" Ryan asked, needing to hear it as much as Nate needed to be reminded.

Nate took a long draw on his beer, then nodded. "Yeah. She's sore. And pissed. But she's going to be fine."

"Pissed?" Ryan asked, feeling like a lead ball settled low in his stomach. It was his fault Emma was hurting. Of course she was pissed at him.

"I told her she's gotta take it easy. No dancing...and no yoga for a while."

Ryan frowned. Emma wasn't going to be able to work for a while because of him. Dammit. He wondered if she had any short-term disability insurance. If not, he was going to have to tap into his savings account to help her out. And somehow do it without her knowing. Emma Dixon was not the type to take charity.

"She can't possibly really *want* to do those things," Ryan said. "She's gotta know that she has to heal and rehab." Emma was stubborn as they came, but she wasn't stupid.

Nate shook his head. "She knows she can't do it. She's hurting too much right now to truly want to. But it really rubs her wrong for *me* to be telling her what she can and can't do."

Ryan relaxed a little at that. He could imagine Emma arguing with Nate simply because it was Nate.

"How long will her recovery be?"

"Six weeks for the bones to heal," Nate said. "Then a few more to really rehab. But she can do a lot in therapy even right now. And I did a hell of a job so she'll heal really well. Plus, she's strong, in good health. She's got a lot going for her. She just has to take the rehab seriously and not mess around." He frowned as he said it.

"She'll take it seriously," Ryan said. Again, Emma wasn't stupid. And if she did mess around, he'd kick her butt.

"Then she'll be fine. She'll get back to normal."

Ryan let those words really sink in. She was going to be okay.

Nate stayed for another hour, then had to get home to check in with his son, Michael. "You're good?" he asked on his way to the door.

"Yeah." And basically he was. He felt like shit about the accident, but the girls were going to be okay and it seemed that most of his friends were still speaking to him.

"Okay, call if you need anything. Or come over if you get bored."

That was a real possibility. He could play video games with Michael or something.

"Thanks. I will," he promised.

He managed to make it through the rest of the evening on his own. Cody called to check in, as did a couple other guys from the team. He called his mom to fill her in, but ended up leaving a voice message. He made dinner. Watched TV. Went to bed early.

As the numbers on the clock changed slowly—too slowly—on his bedside table, he finally admitted that he had been expecting Amanda again.

But she didn't show up.

Until the next morning.

He was up and finishing his coffee when the doorbell rang.

He knew who it was before he even turned the knob.

"Hi," she said, as she had the morning before.

"Hi." God, he wanted her with every fiber of his being. He didn't just want to pull her into his arms and strip her of the silky red blouse and black pencil skirt. He also wanted to make her pancakes and ask her how she was and find out what her day was going to be like.

He should tell her to quit sending babysitters, but he couldn't. That was Amanda. She took care of people, and he was weak enough to admit that being someone she took care of felt damned good.

But he managed to send her away. Somehow.

Of course, she came back the next day. And the next day.

On the fourth day, he propped his shoulder against the doorjamb, crossed his arms, and drank in the sight of her. God, she was amazing.

"How's Olivia?" he asked.

"Good. The doctors say she's perfect. I still don't like the idea of her being home alone all day though."

"You've been taking off work?" Every day she'd shown up on his doorstep she looked gorgeous, like she was ready for the office.

"Just the first day. Everyone else has been taking turns." She shrugged.

He frowned. "You didn't think to ask me?" He'd been off since the accident. He had to be one hundred percent at his job, and the doctor had recommended a few days off before he'd sign the approval for him to return to duty.

She waved her hand. "Oh, it's been fine."

"Who's she hanging out with today?" He'd texted her a couple of times and she'd said she was feeling good, but he hadn't realized they'd all been taking turns—and missing work—to keep an eye on her.

"Doesn't matter. I'm just going into the office for a little bit. I'm meeting with Jill and a couple of her friends."

"Is Jill still having trouble?"

Amanda waved her hand again. "It's fine. She'll be good."

He really wanted to let her in. But he couldn't. He was barely resisting falling at her feet and confessing his undying love. Inside his house, closer to his bed, and he'd never let her leave.

"So, who's with Liv today?" he asked again.

"She's going down to the station for a little while."

"The fire station?" he asked.

"Yeah."

"She's back to work?" That was a good sign.

"No, just hanging out."

"Amanda? Why didn't you ask me to spend time with her? I make the most sense. I'm off work anyway." It occurred to him to be concerned, even hurt, that she might not trust him with Olivia after what happened. But he knew that wasn't it.

She did that wavy thing with her hand again. "You don't need to do that. It's fine."

He grabbed her wrist. "Stop saying everything is fine."

She sighed. "I don't want you to worry about all of that."

"'That'? You mean the people you care about? The people *I* care about?"

"It's all covered."

Yep. He knew exactly what she was doing. She was

protecting him—from the stress, the not-great stuff that he'd told her he didn't like.

"Amanda."

"Are you going to let me in?" she asked. "I brought the pirate slave girl outfit that you wanted." She held up a shiny black bag from the costume shop.

"You bought a pirate slave girl costume?" Well, he could probably let her in for a little while...

"And a naughty secretary outfit."

Yeah, he could definitely find some time—

Then he shook his head. No. He saw what she was doing. He was the guy to play dress-up with while everyone else—especially Amanda—took care of the serious stuff.

Ryan straightened. "I'm going to the station."

"What? Why?"

"To get Olivia. We'll hang out. Her being down there is ridiculous."

"Well, um..." She glanced over the shoulder.

Ryan rolled his eyes. "She's in the car?"

Amanda looked a little sheepish. "Yeah."

He rubbed the back of his neck, half frustrated and half convinced that she was his favorite person in the world. He looked into her eyes. No, he was *fully* convinced she was his favorite person.

"What if I'd let you and the pirate outfit in?" he asked.

"I knew you wouldn't."

"But you still brought the costume?"

"Costumes," she corrected, leaning in and setting the bag inside his front door.

Where it would tempt and taunt him.

He pulled his gaze from the shiny bag and cleared his throat. "You were sure I wouldn't let you in?"

"Not *this* time," she said. "But Liv has the keys with her in case I'm not out in twenty minutes or so."

He shook his head. "Let's go get her." He started to move

past her.

"Are you sure?"

He turned. "Don't."

"Don't what?"

"Protect me this way."

"But you didn't ask for the responsibility and craziness—"

"I want it. Period."

She stared at him, but finally gave him a nod. He rounded the corner of his garage. Olivia was sitting in the car, her elbow propped on the window, twirling her hair with one finger. Her face lit up when she saw him though, and she climbed out quickly.

His stomach clenched for a second, but the moment she was within reach he pulled her in for a hug. "I'm glad to see you, Liv."

She wrapped her arms around him too and squeezed him back. "I'm okay, Ryan."

He took a deep breath and let go of her. "That makes me better too."

She smiled up at him and he looped an arm around her shoulders, looking to Amanda. "She's in good hands."

Amanda looked a little choked up and he gave her an eye roll and a smile.

She nodded. "Okay. I'll be back later."

Yeah, he knew she would. Whether her sister was here or not. And it was going to get harder and harder to push her away.

He watched her all the way out of the parking area.

Finally he went to join Olivia inside.

She was perched on the edge of the couch, shuffling a deck of cards on the coffee table.

"What are we playing?" he asked.

"Garbage."

He loved that game. He settled into the chair perpendicular to the couch. "Okay with me. What are the stakes?"

"Every time I win, you have to tell me something you like about Amanda."

Ryan stiffened. "What?"

"And every time you win, I have to tell you something *I* like about Amanda."

He took a deep breath. "Why?"

"Because I want to make it impossible for you to keep pushing her away." Olivia Dixon was the kind of person who made everyone smile. She had an inherent sweetness that made people like her almost immediately.

But she was sneaky.

"I'm really good at Garbage," he said, after a moment.

"That's okay," Olivia said with a big smile. "I have lots of things that I like about Amanda."

Yeah. That wasn't going to be a problem for him either.

He won four hands in a row and heard that Olivia liked how Amanda donated food and toys to the humane society once a month, how she made the best banana bread in the world, how she knew every episode of the TV show *Chuck* forward and backward, and how Olivia not only knew she could call Amanda for anything, but she *wanted* to because Amanda always knew what to do to make her feel better.

Winning was supposed to be working for him, helping him avoid saying what *he* liked best about her, but it turned out that any mention of Amanda made him crazy.

He lost the next hand.

Olivia sat up straighter. "Okay, tell me something you like about her."

He sat back in his chair. "It's a long list."

"Glad to hear that," Olivia said.

"Not liking her isn't the problem, Liv."

"So what is?"

He took a deep breath. "You know your sister really well."

Olivia nodded.

"You know that she will do anything for the people she

cares about."

Olivia nodded again.

"And she deserves the same."

Olivia sat forward. "Of course she does."

He focused on the cards on the table instead of on Olivia's face. "I don't know how to be that guy."

Olivia reached over, putting her hand on his arm. "Well, there's no one better to teach you how to be there for people than Amanda."

That sounded so easy. And tempting. He pushed to his feet. "You hungry?"

He heard Olivia sigh behind him, but then answer, "Sure, what do you have?"

"Mac and cheese." And whatever Amanda had put in his fridge.

"I love mac and cheese."

Thankfully, Olivia left him alone in the kitchen as he boiled the noodles and stirred in the powdered cheese, milk and butter. He was grateful for the meal prep that he'd done a million times before so that he didn't need to concentrate. He couldn't keep his mind from wandering to his mom. Why hadn't she ever fought for a relationship? The men in her life had been great guys. Ryan had liked every one of them and he knew they'd treated his mom well. Why hadn't she ever tried harder to make things work? He couldn't remember her ever seeming all that upset when things broke up.

He was frowning as he brought mac and cheese, bananas and iced tea into the living room.

Olivia proved her sweetness further by dropping the topic of Amanda as they ate, watched three game shows—Olivia scored more points in two of the games, but Ryan kicked her butt at the rerun of *Family Feud*—and finished the quart of Peanut Butter Passion ice cream in his freezer.

The phone rang as he finished rinsing the dishes.

He smiled as he looked at the number. "Hey, Mom."

"Hi, sweetie. You're okay?"

"Yep. Fine." He filled her in on the accident, his injuries and the girls' conditions. Then they chatted about her most recent adventure—a road trip through the wine country in California.

Finally, Ryan felt comfortable bringing up the subject he'd been dying to talk to her about. "So, I have some more news," he said.

"Wonderful, honey. What's going on?"

"I'm in love."

Karmen laughed. "That's fantastic."

"It is?"

"Of course. Falling in love is the biggest rush in life. You should ride that roller coaster as many times as you can."

And there it was. That philosophy that he'd grown up with, the outlook that had made sense to him for so long—right up until he'd fallen in love, for real, with Amanda.

"What if it's more than just a rush?"

"Well, great. You've got someone you can talk to…those are the ones that can last."

But Ryan knew that in Karmen's world, "lasting" didn't mean forever.

"Why didn't you ever stay with any of the men in your life, Mom?" he asked. He'd wondered, but he'd never asked.

"Oh, Ryan," she said breezily. "That's not how I'm wired. I like the for-better, for-richer and in-health parts. Not the rest as much."

"But if you love someone, don't you want *all* the parts?" It would be incredibly hard to see Amanda sick, but he couldn't imagine not being there if she was. He wanted her to be successful at her work and wanted to have the money to buy her anything and everything she'd ever need, but if things got tough, there was no one he'd rather eat ramen noodles with every night. Could he do for worse, for poorer and in sickness with Amanda? Absolutely. And he'd feel blessed every day that he was the one who got to be there.

"Ryan," Karmen said gently, "not everyone is that strong."

"Strong?" He'd always thought of his mother as strong. She made her own way in the world, didn't need anyone else, did her own thing.

"Strong enough to love another person forever. People mess up, make mistakes, say hurtful things. People are hard to love, son. Some people are tough and can stick it out. I prefer the easy way. I love 'em good and hard, but only for a while."

Strong. That was Amanda. "She's strong, Mom," Ryan said. "It doesn't matter how many times someone disappoints her, or makes a bad choice, or hurts her—she's still there when they need her."

And Ryan was eternally grateful for that. He'd done all of those things, hadn't even told her that he loved her, yet he knew she'd be there anyway.

"I take it you've finally found one that won't let you go," Karmen said after a few seconds of silence.

He took a deep breath, then blew it out. "Seems that I have."

Karmen sighed, but it was a happy sound. "She's the one then."

Ryan felt surprise shoot through him, followed quickly by an emotion he could only describe as complete satisfaction. Still, it was a *really* strange and romantic thing for his mother to say. "The one?"

"Yes," Karmen said with enthusiasm. "Finally."

Ryan's eyes widened. "What do you mean 'finally'?"

"I know there have been a lot of girls, Ryan," Karmen said. "And I know you push them away when you start caring too much. You do it to test them, to see if they'll stick. And none of them have. Until now."

Yeah, he'd done that. Sometimes he'd even been aware of it. And he'd been pushing hard with Amanda.

"And this is a good thing?" he asked.

"Of course."

"Mom," Ryan said firmly. "Have you been drinking your feel-good tea?"

She laughed. "I'm not under the influence of anything other than being a mother who loves her son and wants him to be happy."

"But..." He was confused. "Amanda is the type of girl who wants forever. That makes a guy want forever."

"That's awesome."

Yeah. *Really* confused. "But... We don't... I don't...know how to do that."

Karmen laughed. "Of course you do."

Ryan shook his head even though she couldn't see him. "How would I know how to do that? You and I have never done it."

"Ryan, you've never ended a relationship with someone you love in your life."

His mouth dropped open. "Are you kidding? Dad? Hank? Larry?"

"Ryan," she said, with clear exasperation. "You drove me crazy after your dad moved out because you insisted on calling him and having him a read a bedtime story to you over the phone every night. You talked to your dad on the phone every night for years, even after you outgrew the stories."

She chuckled softly and he could picture her shaking her head at him.

"After Hank left, you insisted that I invite both him and your dad for Christmas dinner and they ended up coming over every year after that. When Larry and I broke up, you taught him to use e-mail so you could stay in touch—after you bought him his first computer. You've bought Hank season tickets to the Husker football games for the past seven years so you can go together." She stopped and took a deep breath. "Honey, you definitely know how to stick with someone." She paused again, then laughed. "You've put up with me all these years and we both know *that's* no small task."

Ryan felt something shift inside of him and click into place all at once. She was right. He hadn't seen *her* make a romantic relationship work, but he'd made *his* relationships work with his dads. And his friends. And his coworkers. He hadn't made it work with a woman yet, but then again, he hadn't been with Amanda until now.

Maybe he did know how to stick. Maybe he could make this work. After all, if Amanda was the one for him, then he had to be the one for her.

"I love you, Mom."

"I love you too." And he knew she did—more and longer than she had anyone else, ever.

He was smiling as he disconnected. His mom was fine. She was happy. That's all he could really hope for.

That's what he wanted for Amanda.

He was just having a little trouble adjusting to the idea that *he* might be what made her fine and happy.

Olivia was curled up in the middle of his couch, watching SpongeBob. He grinned. He was so glad she was here. It felt great to see her, talk to her, help her out—even if it was with dumb entertainment all day.

She looked over at him as he sank onto the couch cushion beside her. "Hey, Ryan, thanks for today."

"Of course. It's been fun."

She turned toward him, her feet tucked up underneath her. "It has been. But it's been even better than that. I'm so glad that you're not mad at Isabelle and Emma, or beating yourself up, or letting my brother scare you off."

He looked at the woman whose beautiful green eyes were an exact replica of the ones he wanted to look into for the rest of his life. "Nothing could keep me from being here for you and your sisters, Olivia," he said, realizing that he meant those words with everything in him.

What had happened had sucked, but they were healing and

moving on, still all together.

He'd never been through a really tough time with someone. In his mom's life, the goodbyes happened when the tough times started. That was the best way for Karmen to avoid the angst and negativity she was so determined to keep out of her life. And he felt sad for his mom in that moment. It turned out that things felt even better, stronger, more solid, when you made it to the other side together.

"Hey, Liv, what time does Emma have rehab today?" he asked, knowing exactly what he needed—and wanted—to do.

"Around three, I think."

It was twenty till three. "Great. Let's go."

"We're going to see Emma's rehab?"

He'd been dying to call Em or stop up there all day. "Yes, definitely. I have a feeling Em could use some Oreos after her workout today." Emma would do almost anything for an Oreo. If he brought her the ones with the mint cream, everything would be right in the world again.

"I'm with you," Olivia said, grabbing her shoes and slipping them on.

Ten minutes later, they pulled into the parking lot for St. Anthony's Rehab Center. He knew exactly which vending machine to go to for the cookies, and they arrived in the therapy gym as Emma was wheeled through the door.

For a moment, seeing her in a wheelchair made his heart clench. But then she saw them and her face lit up and Ryan knew he'd be spending more afternoons down here in the next few weeks.

Amanda wasn't going to be able to keep him away from the craziness or complications. He was going to dive right into the middle of it all—exactly where he wanted to be.

When she walked into the rehab center at four thirty, Amanda realized that she wasn't surprised that Ryan was there.

She'd had a moment of anxiety when she'd gotten the text from Olivia telling her where they were.

She'd tried to be strong. She'd tried to trust that his feelings for her would pull him through his doubts. She'd been determined to show him what it looked like when someone made a commitment, for better or worse. But she could admit, to herself only, that she'd wondered if he could do it. Maybe he really didn't have it in him. Maybe his feelings for her weren't enough to break through the lifelong belief that everything, even love, had a season.

But as she'd driven to St. Anthony's after her meeting with Jill, she found the worry turning to hope, then excitement, and then happiness.

He was there. Where she needed him.

He wasn't running. He wasn't avoiding. He wasn't shying away.

He wasn't letting her protect him.

He was right in the middle of things.

Ryan and Olivia sat on the edge of one of the exercise tables, facing the wider table where Emma was going through a series of exercises with one of the physical therapists. Amanda paused several yards away, without any of them noticing her, and just watched. Her sister was working hard and Amanda could tell it was painful and difficult. Emma had a look of concentration and determination on her face that Amanda hadn't seen in a long time.

She'd heard from the therapists that Emma was pushing herself, and Amanda was proud of her, but damn... She took a deep breath. She saw patients in much worse shape work on much harder activities all the time. But those patients weren't her little sister. Emma's face was wet and only half of it was sweat. The other moisture was from tears.

Amanda looked at Ryan. Was he okay? She knew him and knew it had to be hard on him to see Em struggling after an accident he was a part of. She wanted to go to him, but wanted to compose herself a bit before she got any closer to Emma.

Finally Emma finished her reps and collapsed onto her back for a break.

Ryan lifted his head just then and noticed Amanda in the huge mirror that took up most of the wall across from where he sat. He leaned to say something to Olivia, who also looked and then raised her hand in greeting. Amanda smiled and waved back. Ryan got to his feet and headed straight for her.

"Hey," he said drawing close.

Just that one little word and she felt better. "Hey."

"She's working hard."

"I can tell."

Before he could say anything more, Nate strode into the room, his long white lab coat billowing behind him like a cape. "Let's go, Dixon," he said as he approached Emma's table. "This isn't nap time."

Emma propped herself up on her elbows and glared at him. "When the hell is nap time? This place is insane. This is my third therapy session today."

"You can nap when you get home. Get moving. We need you out of here so we can give your room to someone who's actually sick."

Amanda frowned. Did Nate have to get Emma all riled up *now*? She was working her tail off. Couldn't he see that she was tired and upset? She started forward, but Ryan stepped in front of her.

"No, Amanda."

"Hey, he needs to lay off a little."

"Just...watch. And trust." Ryan moved in behind her but wrapped his arms around her, keeping her in place.

Which felt really good. She sighed and did what he asked—she just watched.

Emma pushed herself up to sitting. "You know what I think, Doc? I think you're worried that I'll lie around here and my butt will get big and mushy. I know how much you like looking at it. You just want to keep it in shape."

Nate ran a hand over his back pants pocket. "Speaking of butts, I'm feeling a major pain in mine right now."

"Oh, you have no idea," Emma told him. "I have your personal cell phone number now. Your nurse gave it to me. I have a feeling I'm going to have a lot of emergencies at about three a.m."

"And by *emergencies* you mean the overwhelming urge to thank me over and over for doing such a great job putting you back together?" Nate asked, tucking his hands into the pockets in his lab coat.

"I mean the overwhelming urge to tell you all the ways your bedside manner sucks," Emma informed him.

"Oh, so you'll be calling me with more of your incurable and incessant whining and complaining then?"

Emma glared at him again, then pulled her T-shirt off and wiped her forehead with it before tossing it away. Clad in only a black sports bra, she added a two-pound weight to what she already had on her ankle and started moving again. "You better watch it, Doc. I might be a little slower on my feet right now, but I can, and do, keep grudges for a very long time."

Nate shrugged and turned toward Olivia. "I'm not worried."

"You should be," Emma said. "I know it's hard to believe but I can be a real bitch."

Nate chuckled as he checked the bump on Olivia's head and made her follow his finger with her eyes. "How you feeling?" he asked the youngest sister.

"Fine. The medication helps with the headaches. Otherwise I'm good."

"Glad to hear it." He gave her an affectionate smile, then turned back to Emma. "You wouldn't be a bitch to the guy who controls when you're getting out of here and how often you can refill your pain medication prescription, would you?"

"I'll leave whenever I damned well want," Emma told him.

"Or the guy who was with you in the recovery room," Nate answered, turning back as he reached the door. "People say the craziest stuff when they're coming out of anesthesia." He hit the door with one hand and, with a big grin, walked out.

Amanda turned in Ryan's arms. "Wow."

"He's good," Ryan said with a nod.

"He handles Emma anyway." She put her arms around Ryan and leaned into him, absorbing the feel of him—solid and strong.

She felt Ryan sigh, then one hand on top of her head, stroking down over her hair to the middle of her back. "I love that you'll lean on me physically," he said. "And I really hope we're getting closer to you leaning on me in every other way too."

"Olivia!" Emma called. "Tell someone I need some AC/DC."

A male therapist and another patient—also male—both lunged for the stereo system.

Ryan chuckled and Amanda soaked in the sound and feel of it. God, she loved him.

"You sure you want to be fully entrenched in all this with me?" she asked him.

He pulled back and looked down. "I know I said that the people who are close to you shouldn't be the ones that give you stress, but I realized something really important—walking away is the easy way to go. Unless you love someone. Then walking away is impossible."

Her heart sped up and she blinked hard, fighting tears. "My life is crazy."

"Well, your life has something in it that I'm very interested in."

"The dill pickle chips, right?" she asked.

"Hell, no." He gave a mock shudder.

"Ice cream sandwiches?"

He paused. "Well..."

She laughed and squeezed him.

"*You*," he said sincerely. "It's all you."

Happiness raced through her at that one word. "Good

answer."

Just then Emma swore, ripped off the leg weight and threw it. She slumped back onto the mat, covering her eyes with her forearm.

Amanda instinctively started forward.

Ryan held on. "Breathe."

"No."

"She needs to do this. On her own. She's okay."

"She's not okay, Ryan." Amanda hated this. Her sister was hurting. For so long it had been Amanda's job to keep that from happening or to at least to fix it when it did.

"Okay, but she will be," Ryan insisted. "She will be fine. She needs to know she can do this."

"Then I'm going to go talk to Nate. He doesn't realize—"

Ryan sighed, then spun her, cupped her face and kissed her. And kissed her. And kissed her.

By the time he lifted his head, she could only vaguely recall where they were and was fuzzy about why.

She pressed her lips together and shook her head. "You're trying to distract me."

"Let's go play spies in the other room," he said.

Tempting. Very tempting.

"You think someone here is a spy too?"

"I think someone planted a bug on you."

She raised an eyebrow. "Me?"

"Yes. I'll need to frisk you. I'm sure you understand."

She started to smile, then fought it. "I'll cooperate fully. I have nothing to hide from you."

He grabbed her hand and they made their way to the surgery consultation room two doors down. Ryan put her hands on the wall and started sweeping his hands over her. She loved the play, she tried to focus and forget about real life, but she couldn't ignore what was really going on.

"Thanks for distracting me," she said as his hand slid over her breast to her hip.

He pressed his lips to her neck. "I'm *protecting* you."

"Protecting me from Nate?"

He laughed lightly. "No. Protecting you from fixing things for Emma and keeping her—and you—from seeing that she can do this."

She froze for a moment, then turned to face him. "You're protecting me from myself?"

He nodded. "And Conner and your sisters from you."

Amanda narrowed her eyes. "How's that work?"

The door behind Ryan opened, and they both looked to see Conner step into the room.

Her brother's jaw tightened when he saw them standing so close. "Olivia said you were in here."

Ryan straightened, but stayed right beside her. "I'm going to take Amanda home. Was thinking you could take care of Emma and Olivia."

Conner looked back and forth between them. "Okay."

Amanda shook her head. "No. That's okay. I'll stay." Conner would *hate* seeing Emma struggling like this. "Olivia wanted to stop and get a new—"

"I'll take her," Conner interrupted.

"But I—"

"Amanda," Ryan said quietly. "Let him do this."

She looked up at him. "You don't understand."

"I do. You protect Conner from this stuff. But you both need to realize that not all of this is on you. Let him see Em working hard. Let him have that. You haven't let him see how amazing they are because you keep him away from the bad stuff. But it's in the bad stuff you realize who people really are."

She stared at him. Wow. He was...something. And he was all hers.

"What?" Ryan finally asked.

"And I thought I was in love with you before."

He gave her a huge, sexy, sweet grin. "And this is just the beginning."

Conner cleared his throat and they both looked to him. "So, I'm going to be with the girls. What are you going to be doing?"

"Talking about the enemy's plot to infiltrate the top levels of government by posing as costume shop owners and how we're going to stop it."

Conner frowned in clear confusion. "A costume shop?"

"Yeah. We're going to have to go down there and see what we can find out in person."

Conner's frown deepened as Amanda worked on not laughing. Conner must have decided that it wasn't worth delving into or that he didn't really want the answer. "I'm going back to the gym. You'll be here with Amanda?"

Ryan pulled her close. "In fact, I'm never leaving her."

As the door shut behind Conner, Amanda looked up at Ryan. "You haven't actually said that you love me, you know."

He smiled and ran his hand up and down her back. "I prefer to show versus tell."

Heat and excitement for what was to come coursed through her. "So, let's get on with this showing thing already."

"I'm ready. But we're going to have to go back to my place."

"Gee, what for?" she teased.

"To spend the night together. Finally."

"You think we can finally make it a whole night?"

"Yes. And it will be the first of many."

He said it with such intention that her heart squeezed with desire and love she'd never dreamed of experiencing.

"Oh, I'm counting on it," she told him. "I am definitely counting on it."

About the Author

Erin Nicholas is the author of sexy contemporary romances. Her stories have been described as toe-curling, enchanting, steamy and fun. She loves to write about reluctant heroes, imperfect heroines and happily ever afters. She lives in the Midwest with her husband, who only wants to read the sex scenes in her books; her kids, who will never read the sex scenes in her books; and family and friends, who say they're shocked by the sex scenes in her books (yeah, right!).

You can find Erin on the Web at www.ErinNicholas.com, ninenaughtynovelists.blogspot.com, on Twitter (@ErinNicholas) and even on Facebook (facebook.com/erin.nicholas.90).

It's all about the story...

Romance

HORROR

www.samhainpublishing.com

CPSIA information can be obtained
at www.ICGtesting.com
Printed in the USA
LVOW12s0231141116
512848LV00002B/147/P